THE PRINCESS OF
THE WIND AND
THE SON OF MAN

THE PRINCESS OF THE WIND AND THE SON OF MAN

NARAYANAN MOHAN

PARTRIDGE
A Penguin Random House Company

To order additional copies of this book, contact
Partridge India
000 800 10062 62
orders.india@partridgepublishing.com

www.partridgepublishing.com/india

CONTENTS

DEDICATION

This book is dedicated firstly to the late Shri Balakrishnan, the person who discovered the flair for writing in me, to my friend Shri Satyanarayanamurthy for his appreciation and encouragement in my written endeavours, Shri Krishnan for patiently going through this book despite my constant 'pestering,' for his quick insight and offering his encouraging response and suggestions as an informed reader, as also my wife Meena who went through the manuscript.

I very much owe it to Shri Charanjit Ahuja, a print media professional who even though was totally unknown to me, took out time from his busy schedule, to read my manuscript and in giving a very encouraging response to it allaying my fears and frayed nerves about the book. I must thank my mom for her support in my pursuit of the arts and for putting up with me while engaged in writing this book. My special thanks to Ms. Karen Jimenez who insisted that I publish this book, in introducing Shri Charanjit to me and her helpful attitude and approach in materializing publication of this book.

CHAPTER I

At the break of dawn, the cow and the calf lowed as Manu opened his eyes. Oh! It was feeding and milking time for the cows. It was already light, yet another fine young morning, and here he was, still asleep. The very thought of a beautiful morning and all those tasks awaiting him catapulted him out of his bed. It was that time of his life when the here and now dominated his life. There was no past to recall and no future to worry about, no nightmares that haunted him or wistful dreams. Only the current occupied him.

He folded the sleeping mats and the bed sheets, along with the pillow into it, picked them up, and placed them at the far corner of the room meant for piling on the bedding. It was twelve-year-old Manu's daily task to wake up first in the morning, set up the huge brass pan for the cows, filling it with water, and empty a bucket full of leftover rice gruel, a few peels of bananas, de-oiled cakes of oilseeds, usually sesame or coconut, at times even cotton seed, mixing them thoroughly in its wake for the cows to have their fill. And then he would let the calf have its fill of his mother's milk, though not quite let it have it all, before tethering it. For if he didn't, there would be nothing left to milk! Having thus induced the cow to lactate, it was time to pull hard at the bridle of the calf to keep the calf just beyond the reach of its mother's udder so that Manu may milk in peace. Deftly he would take a little ghee or butter between his fingers to apply it over the teats by smoothing it over.

'Ammu, come on, move a little this side,' he said to the cow, patting gently. He led her down and out of her shed into the porch, tethering her to a tree, and her calf not far from her, and when finished, he said, 'There, you are a good girl.' Then sitting on his haunches, keeping the pail between his feet, he would gently squeeze the teats between thumb and forefingers, sliding it gently down. Slowly, the pail swelled up with frothy warm and sweet milk.

Milking over, he kept the pail carefully aside on the porch; he sat down, bent double a little beneath the cow by the side of her teats and tugging at it

1

and turning it round towards his mouth and pulling at it, squirting a little milk into his mouth. Ammu was somehow indulgent, as they shared a special relationship. He then got up, picked up a broom, commanding, 'Move this way, Ammu.' Just then Ammu lifted her tail up and disgorged steaming chunks of cow dung and a clear pale yellow stream of *gomutra*, as they called it there, literally meaning 'cow urine'. He waited, moving aside for her to finish with it, and then with the broom swept away the dung into a heap at the side of the tree.

He would transfer it later to the pit by the side of the cowshed filled with all the dung and urine swept out along the channel alongside the wall in the shed and through a hole in the wall on to its side. This pile would, in time, slowly turn into compost for fertilising the plants and the coconut palms in that estate.

As Manu got busy cleaning the shed, the calf by now, being let free of his tether, was quickly by his mother's side, kneeling down and having his fill of what was left of the milk, as Ammu was a clever mother, still holding back some milk when Manu was milking her and stocking up milk aplenty for her calf. Ammu, having long finished the brass pots of gruel and titbits, now began munching on the bundle of hay that had been untied and lain before her by Manu.

Manu, after cleaning up, came out of the shed, went out into the porch, picked up the pail of milk, and swiftly disappeared into the house. He went into the kitchen. 'Amme Paale! Mother milk!' he cried out. His mother was lighting up the hearth with twigs, dried coconut leaves, husks, and shells, having set the tea kettle to boil.

Even as Manu handed over the pail of milk to his mama, she queried, 'Have you cleaned up the shed?'

'Yes,' he replied and turned to go.

'Have the tea and then go,' said his mother. She then set down the big boiling bronze kettle, taking it off the stove while setting a small pail of milk in its place to boil. The tea was poured into steel tumblers sugared, and later milk was poured into it. She stirred it carefully and handed Manu the tumbler. 'More firewood is needed. I think some leaves have fallen off the coconut tree at the southern end. See if you can pick them up.' After he finished his tumbler of tea, he picked up a chopper knife from the wooden cross-beam over one of the pillars supporting the roof of the veranda to the side of the porch and ran out to the southern end of their estate.

For him, working in his farmhouse in his village was pure excitement. Today was an off day for school, meaning he could do much as he pleased! Nothing was more pleasing to him than rummaging around the trees and plants around his house. He bounded off amongst the trees along the direction his mother had suggested to him, looking for that coconut tree. He found the tree and the fallen leaves. Just as he was to lift the leaves, he saw something crawl out—a scorpion! He froze a few seconds. Regaining his composure, he chased the scorpion out then checked carefully beneath leaves.

With one arm around the base of the leaves, he dragged them into the backyard beyond the porch. Using the *vettukathi*, a kind of chopper used in those parts, he shaved down the sides of the huge coconut leaf fronds, bringing down the blade, letting the leaflets fall into a heap till the stem became a long pole denuded of the drying leaflets with a fan-like base. He then swiftly chopped off the broad fan-like base, cut the rest of the stem up into smaller pieces, and stacked and tied the leaflets into two, three small handy sheaves to be used as 'logs' of wood to burn in the hearth. He then picked up the wide fan-like base of the stem and cut it up into narrower pieces.

The sun was already up, light streaming down between the trees and foliage. The atmosphere being quite cool yet electrified by all the signs of life around waking up, languidly, like a beautiful damsel rousing herself from a dream-filled slumber to the ecstasies of a wondrous morning.

For quite a few minutes, he stood there looking around and up at the sky, watching the magic of the riot of the morning colours, the green screen of the trees against the bright cobalt blue backdrop of the sky getting brighter and brighter, the streaks of yellow and silver streaming between the green foliage, lost in the melody of the humming of the birds, the squeak of the squirrels, the rhythms of the chirping of sparrows in unison. The music of another great morning, as each morning was to him, welcomed him. There he heard the persistent coos of a cuckoo. He mimicked in reply, which was returned even more vigorously, and the exchange went on for quite some time. It was fun. This was a little game he enjoyed playing with the cuckoos. He then watched it settling now in this branch and then on another and then flew into the open sky, up and up and away free. *If only I had wings,* he mused.

In the distance a clear and strong 'ooh' broke out. It was no cry of pain or surprise but a deliberate call of the fishmonger carrying his baskets laden with his morning catch of fish, in baskets on either side of a bamboo pole balanced deftly on his shoulder. At a good distance out into the street across the farm, one could see a couple of women from the neighbourhood rushing out of their homes into the street, calling out to the fishmonger, stretching their bamboo baskets.

In the distance along that street at the corner moved a tall figure of a man with a slight swagger, rather dishevelled, wiry, and tough-looking, wearing a lungi. It was Brandhan Murali, the madman Murali, wandering around and ambling towards the riverside for his morning routine. Women giggled at his sight and men frowned at him. But children loved him. He rescued a child once from the flowing waters of an overflowing river.

Manu meanwhile took out the sheaves of leaves that he had bundled up and reached the porch close to the kitchen. Then he called out to his mother even as he placed the bundles on the raised veranda by the side of the wall. Just as he turned around eagerly and excitedly to make his getaway for his usual fun and frolic by the riverside with his buddies for a bout of diving, swimming, and bathing, his mother came out, calling, 'Good work. Your father wants you to help him water the palms.' Apparently, Manu's father had finished reading the newspaper, the first thing he did every morning.

'There goes my plans,' he said to himself, irritated. He picked up a long-handled spade lying on the corner of the courtyard and hurried off. A lissom, handsome brown lad growing taller by the year in a family of five with a brother and sister, all younger to him, he was in that part of India which was still partly rural, but becoming modern, though many social attitudes, traditions remained largely unchanged. But a firm conviction had taken root in those parts that the three Rs were a must for each and every child. Electricity was nearly ubiquitously available, and motorable roads reached the remotest corners of that state. Though the idea of distributive justice as a political ideology had taken firm roots in most minds and for many it had become more of a religion, for most the mind clung to age-old mores, comfortable as they were like old clothes and shoes, providing security and comfort in an otherwise uncertain world.

But distributive justice had struck deep at the roots of even Manu's family. Manu had only a vague idea about how it had changed the world for his family.

He remembered when he was much smaller his grandfather and even his father talk about the parcels of land much bigger than what they had now was at their disposal with quite a few acres under cultivation and the granaries overflowing with grain. That was enough to keep the family going well, and they had a name and place in society. But his great-grandfather had seen the brewing storm long back. He had insisted that every child of the family should get his education and every male must be able to earn a job. As soon as his grandfather managed to finish his schooling, he enlisted in the British Indian Army while still in his teens. And that was something that his great-grandfather hadn't quite bargained for. Yet he did not demur. After all, there was nothing really by the name of jobs here around. So jobs could be had only far away from here.

His grandfather had served in the British Indian Army and would regale them all with the tales about the adventurous journey that took him from India to Mesopotamia and Egypt, about how those distant lands looked and people lived, the Bedouins and the Arabs, and how magnificent the ziggurats and pyramids were. But his grandpa could also see how harsh the life there was and how hard they lived. These distant lands in many ways gave a glimpse of what he saw around in his own land, the bazaars, the attire, the food, and so on. Nevertheless, his grandfather's life in the army was not exactly a fairy tale. It was a hard life in the British Indian Army. They were meant to be cannon fodder, but destiny willed otherwise. His grandfather would say that he was alive only for regaling them all with stories. Each time a battle erupted, there was no certainty that he would return home alive, and there were times he wished he was back home amidst his own people and family in peace. In those distant lands, despite striking friendships, he was to be a kafir to them. Having taken an early retirement with a small pension, he came back, married, and settled down and with his father, i.e., Manu's great-grandfather, began to manage the farm. For Manu hearing from his grandfather about the ziggurats, the pyramids, about Al-Qahira, or Cairo, Istanbul, or the Palmyra in Syria, about the Turks, the Germans, the Italians, and the French were nothing short of a fairy tale. These tales were a journey that took Manu around in a dreamworld of his own

But barely a few years after settling down, his great-grandfather found the new revolution take away whatever lands they had, with only the estate surrounding their home left to them, when communist governments took over in the region. His brother had settled in Bombay as a clerk in a company. His grandfather often said that they were still lucky to have been schooled and be employed and so didn't have to depend on the land entirely. But lots of other families couldn't make the change and struggled. In effect, the revolution succeeded in bringing a kind of equality in the sense that at least those better off were brought down to poverty like all others. Manu didn't quite understand the politics of the revolution here that his grandfather had spoken about except that there would have been a bigger estate, more space to run about, more bananas, more jackfruit and mangoes to eat. The more the merrier! Of course, that was some loss for a child! Oh, how much he loved to be around in these estates!

Manu's father wasn't entirely so lucky as his father. These parts of the world though saw a revolution of sorts in schooling; it was still a rural society by and large. Even the few industries that were there were struggling, and things looking increasingly bleak in a hostile climate, it was seen as a means of 'exploitation of the workers by the capitalists'. When you did nothing, there could be no exploitation. With difficulty, he landed himself a job at first as an accounts clerk in a timber shop a few kilometres away. There was a labour dispute, unions intervened, and that enterprise shut shop. He landed another job as a temporary clerk at a state-run liquor vend for a while but didn't like to continue too long. Anyway, the position was only temporary. In short, he did not get the much-sought-after position in the government or land something substantial elsewhere. He was essentially a rolling stone, squeezing this piece of land and occasionally making something out of odd engagements. More than anybody else, it was he who was anxious that he should make Manu a successful man.

Manu's coming into this world was celebrated, as a miracle, as he took a long time in coming for a couple that remained childless for years. But once he arrived, his siblings followed and things in general looked up for them. The family astrologer told his mother that he was a boy gifted with some extraordinary vision but stopped at that. But his mother did not know how the astrologer, when casting the horoscope of Manu at his birth, found something vague and unexplained. He could see that this boy would go far and wide and there was something listless, restless, and unsettled about his life. He could see that the boy was endowed with powers of looking into the past and into the future. It showed that he was in fact hundreds of years old from much before his chronological date of birth, endowed with experiences of things that no human could have accumulated in a lifetime. It was clear that this boy would be a visionary, if one may so—that is, he would see, literally see, visions of things far and wide, of things in the past and well into the future. But that would need some trigger, maybe some divine push. There would be some event that would open up this unique gift of his. But when it would occur, it was unclear.

The old wizened face of Thirumeni was in an expression of deep thought as he stroked his flowing white beard, his forehead creased in doubts. He cast and recast the position of the planets, recalculated it back and forth, but the precise cause and effect eluded him. What he could see ever vaguely was a life of struggle to find something, and the experience possibly alloyed to this struggle, a struggle and experience stretching into centuries. He finally gave up, sighing, thinking that maybe the horoscope was OK and just that age was catching up with him. Yet he did not voice his concern over the grey areas in this boy's horoscope, and none were the wiser for it. Here among the family it was just taken to mean that the boy would be extraordinarily successful, in a worldly manner, as everyone usually wished. It could have meant anything: money, plush comforts, fame for the family, and so on. Nobody paused to think if it really meant those things they assumed.

But that didn't entitle Manu to any privileges or concessions. Being the eldest, he was already being seen increasingly as part man, as an apprentice on his way to shouldering greater responsibilities—in short, a pack mule readied to be loaded. Though struggling, yet theirs was a fiercely proud family that liked to be seen as an upcoming family in these parts. And now there he was, directing water on the plots around with the spade. 'Look there, you fool! Fill in that breach quickly! The water is getting away!' The sharp command from his father jolted Manu into action. The water, pumped furiously into a cemented tank, was flowing out of it along a channel carved on a raised ridge of packed clay soil, snaking through the entire length and breadth of the orchard, passing by every coconut palm and banana plants. From these ridges were smaller channel diversions leading up to the round beds around the palms and the plants.

As the water streaked through the raised canal, the dry, thirsty, and parched earth greedily drank it up till a fresh wave of water flowed through with ease. But this too had other predators in its wake. Although the ridge was hardened by the grass binding it in place, there were crab burrows and pores of the like, into which water blundered. Manu had to watch out for these and plug them as he made them out. He had to see where the channel lacked depth and dig out the mud or the grass obstructing the flow of water and where the walls of the canal were weak.

It was fun for Manu to cut a channel on the side of the ridge to channel water to a coconut palm or a banana plant and dam the onward flow with those spades full of mud. As soon as it was done, he would close the breach, lifting the barricade across the ridge by scooping back spades full of mud and ramming it tight on to the sides with the flat of the spade. Thus the water flowed onwards to the next parched palm or plant. This way only a part of the farm could ever be watered in a day. It needed four days at the least to reach all the plants in the entire estate. Usually the watering was rotational, with each segment attended weekly at least once in the height of summer before rains came down.

While father and son were busy at the farm, his mother was churning the curd in a huge bronze pot with a churner made of wood with a mace-like hemispherical head having a long, slim grooved wooden handle like that of a screw. This slim grooved handle was looped into an appropriately thick white rope through an iron ring fastened to the wall. With both the hands alternating in releasing and pulling the ropes, the churner was rotated. It took a half an hour's effort to get the butter up floating, which was slowly gathered into a ball, with fingers dipped into the butter milk and sieving through it. Then in preparation for lunch, she had to grind the coconut which Manu had already de-husked, neatly broken into two halves, and grated into a plateful. On a huge granite slab with a matching round granite pestle, she rolled or rather slid it over the small pockmarked slab, crushing and grinding the grated coconut underneath it. The pock marks provided the traction and friction required for the grind.

'Congee!' came the sharp voice from his little brother, Ramu, now walking, now running up to him and his father, with the weight of the vessel filled with rice gruel. The vessel was set down on the grassy patch, and glasses full of warm gruel were handed out to each of them. Warm, slightly salted rice gruel seasoned with butter milk, with crunchy popadoms and pickles to go with. Sometimes it was accompanied by boiled whole green gram with a little turmeric powder and salt, seasoned with fresh grated coconut, a little coconut oil, and fried mustard, red whole chillies, and a few curry leaves. Sometimes it was boiled yams seasoned in the same manner. Manu loved it. This was the usual breakfast on holidays, especially while at work on the farm. All were thoroughly enjoying it.

'Paambe, snake, snake!' the terrified shrill cry of Ramu arose, the glass of gruel dropped from his hand. An alarmed 'Where?' rang out of his father's throat as he whirled around.

But Manu, unruffled, unaffected, turned on his heels swiftly, glass still in hand and eyes intently searching into the surroundings, alighting on the thickets a little to his left and latched onto a thick, stout viper that was creeping towards them out of the thicket. In a flash he dived towards it and had the snake by its tail. In a trice he pulled it out and twirled it around in the air vigorously before letting it go. It fell writhing to the ground, its back broken, breaking into spasmodic leaps. A single blow with the spade by his father did the rest. But his father was far from pleased. 'You idiot, what do you think of yourself? As a hero? Who asked you to handle it? It could have coiled back to bite you!'

All those who were there, his father and kid brother and sister, stood rooted to the spot, even as his mother came out of the house, rushing towards him, hearing all the cries, anxious. She scanned him through along his hands feet with her eyes. 'Anything happened?' And then she gave him a hug.

'Don't worry,' Manu comforted her with absolute nonchalance.

'Come on, there is no time to waste,' commanded the brisk voice of his father, beckoning him to follow.

After the watering session was over, father and son repaired to the riverside for a bath. As they proceeded, Brandhan Murali was shuffling away from the bathing spot, slowly, alongside the banks of the river. Manu's father rather gave a glowering look at the receding figure. Manu was told to keep off from him without explaining why. Anything and anyone unfamiliar could be dangerous, as goes usually the human nature.

Tired as they were, they did not take too long to finish their bath and returned quickly through the banana plantations.

A flame of hunger spread across his stomach as his nose picked up the aroma of the popadoms being fried and of the other dishes being finished as he neared home. That quickened Manu's steps. He entered the home after washing his feet off its mud, took off the thin wet cotton towel wrapped around him, and changed into a crisp white mundu. It was a broad piece of cotton cloth tucked at the waist extending down to the toes with horizontal colour slashes along the length at the top edge and the bottom edge and vertically along the breadth of the cloth waist down.

Puzhakkara

Father and son then sat down on a piece of wooden seat, each oval in shape with a tail on one end to grip, while his little brother and sister also sat down with a banana leaf each before them. They also had steel glass tumblers full of water placed before their leaves. Both of them sprinkled some water on their respective leaves before wiping the leaf carefully from the centre of the stem upwards along the veins, taking care not to split the leaf along the veins to render it useless. When it was done, they just lifted the broad end of the leaf, letting the water runoff from its tapering end before setting it down.

Just then his mother came up with a bronze pot laden with cooked rice. Then came *kaalan** to go with the rice. And then came the popadoms, a piece

---

* A thick soup of raw bananas boiled in buttermilk, salt, turmeric, and crushed black peppercorn, garnished with grated and ground coconut, finally seasoned with fried mustard, fenugreek, and curry leaves.

of crunchy thin flat roundels of dried paste of black gram fried in oil and the olan* as side dishes.

Manu quickly ladled out the olan on the tapering edge of the leaf while his mother had already placed a spoonful of cut mango pickles at the farthest end of the tapering edge. Serving food and eating on banana leaves had to follow certain conventions. How he relished popadoms! So much so that his mother would keep admonishing him, 'Have your rice and kaalan. That's the main dish, not the popadoms!'[†]

· ·

Two days later was Independence Day, and Manu had to get to the school to participate in the celebrations, although an hour later than usual. This meant that he had the luxury of a good small meal his mother had cooked up with rice and sambar[‡] and the ubiquitous popadoms. Usually he had only porridge of split wheat with milk before leaving for school. Normally, every year Independence Day celebrations was a routine affair defined by flag hoisting, singing some patriotic songs, having toffees, and dispersing for home in a short period of a couple of hours. But today it was different. A young schoolteacher newly posted there and with interest in the dramatics mooted the idea of an abridged re-enactment on stage of the famous Dandi March culminating in the Salt Satyagraha, protesting the British imposition of tax on something so mundane as salt being consumed by even the poorest Indian. But there were strong opposing voices wanting depictions based on Marx and Lenin and the dreamworld of socialism that had fast become the staple here. But eventually everyone agreed to the Dandi march at least as a change, as nothing like it had been enacted in a long time.

Manu quickly left for school. After the usual flag hoisting came the time for the dramatic enactment. A small boy was chosen to play the part of Gandhi, the Mahatma, to lead the procession enacting the Salt March. Manu was a

---

*　Made of thin flat rectangular slices of ash gourd and pumpkins boiled with salt and garnished in coconut milk and green chillies.

†　Flat thin roundels of dried lentil paste fried in oil.

‡　A fragrant soup of lentils, potato cubes, small or large onion cubes, cubes of aubergines, cooked in tamarind with a pinch of salt, turmeric, asafoetida, and seasoned in the end with a coarsely grated paste of freshly ground coconut, lightly fried coriander seeds, fenugreek, and red chillies.

participant as one of his followers just behind him. The children, all nervously glancing, giggling, were jostling around, though they were asked to walk in a file one behind the other, with the small Mahatma leading them. Even as the small Mahatma was nervously tugging at his waist to keep the dhoti in its place, which was refusing to stay put, Manu quite accidentally stepped on one end of the garment hanging loose and trailing to the ground. That just undid the whole dhoti, and the poor Mahatma was left in his knickers. A roar of laughter went up even as the Mahatma began weeping. Thus the drama ended. But the excited children and the siblings of Manu ran home, screaming, 'The Mahatma's dhoti came off!' But his father was not quite amused to hear it and enquired as to what the matter was. When the excited children told him what the matter was, he could barely conceal his mirth!

• •

For Manu, Friday evenings were always special! A visit to the temple! It was something Manu looked forward to eagerly. Temples held for him a certain undefined mystery and thrill, and the one nearby was even better, for it did not have much crowd and jostling, giving a peaceful access to all he wanted to experience. It had a large setting, placed in a huge plot of land a couple and more acres big surrounded by huge and thick walls. As he entered it, he would feel as though getting into a unique, ancient, and primeval world, slowly getting away, cut off from this world. Inside there was in the midst a gabled structure surrounded on four sides by stone walls with metal cladding, consisting of rows of metal lamps stacked from top to bottom that were lit on special days with sesame oil and cotton wick.

And what a sight it would be to watch! At the entrance to this was the huge multi-tier stone lamp in the shape of lotus petals, behind which was another stone pillar several feet high clad in brass, which was the standard bearer of this temple. This pole was at its shiny best with a brand new flag aloft when the anniversary of the day when the temple was consecrated was celebrated annually as the temple festival.

Inside the gabled structure lay the sanctum sanctorum, in which the stone deity was barely visible amidst the lit oil wick bronze lamps that hung from above. Manu, as did everyone, had also to peer carefully close up into the sanctum sanctorum for a glimpse of the deity. It had at its front a flight of ascending steps in stone amidst open doors carved out in heavy wood barely six feet tall. Even then the god, his or her visage would be visible only on intense focusing. Occasionally the priest smeared the black granite deity with sandal paste, carving out the features of the face when his artistic inclination so dictated. At times face masks of stamped silver marking the eye etc. were superimposed on the layers of sandalwood paste on the idol, bringing it alive. Jewels and necklaces or earrings adorned the god, which made him more visible and pleasing. That certainly added to the aura of mystery surrounding the deity and temple.

His mother told him that the image of the god was located in the Bhugarbhagrihaa, literally meaning 'the womb in the earth'. So the image of the god was located safely, securely, and mysteriously in a womb. He always felt a charged atmosphere therein, noticing how all stood there silently with folded hands, anxiously staring at the idol as though the god was about to appear in person. Apart from the god himself, there were standing figurines carved at the entrances to the sanctorum. Then there were strange lion-like heads with open mouths, baring the teeth, appearing at the top of these entrances. Each time he came in there, he was always drawn to gazing at them almost endlessly. They had their own myths and legends, each appearing so real to him. Besides them, there were panels on the walls of the sanctorum painted or carved with the mythical figures from the *Mahabharata*, Krishna or Bhima, or from the *Ramayana*. Each time he saw them, all their legends seemed to play out before his very eyes for real.

The doors of the sanctorum were suddenly closed with the priests closeted therein for their rituals and worship, chanting sacred mantras in Sanskrit. It was a long while till the doors opened amidst peals of bells clanging in unison at the appointed sacred hour in the evening. Then amidst the din of the bells ringing came a priest with a brass multi-tier lit oil lamp in his hands that he brought round and around, time and again, lighting up the facade of the idol, while all watched, chanting prayers on their lips with folded hands, focusing intensely on the god. Once the ritual was over, the priest emerged from the sanctum sanctorum, bringing the lamp closer to the devotees, who, with their outstretched and downturned palms, placed it over the open flames and then cupped their closed eyes with their palms as if to invoke the blessings of the lord carried in those flames. The priest, after that, tilted a long-necked bronze vessel with a long nozzle, dispensing the holy water and milk 'as blessed by the deity' to the outstretched palms of the devotees, who partook it. He also threw at their palms a pinch of sandalwood paste and some pieces of flowers.

A temple in Kerala in Puzhakkara

It wasn't just the temple but the festivals coming up there that fascinated him, especially the masked dance of Kathakali held in the precincts of the temple on the raised and pillared mandap viz, a gabled quadrangular platform erected for the purpose inside the temples since ancient times. On this were various dances performed as an offering to the gods, including Kathakali. But Kathakali fascinated him to no end. Kathakali literally means 'to enact or play out a story', i.e., through dance, drama, and music. The masked dancers with colours of black, green, or blue painted on their faces had a circular white paper-like wedge beginning along the sides of their faces and going around the chin, depicting beards in men. The eyes were heightened by thick blackened lashes, and painted eyebrows and eyes reddened with seeds of certain plants transformed into red-hot coals spewing fire in the background of black painted eyelashes. A fan-like decorated headgear was worn as a crown, with long-armed upper garments in red or black and thick jewelled bangles and a billowing skirt usually in white with exaggerated rumps formed the lowers. The dancers moved about with stylised movement of arms and fingers held in mudras, stylised symbols exaggerated by rhythmic gestures of the eyes and hand movements. Set amidst steady drumming and verses sung by two accompanists on stage that described the denouement of the scene taken from *Mahabharata* or such like epics, these held Manu spellbound.

The setting of these Kathakali dancers in the darkness of the temple with only oil lamps to light them up as in the olden days, with electric lamps complementing them, now added to the mystery and electrifying atmosphere to no end. For him their character and deeds were real and heroic. How wonderful it would have been to be in those times, he wondered! He was no stranger either to the mythologies surrounding these performances, as he was in attendance whenever expositions on them were held. Many a story teller would relate to these in the most lively manner as though it were just happening, and he discovered that all the characters had, like him and others, passion or anger, jealousy or greed, compassion or love. He loved hearing the description of the drama of how Bhima beat up his opponents or how Arjuna shot his magical arrows to vanquish his enemies. They were talented storytellers indeed. How they made him wish he were part of those myths and saw his heroes for real! How awesome the wooden images of Bhima and other Pandavas looked where it was set at the Navaratra ('the nine nights', literally) in the city on a visit to his uncle's home. But he would grow to appreciate them better as he grew older.

But as Manu grew, his doubts also grew. He didn't quite understand why grown-up people should fight and steal from each other, cheat or lie, or quarrel with each other as he found many a character in these mythologies do! Indra was always up to some mischief, and yet he was the king of gods! Did these divine creatures have nothing else better to do but scheme, fight, and cheat? At home he and his siblings were never allowed to drink tea or coffee. 'Children should not drink it,' his parents would say. Yet his parents were constantly found drinking coffee or tea! He was always taught at school how one should be punctual and honest and not conceal things. But he found that teachers often came late and elders less than honest. While they were lectured on good habits and manners, his lady chemistry teacher was found at times nibbling at her nails while putting up her feet on the table!

When he could no longer resist, one day he asked his Sanskrit teacher, 'We are asked to do things which elders never practise!' His teacher smilingly replied, patting lovingly Manu on his head, 'Do what your elders tell you to do and not what they do!' It was a clear message: regardless what the elders did, you had to follow the norms made by them in this pre-ordained world!

At another occasion, while quite a young boy, possibly the only occasion he had quite innocently asked as to what clothes gods wear. Did gods of different religions wear different clothes? He received a sound thrashing at that, never venturing into such imaginative queries. He learnt painfully that elders had a very blunt way of dealing with questions that startled them, those that they never had an answer for. Spanking! All that mattered was for you to fit in with the pre-ordained world that the elders had conceived. It was not your business to ask why! These seeming incongruence of the elders troubled him, between the myths of a moral dreamworld and the ugly realities.

He was still in the primary school when the first atomic device was tested by India and in the middle school when the emergency was imposed. Occasionally current newspaper reports and politics became topics of discussion in which Manu would eavesdrop. There were intense discussions among the elders about news reports about the Middle East, the continuous bombings of Beirut by 'phantom fighter jets' from Israel, or some or the other action by 'Palestinian guerrillas' that were current. It was a matter of small jubilation for his elders when Saigon fell and the Americans withdrew. None quite understood why the poor Vietnamese were getting bombed!

And then one of the brothers of his friend, a professional college student, disappeared into police custody when the emergency was imposed in the country. It had become a political sensation. The young man was reported to be a member of an extreme leftist group that were known for violent campaigns against landlords by tenant farmers in the verdant hills of the Wayanad in the western ghats, around 300 kilometres north of Puzhakkara in their quest for equality by building a regime of, and for, the proletariat. It was a hot topic of debate among his family elders. Manu barely understood the import of these happenings in politics except a vague feeling of the suffering of the people. While the happenings in distant lands sounded more like some fantasy, hardly real, he could feel the pain of his friend and their family at the disappearance of their beloved son and his friend's brother.

Disquieting things did happen in those times! But he was yet to step into the realm of nightmares. As for dreams, the closest he came to a dream was when a circus visited the town nearby his village when still at school. It was for the first time Manu saw jugglers, clowns, tightrope walkers, and of course all kinds of animals performing what for him were an amazing spectacle. It was to him closely akin to the mythical skills of Arjuna or other warriors that he never saw but only heard about. But here he could before his very eyes see something of it, a glimpse of that mystical and mythical world. It was a sheer pleasure, an ecstasy to watch them. It so impressed him that for days he would recollect each and every act of the ensemble. It was so irresistible that he managed to watch it, on the sly, a half-a-dozen times. He imagined it to be such a perfect fun-filled world that he even wanted to just run away from home and go with the circus. Only just so he did not do it. It was like a dreamworld, a flight to freedom, like his wish to fly like the birds he saw flying every day, carefree.

•••

In the final year of his secondary school, Manu was in the very last phase of writing his last examination paper. Well prepared and having put in hours of labour; he was thoroughly exhausted by these efforts as he finished the last paper. At the end of it he was relieved and happy that he had done his best and thrilled at the prospect of a vacation when he could freak out at will. It was nearly the end of April and the beginning of the hot yet fun-filled rewarding summer months. There was no dearth of adventures and fun for boys, with the river flowing right by their homes, with the mango trees growing heavy with fruit, as were the jackfruit and the cashew trees.

It was a Thursday morning, a week after his exams were over, as he stood watching a squirrel gouge out a ripening jackfruit high up in the branches of a tree in their estate. 'Manu, hey, what are you doing?' came the clear and loud call of one of his friends. He turned around only to find a whole group of his mates hurrying towards him.

Manu, without even turning his attention or head away from the jackfruit, simply pointed his finger at the tree and the fruit. Everyone looked up.

'Yedao (hey, you), get that down, Monkey. We can all have a nice time.' Monkey was one of the favourite names his friends had for him as he was an excellent climber of trees with his long limbs. There was hardly a tree he hadn't climbed in the surroundings, even the reasonably tall coconut palms—mostly surreptitiously, for his parents had strictly forbidden climbing. Without a second thought, squeezing a knife at his side by the waist between the tight roll of dhoti around his waist and his body, he quickly climbed. As he reached the tapering end of the branch, he slowed down, cautiously slithering towards the fruit. But alongside, a few red ants were also clambering around the branches and also unobtrusively creeping into his trousers. And these were fairly big red ants with a painful sting!

'Ooh!' A scream rent the air as Manu's left hand quickly let go of the branch, swiftly moving it to his bottom, where the ants had him at their mercy. All his friends standing below were for a moment left frozen, head and chin turned up, wondering and amused in turn. There was a sudden rustle of leaves. The movement of his hands and the sudden shift of his body weight affected Manu's balance, causing him to roll over in a moment on the branch, rustling the leaves. Yet he managed in a trice to hold on to the branch with the other in a tight embrace.

But misfortune struck. These swings and jerks proved just too much for the old branch as it cracked and snapped. The jackfruit, the branch, and he fell. His shoulders and back struck a whole thick cluster of branches and leaves, as his hands went leaping and flailing to get hold of it. But he managed just to tear off fistfuls of leaves.

He fell, landing first on his feet and then on his rump with a thump along with the jackfruit. For a moment he didn't move. His friends came bounding towards him. Bending over, they cried out, a little concerned. 'Hey, what happened? Are you OK?' they whispered.

Then slowly he opened his eyes, trying to move his limbs, feeling his sides and back. Attempting to get up on his own was quite difficult for Manu. Even as his friends helped him up on his feet, he was groaning and grunting in pain and discomfort. But after a while, he seemed much better, walking all right though with a slight limp. But it seemed there was no serious damage, and that came as a big relief for one and all there. At least things would not travel up to Manu's parents.

Up on the next day morning, he was on to an adventure of a different kind, climbing, this time, up a coconut tree. Just after his morning duties, he headed straight towards a coconut tree, a fairly short one. With a coir loop around his feet to prevent them from drifting apart, he clambered onto the stem of the palm, with his long arms clasped into a lock around the tree trunk. It was usual for professional climbers to use a short rope doubled up around the tree and gripped on either ends by both the hands to winch oneself up with the hands while propelling oneself up, with the feet pushing down on the trunk, with the arches of the feet pressed close to the tree trunk. But Manu used only his bare hands to clasp. The circular rope around his feet was only occasionally used by him as a matter of ample caution. He quickly clambered up to reach up to a tender coconut, gripped one after checking a few for suitability, before latching on to one. He twisted it furiously before it snapped free from its stem. He then dropped it down below. Quickly climbing down, he picked it up then, with a few slashes of the chopper at the top of the nut, cut a penny-wide opening. Then he slowly drank the cool, slightly effervescent, and mildly tangy coconut water.

With plenty of mangoes this season up in the trees and the cashew boughs laden heavy with the cashew mangoes and the nuts, every boy and girl around were having a busy summer vacation! And Manu was equally busy. But in the past he was usually off to his grandma's place or to one of his uncles in a fairly far-off city. Nevertheless it was fun.

Every time they were at their grandma's place, it was time for a virtual feasting. It was the time for huge jackfruits to be taken down the trees then allowed to ripen and then cut up first with a chopper then into small roundels and into further quarters. But this also needed lots of preparations. One had to smear the hands and fingers with coconut oil lest the white gum-like latex oozing from the stem and stalk should stick to the hands and fingers or even the blades of the chopper. The stickiness of the gum was legendary. Then with a similarly oil-coated knife, each of the whole fruit, nestled amidst a bed of thick flat white bunch of fibres, tightly packed, was gouged out one by one. The whole air smelt of ripe jackfruit as children ate many handfuls of it. It was a time when even after children had eaten, their stomach full of the fruit, too much was still left as jackfruits, one after the other, were brought down.

Manu loved it. But eating too much of the ripe fruit also sent the children often scurrying to toilets with an upset belly. With so much jackfruit remaining, jackfruit jam had to be made. In a huge bronze *uruli* (dixie) several lumps of jiggery was set to melt in a basin of water as fire burnt underneath, and then the jackfruit were cut, gouged out, cleaned and the seeds taken out, and put into the boiling cauldron. With a huge bronze spatula, this concoction was stirred for hours, at times for over a couple or more of days, with clarified butter poured into it till it had become a thick, tight, dark-brown paste. The aroma wafting around was overpowering for Manu and the other children. They all would sit around, watching expectantly their dear grandma and ma stirring the cauldron for those two or more days till it was done. And how it tasted when finished! There was no limit to the licking of the fingers! And then there was this delicious dessert with this jam! This brown jam was melted in water with lots and lots of coconut milk poured into it and set to boil till it acquired a creamy consistency. With the aroma of the dessert cooking filling up the home, the children would circle around in excitement. And then the remainder of the jam was stored in airtight jars or steel containers for future use. These jars were hidden at some secret locations away from the prying eyes of the children, usually in the granary.

But the children would one by one steal into the secret of the granary, a completely wooden room that was tightly sealed off to keep off rats or other vermin. Somewhere inside the granary was the jar of jam and other tasty titbits that grandma kept. It was the job of these children to scour for these and ferret them out. But if caught in the process, a scolding or a pinch of the earlobes awaited them! But the granary was also another source of fun for them, a place to hide when playing hide-and-seek. In that dark storeroom, one often bumped into whole pumpkins and ash gourds or a whole bunch of bananas left suspended from the ceilings in rope loops if one wasn't careful. But this wooden granary inside that storeroom was darker still!

But for once the ploy of hiding in the granary almost boomeranged. He still vividly recalled how his little sister was hiding in there when his cousins had come over and were all playing hide-and-seek. As each went into their own corner, his little sister went hiding into the granary. Some time passed with each of those hiding waiting, watching with bated breath. And then there was some slight screech, maybe a rusty window hinge creaking as a gentle breeze blew around or something of that kind. The poor girl, already suffocating from the musty smell of this wooden room, was frightened to her wit's end as she heard the screech in the darkness, which set her screaming and was soon found out. And what a smack she got from her father for the din she raised! 'Poor sis,' sighed Manu.

But there were other times when they went off to the city to be with one of their uncles. It was fun, especially during the Navaratra, when they got to see the huge wooden statues of the Pandavas assembled and lined up one by one and one behind the other as per the seniority of the brothers, starting from the youngest at the back and the elder ones at the front till the gigantic figure of Bhima came up. It sent a thrill and awe among them. The huge figure with a stern demeanour, large eyes, muscular arms, with his right hand bent at the elbow, carrying a huge wooden mace and curled moustache, topped by a huge crown, cut quite a formidable figure at least twenty feet high. He could go on staring at it for hours. These wooden statues were lined up before the main pagoda of the temple.

But there were other attractions too. On one side of this line was a beautiful gabled palace of wood, woodwork, and tiles with a clock tower that had the bearded head of a man (stated to be *maethen*, or a Muslim) with large eyes, an imposing beard, and piercing eyes, who opened his mouth every hour and as many times as the number of hours the clock struck. When he had opened his mouth sufficiently wide, the two goats on either side would jump up and butt their heads to close it shut! But his cousins didn't seem nearly so excited by these sights. Maybe, as they say, familiarity breeds contempt. But then his cousins didn't seem to think much of them either. For them, Manu and his family were more the country bumpkins and they themselves the city sophisticates, taking pride in all that was around the city.

The few occasions he visited at his cousins' he also saw a few disturbing scenes. There were marriage halls inside the fort where a large number of homes were found within its precincts. Occasionally grand marriages were celebrated there amid drumbeats and clarinets, followed by the sumptuous feasting. But he noticed often, after these celebrations were over, the banana leaves with leftover food were dumped in the enclosure built for the purpose just outside on one side of the entrance. They were many people, young and old, crowding into the enclosure, scrounging for the leftover food even a couple of days later. He was a young child, yet it pained him. He could not understand they were poor and probably homeless. Yet it occurred in his mind, why did not these city sophisticates ask over these people for a nice dinner post marriage? They numbered, after all, just a few. Back at his village, at every temple festival, all in his village, the rich or the poor, got down to be seated on the floor of the temple along the paved stones of the perambulatory in long lines around the temple and be served on a banana leaf a sumptuous meal as prasad or some gift blessed by the Almighty. Indeed, there used to be a practice of feeding the poor near the Padmanabha Temple by the kings, he was told.

In one particular year, while still a kid, something exciting and memorable happened when he visited that city. He always remembered that so vividly. The country's prime minister was on a visit to that city, and while she was on her way from the airport, she stood in an open jeep, waving to the crowds, and went past the people lined on either side of the not-so-wide inner-city road parallel to the huge temple wall. Little Manu was among those lined up along the road, and he saw a fair lady with a royal demeanour, in dark glasses, smiling and waving and looking down to everyone and to him. She appeared so close to him when she went past him that he felt he could almost touch her.

On another visit to that city, something more sensational and disturbing happened. 'There was a body found floating in the huge temple tank,' reported a neighbour. It took at least a day for the discovery to be made, and at least for another day it remained there till the partially submerged body emerged, transformed to a fully bloated body. Speculations were rife. 'Was it an accident?' somebody asked, as people were found usually bathing there in the mornings. 'More likely a suicide,' said another. 'Or was it a murder?' questioned a third. Nothing was clear. Investigations went on and on and the incident forgotten.

On another occasion, another sensational incident occurred. Outside the east fort, at the junction of three roads and right before a Ganesh temple, was found a man sprawled on his back with a knife handle jutting from his stomach, with the oozed-out blood coagulated on the tar road. It kept the city quite buzzing for the next few days. It was clear that it was a case of murder. It was speculated that the man was actually a pimp and some deal must have horribly gone wrong.

Manu was always fascinated as a kid to see policemen there in those times, wearing shorts that was so broad and had such a wide bottom, stopping just over the knees. He felt it was broad enough to shelter him beneath and had this urge to try getting underneath it but just didn't muster the courage, given that most of them had fearsome-looking moustaches.

But the times he went and stayed with one of his uncles at Madras (now Chennai) was also a lot of fun. They were in the suburbs not far from the suburban railway station. As he travelled by the train down these railway tracks, he could see the vast expanse of land, stretching before on either side of the tracks till the horizon that was only occasionally interrupted here and there with brambles or small hillocks where sometimes quarrying of granite could be seen. When the train approached the airport side, the runway was clearly visible, and sometimes he was thrilled to bits looking out, watching a plane land and the train keeping up with the aircraft running along the runway. And once they went during the monsoons. The house of his uncle was in a neighbourhood with plenty of empty spaces around, and at one end of a street there was a huge empty rolling plain leading up to a hillock about three kilometres away, on which was a sanatorium—in reality, a TB sanatorium.

At right angles to this street alongside one side of his house ran another street which after a great distance ended at the temple pond. The pond overflowed with water as it rained for the last few days and was flowing through the storm drains along the streets, spreading over the streets into a sheet of water. Surprise of surprises, he saw silvery flat fishes struggling along the street surface and the kids out there striving to catch them and putting them in a glass jar filled with water.

But most summers Manu just spent time at home. There was so much here to keep him busy. There were so many of the ripe mangoes in the trees that every minute a couple of fruits kept dropping. There was no need to climb trees and risk one's bones and limbs. Manu and his friends were having a field day. There were times when entire trees would be 'sold off' to market middlemen for a tidy sum in return and also a specified quantity of the mangoes for the household for their own use. But other times it was left for the kids to enjoy.

There were also now the cashews and cashew mangoes. When the cashews bore fruit and matured, one could see any number of yellow and red bells of ripe fruit hanging from the tree to which beige or pale-green kidney-shaped kernels were attached. Now it was the pastime of these youngsters to gather around these trees, searching for fallen fruit and nut or bring them down high up from the boughs with sticks or stones sent whistling past them or with a long bamboo pole. And they would only as a last resort climb them, for they feared the ubiquitous red ants. After each had his fill of these cashew mangoes, as they were called, the nuts were collected into a heap, allowed to dry out in the sun first. When it was enough to fill a big iron pan, it was then placed on a few stones, brick pieces right amidst the trees, and with dried coconut leaves, stems, and coconut shells, a big fire was lit, heating the pan. The iron pan was filled with lots of sand at first along with nuts, which allowed the even spread of heat on these nuts. As the heat rose, these whole nuts were stirred till they turned brown, and the acrid smoke of the oil from the blackened shell of the nut burning and flames flaring out filled the air even as the burning and flaming oil from its shell was oozing out. One had to be careful to see the shell didn't turn too black so that it didn't char the soft cashew kernel inside. On the other hand, if it was not sufficiently browned, the oil would still be there when the nut was cracked and stick to the kernel, which could burn both fingers and mouth. It was a delicate task. When the nuts were cracked open with stones, it would reveal nuts raw and soft, still coated with the tongue-biting oil or tasty browned bits or blackened pieces of charcoal, as one's luck permitted and depending how carefully it was done!

By the time these guys got through the entire lot, their hands were blackened with daubs of soot, even on their faces. And with the oil sticking to their fingers not coming off even after repeated washing with soap and water, it kept peeling the skin off from the fingers even days after.

In the vacations, bathing in the river was so much fun! It wasn't the usual dip and out. The guys lolled in the water for at least a couple of hours, diving from high points, swimming, splashing water, bantering, and having a thorough oil massage before getting into the waters. Soiled clothing were soaped and then banged on flat stones smoothened by years of use and then jogged and squeezed against the stone before being washed in the flowing river.

CHAPTER II

'Ammae!' came the excited screaming voices of the children. 'Manu Chettan first classile passaee! District firsta!' Which meant that Brother Manu has passed his exams with flying colours and topped in that district. The children ran like mad towards the house; their mother, just coming out of the house, stood rooted to the spot even as an 'Oh' escaped her. She said nothing, and then recovering from this shock of joy, she asked, 'Where is Manu?'. The children, still panting, pointed out far from the house towards the gate. There was Manu, amidst a bevy of his friends and classmates. The whole party was slowly inching towards the house, laughing and chatting, and then he looked up in the direction of his mother, who smilingly beckoned him to hurry. As they came up to the house, all were invited to have some tea. Tea and a plate of some jackfruit chips was passed around, with Manu helping out as the friends sat along in a row around the long, thick low wall of the veranda while he sat on a small chair, the only one there. Tea flowed, and so did the conversation.

Manus family home at Puzhakkara

It was for the family the event of the year of sorts. By the weekend, a large number of the clan had assembled at Manu's home, his uncles, aunts, the cousins, and so on. Those assembled there wanted to get a slice of the success, even if by proxy. While his mother proudly gushed at how the temple priest, Thirumeni (his holiness), who was also an astrologer, foretold them about the success this boy was to bring them, and his uncles and aunts were full of advice and opinions for the next course of action as to what should be done about him. But for now for this family, the goose had lain the first golden egg. The whole household was abuzz with activity. 'What should he do next?' was the question. His uncles, aunts, even his grandparents, all got together in a grand family reunion and feasting to ponder over this great question.

To have a university graduate among them was the pet obsession, a dream come true of those assembled, a sign of having arrived. In the good olden days being a matriculate, viz. a school-leaving certificate, was the high point of education for anyone. Those getting into a university were just thought to be exceptional. But now graduation was the new benchmark.

But his father had other ideas. 'What will just a graduate do? Roam around with a degree, jobless? Jobs are hard to come by, even for graduates these days. I don't want him to become another Bhrandan Murali,' he said in disgust. It was the first time a mention was made about that character in this house, who had for some unfathomable reason become something of a taboo figure in the house. He began wondering what it was about him that got his goat. Somewhere in Manu's mind, it stuck that he should get to the bottom of this mystery.

Manu's father alone among them thought that his son should be better off learning a vocation, maybe get a diploma at a polytechnic. A man should start earning and start supporting his family as soon as possible, and if he is the eldest, more so. That was the prevalent view. Manu's father knew the pinch of having an education but being without a vocation in life more than any other in the family. He did not want to risk and repeat the mistake that he felt he had made. It was then decided that he should enrol in a polytechnic not very far from his place.

The family finally gave in, albeit reluctantly. Polytechnic diplomas had the tinge of the blue collar that was not the fashion here. Though they liked the steady money it gave, it wasn't quite like being a graduate. A clerk was better than a factory worker, and a civil servant even better, as he had both security, income, authority, and social standing! Nevertheless, the family gave in to the wishes of Manu's father. Here it was always so that family elders decided on such matters and the younger were just expected to follow suit, as Manu did. But somewhere inside him there lurked a musician, a painter, an author, a dreamer at large. But his father never quite approved of these things, which he thought were the pastime of the rich and the idle that would lead a studious child astray. He thought nobody could make anything of oneself by pursuing these. Cinema was seen as undesirable, even wicked, and music and the arts were for the dissolute. Not that Manu believed in these. He was still only coming to grips with the contours of a deceptive world that things didn't appear always as they were made out to be.

The time he spent in the polytechnic were proving to be quite momentous. Besides his studies, he was learning the value of diligence and discipline, of logical analysis and reasoning—in short, he was beginning to have his own mind and learning to use it and take note of it. His focus now increasingly being on his studies, his responsibilities at home were increasingly delegated to his younger brother. His parents were really focused on how he made the best of what he had and get a job as good a one as he could. But Manu's focus did not remain confined to academics. He was into sports, art, even participated in debate, things that his Panchayat school, and father didn't quite let him. At school, shortage of equipment meant that often two sections of the same level played a game of football with either team consisting of at least twenty-two players. They would end up kicking at each other's feet more often than at the ball. But this didn't deter the boys from applying themselves diligently and vigorously in playing games whenever or however the opportunity presented itself. The PT master at the school was more often than not absent at the playground as he was engaged in other pursuits. And about the music teacher, the less said the better. They were the usual rounds of patriotic songs, especially around the time of Independence Day celebrations or the Republic Day celebrations, but nothing beyond. And then all fell silent on the musical front. Year after year, it was the same. But Manu's ears picked the stray lyrics of cinema soundtracks here and there. He enjoyed humming a tune here and there, and soulful lyrics moved him to no end, though he learnt to appreciate them better much later. At times at night he could hear the melodious strumming of a guitar or the soulful tune of a violin from the direction of the riverbanks, wafting towards him, which mystified him to no end. This had happened so often that he decided to investigate for himself the source of it at all on more than one occasion but kept putting it off each time.

But here at the polytechnic he slowly made a place for himself too. While he had many of his old schoolmates there, he also made new ones thick and fast. The first-term exams nearing their end, they had to complete a certain project on engineering drawing needing to be done. His old schoolmate Rajan sought his help. 'Come on, let's have a combined study at my home,' he pleaded. And so began a routine which ended continuing right through the rest of his course. With Rajan residing in the neighbourhood not far from Manu's house, every day they would repair in the evening to Rajan's house. There was nothing but drawings and discussions, problems and solutions, questions and answers, mathematics and physics, engineering and English far into the night, long after all had hit the bed—except of course Rema, the doe-eyed sister of Rajan.

Initially it was a bit of a curiosity that drew Rema into hearing and watching as to what her brother and his friend were discussing. But she didn't keep up with them till late. She had her own class lessons to deal with, and she was in the habit of seeking her brother's help. But more than her brother, Manu was often found clearing her doubts and explaining things to her. Slowly she found Manu fascinate her; though much of the discussions they had over their subjects passed over her head, she found their animated gestures to be so lively and absorbing. She liked the calm, confident, manner in which Manu conducted himself, answering every question posed to him, thoughtfully pondering over things that were posed to him. Gradually she too took to the habit of keeping them company till late as their exams neared, sometimes even making them a cup of tea. Manu even, at times, wrote small pieces of poetry, to which he treated Rajan, with Rema overhearing. Rema's eyes and ears attentively followed each and every gesture and word of Manu. Her large eyes were literally glued to him, catching and collecting every bit of his actions and words, savouring them like some sweet drop of nectar, carefully storing them away like pearls of wisdom in the safe and secure vaults of her mind.

As his regular visits continued thus, one night, returning from his session at Rajan's, he heard the soothing sonorous tones of the violin wafting around. The half-moon showed bright in the sky. As though on cue, Manu was drawn slowly into the direction of the sound, which led him through the farm, the thickets over the ridges, till he found himself by the riverside, and going further up along, he found none other than Brandhan Murali seated on a rocky ledge, with feet planted on the sand, with the violin in hand, playing steadily. So that was the source of the music all along. But Brandhan Murali played on, unmindful of anything, appearing even ignorant of Manu's presence. It was quite late in the night and there was much preparation for Manu to do on the morrow, so he decided not to interrupt the musician and hurried back home.

In time the exams were written by Manu and Rajan, and the results came out excellent, as usual, for Manu.

One evening, when his second term had begun after the summer vacation when a wave of rain had lashed those parts, he came back home earlier than usual as his last period was free. After a change of clothes and a cup of tea, he wandered off into the coconut grove, wondering if he could have a nice swim in the river. Brooding over it, he suddenly decided he should have a tender coconut. He picked up a short rope to facilitate his climbing. He then scanned around, looking for a suitable coconut palm that was within reasonable reach and had the best possible pick. There were a variety of palms which had different kinds of nuts. Some green and big, some small, some pale yellow with a sandy-hued husk, some red hued and with small nuts whose kernels were hard and the water not so sweet. His eyes landed on one, and he went up to it, folded his dhoti over his knees, and quickly clambered up, resting for a few moments. He selected a tender green coconut, reached up to it, and twisted it till its stem snapped. The coconut was set free, and then he dropped it down.

With the job done, he clambered down swiftly, touching down on the ground softly. Then with a sigh of expectant pleasure, he turned his gaze around to the spot where the coconut had fallen or at least should have fallen. Ah, to find the object of his sweet soothing quencher of thirst! But, but where was it? He turned to his left his right, looked in front and then back—where did it go?

Eh! Did he hear something, a muffled tinkling of a suppressed giggle and laughter? Yes, there! From behind that tree was peeping out a lovely sweet face with a gleaming, glittering pair of dark eyes. Rema! The laughing, teasing, bright, riveting eyes drew him to her, nearer and nearer, till she and he were face to face. Silently he watched her, with a sense of novel discovery. It was as though he had met her for the first time in his life in her own right, not as Rajan's sister! At that instant his gaze scanned her face, eyes, hips, lips, sides, her bosom; her whole person seemed to have acquired a curvaceous lusciousness of life, a fullness of appearance, a demeanour of feminine charm, her voice a rich husky weight that had gone hitherto unnoticed. There they stood in mutual admiration, with the space around and between them charged. Not a muscle moved. A gust of wind dropped a leaf between them. The trance broken in a trice, Rema suddenly hid her face, flashing a shy smile, and then bolted from the scene in a bound, giggling. There lay the tender coconut, hidden in the tall grass, waiting for its discovery.

The summers and monsoon having gone by, the winters were setting in. The winters in the southern part of this subcontinent don't quite mean cold wintry days but only relatively cooler, with plenty of cool breeze blowing around. These were the times right in the midst of festivals in most parts of the subcontinent. Yet there was something unique about the temples and festivals here. No temple or festival here was complete without an elephant. These temples built of wood and stone foundations were austere and simple but spacious in comparison to that elsewhere, sombre in atmosphere, surrounded by high walls, creating a feeling of isolation and withdrawal from the outside world. It was usually set in grand locations with a commanding architectural presence in verdant settings and with an unobstructed view, occupying the highest point in the vicinity. The sombre atmosphere, the high walls, and the commanding presence created that aura of old-world mystery, a feeling of a world apart that more than made up for any lack of lavish ornamentation. Anyone entering the precincts instantly sensed the charged atmosphere there.

For ten days now, every day, early in the morning at 3 a.m., at the auspicious hour, there were special prayers or poojas. The priests, after their morning bath in their fresh new mundus, were closeted in the *garbhagriha*, the sanctum sanctorum, in its dark, dingy, humid environs, engaged in rituals. And then they would open up the doors to the sanctum sanctorum to chanting and vigorous bell ringing, with the black idol appearing bright in the looming darkness, amidst the glow of the oil wick lamp lighting, the multi-tiered, multi-wick lamp held up to it and the light reflected from the lotus petal mirror behind the idol, even as the devotees craned their necks to view it. The idol smeared in sandalwood paste looked resplendent decked in silk finery, gold jewellery.

By dawn more devotees began to throng, but two or three hours after sunrise, usually the morning engagements ended with a burst of firing, usually a *kadhana*, a short thick iron cylinder several inches thick plugged with explosives used in fireworks. In the afternoon, an image of the presiding deity was usually taken around the temple on an elephant with the priest ahead and a drummer behind.

Come evening it was time for the more colourful events, musical concerts of local or more accomplished musicians, dances, Kathakali, discourses, and so on. There was a *thayambaka*, an ensemble of specific types of percussion instruments, a variety of drums that rolled. Some men drumming had specially carved curved sticks in one hand, while on the other they played with thimbles on their fingers, performing. It was fun for Manu as for the others to watch the men dressed in their dhotis, their upper bodies bare, with the drums hung over their necks, weaving patterns of rhythms stretching from the barely audible touches, brushes, and scrapes with the fingers and sticks to the highest tempo of fast rippling rhythms. They performed under an elephant canopy, a huge, tall pillared and shaded quadrangle at the entrance to the inner shrine, built for the purpose of accommodating even a couple of elephants underneath it.

On the concluding day, there was a grand parade of elephants in caparison, with the tallest elephant at the centre, carrying the emblazoned image of the god in gold held by a man seated on top and two others behind, one carrying Fly whisks and another two big and round fans of peacock feathers. They were in theory doing the honours to the god before them, fanning him from the heat and keeping him free from the flies! There was yet another just behind the one carrying the god's plaque who held up an ornamented and brightly coloured umbrella. Then there would again before these elephants be an assemblage of percussionists, cymbals, bugles. The vigorous drumming and trumpeting and crashing of cymbals to the swaying elephants, with crowds thronging around, built up to a crescendo and then into lows. Taken together, it was a wonderful spectacle.

But this particular year, something unusual and something inauspicious occurred while the image of the god was being hoisted on the principal elephant after its due consecration by the priests. It slipped from the hands of the handlers and fell almost on the chest of the mahout, who with others somehow helped to break its fall. But that didn't go well with the priests, who feared it to be a grim portent of things to come.

But soon after this incident, Manu watched the deity being safely mounted on Govindan the elephant while others climbed up one by one from behind, carrying in turns the umbrella, the fly whisks, the peacock fans. The principal elephant was flanked by other caparisoned elephants all in a row. The men atop with the whisks, at regular intervals, brought up the fly whisks, twirling it round, with the fluffy off-white tufts of hair unfolding. They then brought it down gently in unison. The umbrellas held over all other elephants were also twisted gently and at intervals kept changing, varying in colours and patterns. And before them the assembled musicians were performing vigorously. Well after nightfall, the drums fell silent and the spectacle came to an end. And now it was time for the grand finale, viz. a display of fireworks.

The fireworks were lined up at some distance 200 metres from the temple in the paddy fields nearby, and people gathered in numbers to watch them. The fuse was lit and it snaked over the line of powder over the field, leaping towards the lined-up crackers. The first to go up were the fire fountains, hurtling into the sky, colourful spangles and patterns interspersed by firebombs that made deafening noise and culminating towards the end in a frenzy of explosions. The whole sky and the surroundings lit up in a big flash with the bursting of these crackers in unison, blinding, dazzling, and deafening one and all present there, so much so that they failed to notice that few of these missiles were straying the course and falling into the crowd. There was absolute mayhem with people running helter-skelter. The celebrations melted into wails and tears. Two died and six were injured. Three of them were maimed for life. 'Didn't I say something was wrong?' sighed Manu's mother almost to herself, stunned and dazed at this turn of events, as both mother and son slowly made their way home. *Carelessness,* thought Manu. But sleep was hard to come by for both. Manu tossed and turned in bed.

Only last year Manu was witness to a hair-raising event. Manu recalled how this temple elephant, Govindan, calmly standing in the temple courtyard, suddenly turned violent. It was a nice morning and people were trickling into the temple to offer their prayers. For over a week now, the elephant had been in must—that is, the time in a year when certain glands on either side of the temple of the elephant was visibly secreting. In this state of excitement, the elephants are tethered in iron chains to trees and the front legs a little loosely shackled to prevent them from running amok. But Govindan was always a little loosely shackled. All of a sudden, something appeared to provoke him and he got violent and slipped out of his moorings and shackles, turning around sharply. And so a cry arose—'Aane virandae! The elephant has run amok!'—among a small knot of people watching as they scrambled and scampered to safety.

The small knot of people, including Manu, who were just watching the elephant bolting from the scene ran helter-skelter. Some ran into the lanes ahead of the elephant uphill along the moss-covered compound walls of houses lining either side of the lane. Others jumped over the wall adjoining the big sprawling compound where the elephant was tethered. Manu was among those running uphill. He ran along till he reached the main road, a broad concreted road along which ran the occasional truck. Elephants, he knew, found it difficult to climb uphill, and so he had confidently run towards that direction. But once having reached the junction at the main road, Manu, turning right, ran further up. After a while, having run some distance, he looked over his shoulder just to ensure he was quite safe and found instead that the elephant too was labouring up the incline and had just reached the junction, pausing for a moment, turning right, following right behind Manu. Manu could not afford to stop, and he ran along till he had reached a huge mansion along that road. Govindan too came along up to a point and thankfully stopped. For a moment, he looked about himself wildly, swaying his big head from side to side menacingly with the frenzied energy of a beast, as though searching for somebody ready to pounce upon. Then he made a move as if to march on but instead turned left towards a huge thickly wooded estate of an old stately tile-roofed mansion just two houses from where Manu stood, stepping over a side fencing of brambles and faggots of bamboo interspersed with stumpy little trees.

The elephant rushed inside, and at a distance behind him ran a small knot of people, including the mahout. Among them was Brandhan Murali, who alone among this entire crowd was actually already around the vicinity, as he had just come over here to make a purchase in one of those small shops. He espied this huge animal rushing in along with the small knot of people someway behind it, and he too peeped in.

Manu recollected how he hesitated between the temptation to get back to watch a rogue elephant being brought to heel and the fear of getting hurt— worse, trampled by the elephant or by the stampede. But curiosity got the better of caution, and Manu scampered back and, along with the crowd, entered the plot adjacent to the mansion. 'The police are coming,' shouted one. 'The local veterinarian is also on the way,' said another. 'It's lucky that the house looks uninhabited,' said a third. 'These days, only the old patriarch, Raman Menon, and the lady are left living here. Maybe they are out somewhere. All their sons and daughters are settled at distant places. The first daughter is in the USA, married to a doctor, the second one is in the Gulf, in Dubai. One son is in Delhi in the civil service, the other is in a bank in Bombay. They have gone to Bombay to be with him.'

But it was Brandhan Murali who alone among the crowd espied a lone female in a corner of that sprawling backyard of the bungalow, busy cutting the overgrown grass, quite unaware of the happenings. Brandhan, without a second thought, sneaked in quietly, dashed across, alerted her to the danger, jolting her into a run towards the wall at the farther end, urging her on, and helping her over it before he jumped over it. It was a plucky rescue only a madman could have attempted, aided by plain luck that the elephant somehow didn't quite notice them. Manu and all those around were left watching with mouths agape, struck dumb.

Manu watched with others the elephant being restless, turning round and round hither and thither, head turning from side to side, furious and looking suspiciously at everything around.

Just then came a posse of policemen along with two well-dressed briefcase-toting men. 'That is the famous veterinarian, Cheeran', pointed out someone. Dr Cheeran was a veterinarian experienced in handling such incidents. The policemen and the veterinarian were huddled low this side of the wall, in confabulation after having a good look at the pachyderm, peeping at it from the shadows of the trees this side of the divide and along the top of the wall, taking care to remain unseen, though it was the back of the elephant that was largely visible. After exploring the side of the mansion with his trunk, the shut windows and all, the elephant had also moved a little away along one side of the mansion away from the wall behind it, behind which wall were the veterinarian and his police team.

The experienced veterinarian sat down on his haunches, set down his briefcase on the ground, and opened it up. One by one he took out a huge syringe, a needle, a big vial. He set the needle on the nearly foot-long syringe. Breaking the vial, he sucked in the contents completely. Then turning to a policemen, he said, 'Be careful,' handing over the syringe. The policeman carefully loaded the tranquiliser dart onto the rifle, while another, with much caution and an eye on the elephant, stealthily clambered up the wall and was motioning to his colleague to hand over the rifle. He then quickly positioned himself at a vantage point, taking cover behind the hedges along the other edge of the mansion at right angles to the edge, along which the elephant was standing. Making sure for a moment that the elephant stood still and aiming right behind the vast expanse of Govindan's back, he fired the dart. He then equally swiftly clambered back to the safety of this side of the wall. Yet everyone there waited with bated breath at the next move of the elephant.

For a few moments the elephant didn't seem to take notice of the dart on its back. It was almost eerie. Everyone standing there was tense with the suspense. And then Govindan exploded into action. Whirling around, trumpeting loudly and angrily, his trunk raised high, swaying his head this way and that, he searched for his assailants like mad but found none. Instead his sights turned to his left to the coconut palm. Quite suddenly, with rage and frustration building up, he stood up on his hind legs and charged at the tall and sturdy coconut palm with his massive head held high and a raised trunk. The palm quivered and shivered under the furious charge, like a leaf hit by a cyclone, spraying the coconuts in many directions. He charged at it again and again. The tree snapped.

Manu and many among those assembled there hadn't quite seen anything like that. It was a spectacle that would remain etched in his mind for the rest of his life.

Spent with the effort and with the tranquiliser now taking effect, Govindan came to a halt. The mahout whispered to two of his assistants and others in the crowd, 'Now is the time to chain him up. Get ready!' The three went across with long sticks in their hand while a policeman accompanied with a rifle in hand. Normally, the mahout had a brass curved hook and pointer that sometimes was used to goad the elephants. But with Govindan, there had never been any such need till now. In a while the elephant was brought under control and tethered soon to a tamarind tree. The drama over, Manu rather felt sorry for Govindan. Even elephants, he sighed, could not be free; however powerful, he was trapped by the wiles of man, conditioned and obliged to do his bidding more than even God's! That was his destiny.

What beautiful moments of his life they were. He sighed! And soon he fell asleep.

Time had gone by thick and fast. Manu worked hard at his studies both at the polytechnic and at home while courting success in most things he did. Night after night as he sat in the veranda, books open on his lap, studying, he would sometimes just switch off the lights only to watch the stars shining in the sky, staring at them long and hard, wondering what mysteries lay in them, how it would look being up there among them!

One day sitting outside in the night, distracted from his books, his eyes wandered, as did his mind, high above into the night sky, to the bright stars, the clear dark sky, the moonlight. Here, far away from the city lights, the night sky was much darker and the stars far more visible. Shutting his books and placing them in his chair, he got up, wandering down the estate, meandering through the trees and the thickets, onto the sandy banks of the river, which emerged as some dark winding tress on the shoulders of a nubile nymph, with many speckles of moonlight showing on them as some diamonds embedded on a maiden's black hair. He walked along the sandy banks, enticed and enchanted by the moonlit night, looking around and up into the sky with eyes agape; he halted his tracks, slowly sank into the mud and sand, first sitting down and then lying down. With his arms folded and the palms behind his head, cradling it, his fingers locked behind, he was engrossed deep in contemplation. What all mysteries did those distant stars that shone in the night sky hold? Would they tell him all that he wanted to know of, he wondered? Something, a hand, touched him. Startled in alarm, he whirled around. Rema! Then it all happened in a blur. He didn't know when he pulled her towards him, how she came into his arms, and for how long they were in each other's arms that night. Suddenly realising how late it was, they parted company in a hurry. Somewhere in the distance, Manu saw the image of a man disappearing into the thickets with what appeared to be something in hand—a guitar? Oh! His heart nearly skipped a beat! Was it the madman, Murali, and did he see them together? Manu entered his home stealthily through the backyard after putting off the lights in the porch, spread out his mat, and lay down quietly to sleep.

In the morning there was utter commotion. There was apparently a house break-in in the neighbourhood in the dead of night. A heavy gold chain was snatched from one of the women's neck sleeping too close to an open window, and some brass and bronze utensils were stolen from the backyard porch left there for washing in the morning. The woman responded very late to the probing hook or a groping hand and the flash of a torch light before she discerned sleepily what transpired and could raise an alarm. Manu's parents were in an animated discussion. His father was a little upset, telling how he often saw that doors and windows here were left ajar and not secured properly, especially at night. Manu's heart nearly skipped a beat. Did his father notice anything yesterday? Thank God nothing happened at his house; else he would have much to answer for.

But in the third year of his diploma, there were other dramatic things happening. There were elections to the students' union in the neighbouring college close to his polytechnic. Manu had many of his schoolmates among the students there. He often visited them for a banter, at times even for a discussion on science or languages. But the students' union activities in these colleges were not simple activities. The rival groups were in some ways shadows of the political parties, but also driven by individual students who loved the limelight and followers. That also allowed these leaders to show off before their girlfriends as to who was the boss.

There was the usual ragging and bullying and tiffs among the groups, with some among these leaders being actually grown-up men who were perpetual students, never wanting to graduate, repeating classes and subjects year after year. Often these led to the charge that there were outsiders meddling in college elections. Manu was not much into politics, though he found some discussions and argument of his friends active in the unions rather intriguing. Once, he found his friend Biju proclaim that Soviet Union was the best place to be in, where everyone was equal and every facility necessary was available. 'Have you been there?' queried Manu.

'No, some of our leaders who went there told us!'

'To how many places did they visit?' asked Manu.

'No, why do you ask so many questions?' replied Biju. 'Only the bourgeoisie have doubts about the revolution,' he added with firmness.

Manu rebutted, 'At least one should verify what was claimed, and how is it possible if there is an iron curtain and you haven't met the common people there far and wide and asked them?'

Biju was silent. These elections usually created some ruckus and excitement born out of rivalry; seldom these went out of hand. After all, they were friends and classmates growing up together. But this year the rivalry got out of hand.

One day Manu, as usual, soon after his lectures ended, went over to the college at the lunch recess. He was with some of his friends, discussing something. Amidst this, a huge uproar and commotion was heard. Shouting and heated exchanges were heard. There was a surge of students gathering and stomping, and then scuffles followed. From nowhere, stones flew, and it descended to a free-for-all. The frenzied crowd gathered there were now divided into groups hurling abuses and stones at each other, with one group gradually gaining over the other and pushing the other into a distinct corner. Though they retreated into the sheltered quadrangles of the buildings of some departments of the college, they were still at the receiving end of the barrage. As this exchange continued more now, the shocked students watched in stunned silence, not knowing what to do, when a shrill voice of 'Peace, peace!' rent the air. What the students saw was a thin, wiry man, their chemistry lecturer, come out of his labs from one of those buildings, pleading with outstretched hands. But the barrage of stones continued without a pause. Quite a few landed in the corner where he stood so that he partly came between the warring groups. Someone from among the lab staff followed him from behind, grabbed him by the waist, and dragged him into the confines and safety of the chemistry lab. But it took quite a little while more before the stoning ended. Quite a few of the students were injured. Mercifully, Manu and his friends were safe, left unscathed.

But all hell broke loose when the news of this mayhem reached the ears of his father, who was furious. 'Who asked you to go to that college?' What's your business there? I have been telling repeatedly to keep off all this campus nonsense and focus solely on your studies. You have been sent to study, and that's your only job. How irresponsible of you!'

Manu told them patiently that they were his classmates at school who were also studious and with whom he often discussed the subjects he was learning. But nothing could satisfy his father.

In a few weeks' time, Manu finished his exams and awaited results. And again it was the time for the family clan to gather for their conference. And there was advice galore on what he should be doing. There was meanwhile a quiet exodus of sorts happening from these parts. Young men, even women, were venturing out of their homes and hometowns, going across the sea to the distant shores yonder in the Middle East. Initially it was office staff, then doctors, nursing staff, midwives, lab technicians, and other professionals. Later even masons, carpenters, construction workers, and the like went. Many a family mortgaged their small piece of land or even sold it off to fund the travels of their son or daughter. Some of his acquaintances advised Manu thus. Where was the money? He could barely imagine broaching the idea to his father.

One of those days, he happened to meet Brandhan Murali, who spoke, for the very first time, to Manu. 'Going to be an engineer, eh?' he said with a smile. Manu replied he was awaiting his results. It was sundown and getting dark, and the two of them slowly repaired to the riverside. Manu didn't understand why he was seen as a madman. It was known that he was an alien in these parts coming down from the hills of northern parts of the state, lived quite alone, was an ex-serviceman. His fearlessness in saving people was known. Maybe that dented the pride of men here. He was aloof, distant, keeping much to himself, not caring for company. Nobody saw him go to the temple. Nor did they see him at the toddy shop or seek an audience to brag around about his Army exploits. He didn't seem to be interested in great wealth or luxury. This aura of mystery around him and the apparent contradictions put people here ill at ease. As none could slot him into their notions of a normal man, 'mad' was a convenient description. They proceeded silently towards his abode. It was a modest place, but well kept and lay out neatly as a soldier's barrack. There were ceremonial mementos on the side table, a few photographs in a soldier's attire amidst his soldier colleagues hanging on the walls. At one corner there was a guitar; at another a violin case. Manu knew Murali to be a good musician and was witness to the proof of his courage a curious combination of guns and music. 'Care to have a cup of tea?' Murali asked Manu, to which Manu nodded. Manu, seated at the table, was gazing at these memorabilia and chatting on how Murali had managed to get his musical training from the band colleagues in the Army. After a while, they had tea and Manu took leave. Manu found a pleasant madness in Murali.

Soon after getting his diploma, Manu found himself scanning the newspapers for job advertisements, responding to them and anxiously awaiting their replies. He kept getting calls for interviews, kept appearing for the same dime a dozen. He did quite well, possibly being among the best in every interview. Yet a job eluded him. There were things such as referrals and references, connections, and those connected a murky world still unknown to him. Having none of these, he had to cool his heels while his father was getting restless and impatient and chafing at this enforced idleness, leaving the family anxious. 'There are girls to be married off and others waiting for their chance in life,' he heard his father murmur. These nearly inaudible murmurs were growing louder by the day, eventually reaching him at first accidentally and then deliberately. It was made clear to him that the whole family's fortunes hinged on him. Being the eldest, he had to show the way by contributing to his family's upkeep, having himself benefitted so much from them!

At long last he landed a job that paid reasonably well at a factory in a city in the neighbouring state. There was joy and relief writ all round and, of course, more elevated expectations. He had in one bound become a man from a child and a boy.

CHAPTER III

More than 200 kilometres separated his city of fortunes from his hometown. As the blare of the siren gathered in intensity, workers slowly filed out as the workers of the previous shift shuffled out in the morning and the workers of the next shift were filing in—among them, Manu. The first few months of his new vocation was filled with the pleasure of discovery as also the frustration and mistakes of a novice learning his craft. It was also time to earn new friends, bond with them. It was also the first time in his life that he was experiencing the feel of economic power and, more importantly, the freedom to spend time and money as he wished—that is, the spare time left after work and money left after sending in his money orders. Late nights spent with friends watching movies and then dining at small restaurants were the order of the day, a way of celebrating his new-found freedom in this small city. He didn't have to now worry about the disapproval of his parents, particularly of his father. He was now enjoying his freedom with gay abandon, but not recklessly. His one room-mate was Thomas. It was fascinating to have Thomas amidst them. He was actually once in a seminary, training to be a monk and a Christian priest. 'It was a matter of honour, a bit of economic compulsion, too, for my family to have me become a monk.' The Church undertook to finance his education, promised a secure future in return for his freedom. Then something happened. His frank views on many things Christian and his excessive love for music and freedom meant he was not so popular with the dispensation in the Church. 'I decided to think over it, sought time, and pursued post-graduation in English and later got employed at the office in your factory after finishing my studies.' Being a trained musician, he was often going around the town with his portable synthesiser, playing in church choirs and for programmes where popular cinema songs were sung, and was paid for the effort. That gave vent to his musical talents, and opportunity to earn enough money to pay his fees and send some home. Manu became now his instant fan, and Thomas his music guru. He pestered Thomas to play music and teach him as well. Many an evening Manu spent strumming the guitar, practising the string exercises, or at times the synthesiser. Manu learnt about Western music and the abstract compositions of Bach, Brahms, Beethoven, Tchaikovsky, Mozart, and Vivaldi from Thomas.

Every morning, Manu got up now to a different routine and to a different sound of morning to the one he was used to at his native Puzhakkara. It was the chirping of the birds that first brought up the morning at his home back there. Late in the morning one could hear the squirrels and then the occasional cuckoo. And then there was Ammu the cow. Here he got up early, but to the sounds of passing vehicles and at times to an occasional sparrow and cycle bells of the morning milk vendor delivering milk. Back there at Puzhakkara, there was a river to go swimming and a big backyard where he could pick up a spade to do something that gave him daily enough physical exercise. Here he could do none of those. He had to contend with room-mates as well. In that shared room, the room-mates had to take turns to have their shower, do their toilets, wash their clothes, and so on. Thereafter he would spend some time in prayer. Then there was this business of preparing the morning breakfast. It wasn't that easy early on. The room-mates often struggled with a kerosene stove just to make a bread toast. While lighting up the stove was a task in itself, the smell of the kerosene in the toast was another thing that they had to deal with. But this was the best they could manage, a kerosene-smelling bread toast. Manu recollected how just a few months back they had welcomed with joy the advent of the LPG connection at Puzhakkara, relieving his mother from the struggle to rub the blackened pots and pans with ash and sand, mud, and tamarind to take the soot off, often leaving many larger vessels permanently blackened. But it took them some real effort to get that gas connection. They were in the queue for years, had to approach many influential 'worthies' having connections to get the recommendations of Members of Parliament and members of legislature on their petitions, even ministers, to use their good offices for a gas connection. But others less fortunate had to literally sweat it out. And finally when it did come, it was sheer joy for the family. But it came with a price. The designated dealer insisted on the consumer purchasing the gas stove that the dealer was selling for giving him the connection. At times, these worthies also demanded a share of the spoils. And then getting the cylinder refills was a feat in itself by waiting for days and hefty tipping of the delivery man.

Manu began his experiments with other dishes, having observed his mother doing things in the kitchen and having himself helped her out at times. The simplest dish one could attempt was an uppuma*. At first all of his attempts failed, getting the mustard either burnt or undercooked. The wheat was either too watery and overcooked or quite raw! The poor blokes often found themselves in the morning at some small tea shops vending hot fluffy idlies† and gorging on those.

On most evenings Manu and his room-mates went around the city on long walks, chatting, taking a different route each evening, exploring the neighbourhood. They chatted up, sharing their day's troubles, travails, and joys, even as they had a nice walk, taking the opportunity to relax and let go. Usually they ended up in some small restaurant, having their dinner together. At times when only he and Thomas were there, he would be beside his obsession, learning to play the synthesiser! And then occasionally they all went for those cinemas. Hollywood or Bollywood, *Goldfinger* or *The Blue Lagoon*. You name it; they saw it.

Thus the days went by when this languid pace of life received a jolt of reality. There was a call for a strike in their factory. The unions had long been demanding a pay hike, as prices were spiralling and wages had remained quite constant. The country had been facing intermittent droughts and food shortages, thereby raising prices and inflationary pressures. They had other grievances as well which, they accused the management was ignoring. It was difficult times which Manu had to go through, along with his colleagues. The strike dragged out for a few weeks, and management was threatening a lockout. It was not just the enterprise that Manu was working in but the entire industrial belt in that town that was getting restive and confrontational.

Meanwhile much as the many workers saw injustice in the attitude of the factory, things were getting desperate for them. So many of them could not afford to be without wages on which their families survived. There were mounting bills to be taken care of, while the factory was also facing a loss of production. Some workers were inclined to join back with whatever hike the factory was willing to agree, but others were adamant and the deadlock continued. Inevitably his money order was delayed and his family quite

---

*   A porridge made of broken wheat, garnished by green chillies, ginger, fried mustard, and curry leaves.

†   Steamed dumplings of fermented batter of rice and black gram.

concerned. His father wrote to him, saying of the urgent need for money for the special poojas they planned to hold for their village deity at the temple in Puzhakkara at the advice of Thirumeni, the temple priest and astrologer, to ward off evil threatening the family. Manu sighed. He did not know what was going to happen. Things really got worse all around in the town when violence entered the scene in other factories in that town. There were barricades, sit-ins, vociferous protests, pitched battles between workers and policemen, serious injuries to some. The prolonged stalemate and confrontation continued, but fatigue was setting in all around for the strike.

Eventually there was some respite. The local labour commissioner mediated to ensure that the factory began to function with most of the demands of the labour met, eventually allowing him to send his money order. That after a month-and-a-half of hard bargains and sit-ins the matter ended amicably was a miracle of sorts. One old factory hand recounted how earlier, years back, when the workers protested against non-increase in wages, it was followed by violent reactions and clashes resulting in several months of lockouts, loss of wages, and loss of jobs, even suicides. But they were luckier this time, he said. Yet there was a price many paid for this strike. Many marriage engagements got broken off, as families of brides developed cold feet at the prospective grooms' shaky jobs. There were fathers who found the sudden cash crunch ruined the planned marriages of their daughters.

Soon after, Manu decided that he should go home to his native village. He had not been to his native home since his being employed for over a year. Despite the novelty of being in a city and the excitement of the discovery of every little wile of a small-city life, he missed sorely the carefree lounge in the backyard, the swims, and his pals back there! But he could not afford to be there for too long, for the work at the factory had just begun to normalise after resumption. But he went back there with a fully loaded suitcase with something or other for every member of his family. There was a nice new dhoti for his father and a piece of shirting, a nice cotton saree for his mother, and garments for his brother and sister. But his arrival itself was reason enough for celebration at home, for it gave the proud family a lot to brag about in the neighbourhood. The visit was over in a blink really. It was back to Mayapuram, his city of fortunes.

At Mayapuram, the monotony of his routine life chugging on at a leisurely pace was broken by occasional exhibitions, bazaars, and fairs held in the huge

Azad Maidan, an open space that was put to a myriad of uses, where hundreds of people thronged on visits. Manu and his friends would go around sometimes in the evenings while in their evening strolls whenever their time permitted and almost always in the weekends. The bazaars, fairs, or exhibitions were a mix of stalls and makeshift shops of handmade, wooden, bamboo, iron wares, clothes, stone or metal utensils, or earthen wares. Manu and his friends picked up something or other for either their daily use or their families back home. The Azad Maidan came to be so called as in the decades before independence, the place was a site for congregations big and small, to assemble for hearing the passionate and stirring political speeches delivered by the various leaders. Of course, it saw even now a fair bit of political rallies and speeches, especially nearing election. But the city's only other pastime besides these was queueing up before the numerous cinema halls putting out the numerous shows that it ran. Manu and his friends were often seen frequenting the Ajanta or the Ragam Theatres, watching films. TVs were unknown then. Of course, there were the liquor-vending shops, before which the queues were as long. It was ditto at Puzhakkara, where he could see similar long queues before the liquor shops and before the ration shops. He wondered how guys who couldn't afford their rations managed these bottles!

As the whine of machines died down, workers moved over to wash and change from their overalls and working clothes to their own. Then they filed out. Manu also finished his shift and filed out. It was the third year of his arrival in the town of his fortunes. Despite being busy, he felt being gradually ensnared by the routine and the mundane. It was just a dreary reality. Nothing particularly exciting was happening. Walking out of the factory, he let out a sigh of relief. It was the end of another work day. Walking down the lane outside the factory gates along the tall walls, he saw neat handbills interrupted by the occasional colourful poster proclaiming aloud in print and colour, 'The grand Circus has arrived here.' A circus in town? That must be interesting! The last time he saw a circus was when he was quite small years back in the town nearest to his village. It was so exciting and so magical that he had nearly decided to run away with them. And how he wished since that he could get to see a circus again, the breath taking trapeze walk, the beam balancing, the vaults high in the air from swings, the leaps from one swing to another, the mid-air contortions and twists and switches, the jugglers, the balancing on prancing horses, the lions performing, and the dogs jumping the fire hoop; the excitement was endless. But for some strange reason circuses never appeared there thereafter. 'A circus in the town! Then it must be in the Azad Maidan!' he quipped to himself and headed straight to the maidan. That's the only place such an event could be organised.

As he approached the maidan, right before him, he saw, were pitched three huge tents with many smaller ones around them in various stages of erection. Quite a few wagons on wheels with caged lions and tigers in them, an assortment of horses, and elephants were stationed at an end of the ground, with a few tents around these as well. So he saw to himself that the circus indeed had set foot here, and they were busy unpacking and setting themselves up there. The whole maidan was agog with activity, with small knots of people engaged in some activity or other, with tarpaulins, poles, tent pegs, rigs, and all manner of equipment, engrossed in their chores while slowly a small cluster of onlookers were joining them, watching. Circuses could never stop to fascinate him. The very first time (and the only time) he saw it as a child it simply was not enough for him. He watched, mouth agape, at the rows of animals lined up by the side of the main tents, at the performers and performances inside the buffoons; everything there was an endless fascination for him. And then when the knife-throwing would begin, it nearly stretched his nerves taut to its breaking point. He was riveted to the edge of his seat, his eyes intensely glued to the knife thrower. Indeed all the artistes seemed imbued with superhuman abilities, so like some mythological men that mythologies didn't seem so distant. They were so real, came alive to him. He was no longer a mere spectator just watching it but an active participant living the experience, becoming a part of the ensemble. It was like entering a completely new world, a world quite unlike anything he experienced. It was no longer simply a desire to watch something endlessly but to become a part of it.

Now when he saw so many at work at the maidan, all these longings and memories came back to him.

For the next one week or so the whole town was gripped by the arrival of this circus. Circuses, as was their wont, camp at locations for months before moving on and take weeks to set up camp before beginning their shows. They had also had to take the approvals of various authorities before doing so. Having just arrived and proclaimed their arrival loud and clear, they had all around them curious onlookers; among them were Manu and his friends.

Every day after work, Manu and his room-mates and co-workers spent their evenings lounging around the maze of tents, some still under erection, among the animals and the performers as he watched them organise their tents, test their various equipment, practise their routines, test out items, preparing for the shows that were to follow.

It would be a week—that is, by the coming Sunday—before they could begin their shows. The whole town, and Manu among them, was eagerly awaiting the show. In this part of the world, with few distractions, anything new, be it the first day show of a new film or fair or an exhibition, was an event to be celebrated, as were festivals. Crowds, dressed to their best as their station allowed, with wives, kids, grandmas, and grandpas in tow, would queue up to a film or a fair or an exhibition in equal measure. There was another crowd around in all these times and places of small vendors of cotton candies, of roasted, salted, and spiced groundnuts and chickpeas on pushcarts rolling on cycle wheels with hot burning coal stove, constantly roasting groundnuts or chickpeas. There were others vending bananas or mangoes or some pieces of fruit. That was their idea of celebration in this small town.

It was a late Sunday morning as Manu and his friends woke up relaxed, leisurely, a day when they could take life at their own pace. Yet there were domestic chores lined up to do: cleaning up their room, washing their clothes, purchasing groceries, and so on. But this Sunday, finishing these quickly was uppermost in their minds, especially in Manu's, for they had the circus. Today they planned not only to laze around the maidan, watching the final preparations of the circus for their opening, but also to lunch at the restaurant and watch a full evening show of circus! Raju and Thomas by this time, who had been out, were back, barging into the house, yelling, 'Hey, Manu, haven't you dressed up yet? I have just finished even my Sunday mass, you know?' Manu, who was just out of the bathroom and was furiously towelling himself dry, replied, 'Come on, give me few minutes and I will be ready.' And ready they all were in a few minutes' time.

The show being hours away, the friends wandered around the maidan, amidst the various tents, watching jugglers, trapeze artists, and other performers practise, sharpening their skills, while others were doing the other chores preparatory to the beginning of the show. Then they spent time snacking at the various stalls and vendors, then sauntering around.

Up there he noticed a young lass walking the tight rope, balancing a huge pole, slowly and carefully, with head held steady and the hands supple, alert, shifting weight and tilting the weight of the pole from side to side. It was at once an arduous task needing intense concentration, strength, and physical effort as it did finesse and delicate skills, which was made to look so simple, elegant, and easy to the spectator by constant practise. Manu could see that the artiste required exquisite skills, a supple and alert mind and body all at once. They watched her anxious intensity with a sense of thrill at the girl. As soon as the girl reached the other end, she threw down the pole with a smile and giggled while dismounting. The tension built up around Manu and company dissolved instantaneously.

Her confident, impish smile, a fawn-like gait, her dark intense eyes, the neat beautiful ivory of her teeth embedded in sensuous mouth, a dark wispy figure stuck in his mind. 'Lost, are you?' whispered Raju in Manu's ears as he tapped him on his shoulders.

After having spent the morning and noon thus, they went off to have their lunch. After having their repast, they returned to their room for a quick rest and snooze. 'It's getting to be showtime, let's go,' said Manu. Manu and his friends repaired back to the maidan and showed up at the ticket counter. A small queue had already built up and now was getting longer and longer. Manu, Raju, and Thomas stood there waiting for the counter to open up for the matinee. The trio were rather getting restive and impatient. In about half an hour they were at last inside the circus arena. But the queue behind them was indeed quite long and would take at least an hour to get in. As they were at the head of the queue, they got in early and now had a selection of the choicest seats. They spent time locating vantage points amidst the stands to settle down into. Finding one, they zeroed in on a few group of seats and quickly took them. Then looking around with an air of satisfaction and also eager anticipation, they waited for the fascinating spectacle to begin. There was an air of impatience to their wait, as it took a long while, which seemed longer with their eager restlessness, for the stands to fill up and for the show to finally begin. And what a show it was for Manu, a mesmerising, memorable evening! But for the whole evening his gaze seemed to be on the lass.

As the show ended and the evening had set in, the trio, sauntering along the maidan and the streets, found their way back home, almost sad that this eventful and eagerly awaited Sunday had come to an end. But in Manu's mind, only the images of that pair of dark fawn-like eyes, that open mouth with luscious bow-like lips opening up like a flower to reveal the beautifully arranged pearls of her teeth set against an oval copperish brown face, the mischievous smile, the aquiline nose and nose ring, the flowing black hair, the full bosom on the lissom, flowing lines of the dainty hourglass figure of a girl remained. She was an irresistible mixture of poetry, mysterious allure, magnetic presence, and delicate fragrance. Throughout that show, his eyes only looked for her, drawn to her as if by some irresistible power.

All the three were now repairing back lost in their own thoughts stepped into a restaurant. Slowly the hot steaming smell of food, whetting their appetite, they ate in silence, lost in their own thoughts and in savouring the food before them.

The friends thereafter slowly repaired to their lodgings. Soon the friends changed, unrolled their beddings, and prepared for sleep. Manu lay down and he too was getting into a slumber. The cool night, deep and dark, had awakened to welcome the first faint milky glow of a half-moon. From somewhere in the distance wafted in the soothing strains of a hauntingly beautiful melody that grew upon him little by little, till it possessed him completely. It led him on like a child lovingly, tenderly, gently by the hand. On and on was he led; on and on he went, by the shimmering brook, over the soft silky grass beneath the star-spangled, dark, deep-blue expanse of the night sky. With the night breeze caressing him, he was gliding on, slow and steady, savouring the gentle fragrance of the mesmerising night. Rows and rows of tall trees, flowery bushes, shrubs stood in their beds, silently swaying ever so gently, a little drunkenly, dizzily, their silence broken only by the gushing flow of the brook. The curved backs of the hills and ridges showed as dark silhouettes in the distance in the moonlight, as a wavy undulating line, broken here and there by clumps of foliage bobbing in the caressing breeze. He strolled on and on till he came to a wide glen by the side of a tree; he sat down, a little tired, still dazzled by this bewitching night. Soon sleep, sweet sleep, took over. He slept on in the lap of paradise while the half-moon shone on him.

Then he awoke with a start. His nostrils were filled with terrible smoke even as his barely open eyes burned. Nothing except a diffused bright light was visible around. He tried getting up but found his hands tied up behind, as were his legs bound. The brook, the meadows, the moon, the breeze, the distant mountains and stars, nothing was there to be seen; all had vanished in that dark grey of the smoke.

Manu sat bolt upright, violently wrenched from his sleep. It was still too dark outside, too early in the morning. Sweating profusely, he tried hard to make sense of it all. Overcome by fatigue, confusion, and sleep, he once again dozed off, still wondering at it all. It was the beginning of his dreams and nightmares.

It was the morning of yet another Monday that he got up to the beginning of another workman's week. And like all Mondays, the dread of another week's work or school awaited Manu. And like all Mondays, the mind was unwilling to yield to the pace of a work life, where the body, still languorously dwelling on the weekend past, perforce was preparing itself for the laborious wrench of the future week, dragging along the drooping holiday spirits of the past week. But the thought of spending the evenings at the circus electrified his being into a whirl of action. He forgot all about the dream and that it was Monday. The day whizzed past in a swift blur; the factory, the shifts, its responsibilities, all seemed such a trifling bother.

As the sirens signalled the end of the shift, Manu's footsteps followed his thoughts swiftly towards the maidan. With all the cares of the day now behind him, his mind and body feeling lighter, his spirits energised, gay, and soaring, as he contemplated of the shows at the circus coming up before him and, of course, of that indelible face. They were busy, the circus people, that is, although Mondays were a no-show day. But it was a day for rest and relaxation, renewal, experimentation, taking care of the animals, cleaning up, setting right the camp and its facilities. As Manu went into the arena, he saw the circus ringmaster busy with the lions. He was trying to teach a few lions some new tricks as also to instil some discipline. Cracking his whip, he made an older full-grown lion sit on a huge stool then get him down to run and jump through a ring of fire, and then get a lioness to do this. A young lion was to follow the same routine. Much as the ringmaster coaxed and cajoled the lion to sit, the lion simply refused to budge and oblige. He seemed so reluctant a pupil, somehow defiant and scared at once. When the ringmaster finally got him to sit, the lion barely sat for a fleeting moment before it bounded off. The jump through the ring of fire was no show altogether. But the ringmaster wouldn't let go of him. He persisted in cracking his whip even as the animal stubbornly resisted by continuing to be seated on that perch. But the incessant cracking of the whip got under his skin, making him restless. Suddenly all hell broke loose as the lion jumped off, knocking down the stool; roaring, he ran around the enclosure, even as the other animals in the cage moved away from their appointed places, agitated. The ringmaster was completely caught unawares. Even as he attempted to get a handle on the things, the young lion, finding an opening in the barred enclosure, came out into the open arena amidst the stands under the canopy. There was utter consternation as people around ran helter-skelter for their lives. It was a most unique and hair-raising experience. It was at once exciting and unnerving. At first he stood his ground bravely, but as moments ticked by, his resolution melted. Discretion got the better of his bravery as he too made his way from the spot, retracting to the safety of one of those smaller tents, peeping out from the safety of the tent, watching keenly the commotion outside.

It was a good hour or so before the wayward lion was finally shut in its cage, all the while with Manu watching. As Manu watched the drama, still peeping out from the safety of the tent, a gentle tap on his shoulders startled him. Alarmed, he turned around, only to be stunned. He hadn't quite bothered to look into the tent to check who or what was inside it. Indeed, if he had looked in a few moments back, he would have found none there. But now there was before him, staring at him, a smiling, hauntingly arresting face with a hint of a question in her wide open and sympathetic eyes. 'Scared, were you?' asked she, even as she motioned him to take a seat and said 'Please do'. For a moment he looked on, open mouthed, before coming to his senses. 'Oh yes!' he stammered, averting his eyes and hastily running his eyes around the tent, taking in the suspended bulb that lit the rather spacious interiors, revealing a couple of cots, baskets, three easy chairs spread out, with huge boxes in the corners, while various kinds of costumes were hanging from the lines at the sides of the tent.

He then turned his eyes nervously to her oval face, meeting her mirthful eyes, taking in her ivory white teeth set in a luscious mouth, curving into an elfin grin. For a few seconds they were lost in each other. 'What's your name?' he asked her, breaking the enveloping silence.

'Pawana,' replied the girl. 'But my father calls me Roohani.'

'Were you resting?' he queried.

'No, not exactly, we were just preparing for the evening practice, and you see this happened. Now we should be into it anytime,' she said.

'Can I watch you all practise?' he continued eagerly.

'Why not?' she replied. The rehearsals began and he watched, absorbed. It was eleven in the night before he returned home, tired, but absolutely radiant. This was a night that was to remain eternally etched in his mind for the whole of his life, and the maidan became the centre of his universe, his life now. But his friends were a bit indignant. 'Where were you?' they asked, as they prepared to go to sleep. 'We were actually waiting for you to come for supper but guessed you must have gone off to that circus.' Manu was sheepishly apologetic.

As each day unfolded, he eagerly looked forward to the evenings spent in the company of the circus and Pawana. Their companionship grew on, she a circus girl and he a factory workman. In her company he slowly got to know the person that she was and about the circus life. Slowly he learnt that her young face belied the wisdom that she had about life, and almost all in the circus was in some way related to her. She was a veritable storehouse of fables, tales, and folklores, mysterious happenings full of age-old and native wisdom. She regaled him often with the varied experiences that she and her group encountered in the course of their journey criss-crossing the country.

After some time he learnt with some surprise that she and her circus folk were actually part of a lost tribe, with a king and his people who had lost their kingdom centuries back and accursed to wander around. But ever since her great-grandfather decided on taking on this circus, their lives changed for the good with hope and happiness coming in. Her father was actually a king and leader of this entire ensemble. But the number of languages she knew and the range of anecdotes that she had to tell were the ones that often kept him gripping when he was not admiring her practising the skills. Often she related to him the happenings of the past. She once recalled how one elder among them, while she was still a kid, related a terrible nightmare he had one night. He had a vision of a great disaster befalling the denizens of that city. He saw in his dreams women wailing, children shrieking, terror-stricken people wandering around. But he could not quite explain the cause. Soon enough, the city was enveloped in a thick blanket of monsoon clouds. People were filled with joy at the onset of rain. At long last there was precious water for parched crops and dry throats. The prospects of an excellent crop and consequent prosperity loomed in the minds of people. But little did they know this was a rain so apocalyptic as to set another Noah on an ark. It rained and rained and rained. The water poured, poured, and poured down from the heavens like there was no tomorrow. Soon enough the entire town was enveloped in a sheet of water—nay, floated in water. Meanwhile, on the advice of that wise elder, the entire circus had packed up, leaving at the earliest. It was a month before the water subsided, by which time a few hundred people had lost their lives, and several thousand their houses and belongings.

Then there were the premonition of the dangers to the circus itself. The old man had felt terribly uneasy a few days before the event yet unable to pinpoint what the danger was. Everyone in the circus became caution personified lest they should by carelessness let themselves down. Alas, all this could not prevent a great fire breaking out in the circus. Terrified animals that were outside, not tethered or caged, ran away from the flames. But the caged lions and tigers roared frenetically. Panic struck one and all. 'The circus people tried saving the lives of the animals, themselves, and their belongings as much as possible. The locals also chipped in,' recalled Pawana. All lives and most of the things were saved. But still some, including the animals, were injured. Ultimately the fire was put out, but not before having burnt down a few tents and shaken every one of them to the core. Manu listened to these with great intent. Pawana thus told him how she learnt to understand her own dreams and learn to interpret them. What would she make of his dreams, he wondered? Slowly he was becoming a permanent fixture at the circus. His friends too were occasional visitors, but they slowly were getting the wind of what he was into and were giving up on him. He could remember it was yet another Sunday morning when Thomas had already got up, folded up his bed sheets and the mat, brushed his teeth, done his toilet, and finished his bath as well. It was his turn today to prepare the breakfast. And this he proceeded to do pretty swiftly—i.e., preparing toast, setting out the jam, slicing and dicing the onions finely and the green chillies and ginger, and tearing up the curry leaves, adding a pinch of salt, breaking the eggs, and stirring the concoction up before pouring it onto a hot saucepan smeared with coconut oil. Meanwhile, the milk was on a boil, nearly spilling over. Hurriedly he removed the pail from the fire and set down the tea kettle instead, setting the water to boil before spooning in a couple of spoonfuls of tea leaves and taking the kettle away from the heat and tamping down the stove. After a little, while he doused out the flame from the stove, sprinkling some water. And then triumphantly he had roared 'Get up, you lazybones' to Manu and Raju. 'Breakfast is ready, get up and have it, I must be off to the church,' he said.

Manu, slowly waking up, had a sudden blast of the smell of kerosene to contend with. 'Oh! That stupid kerosene.' He felt dizzy with its smell. 'What's it for today?' he asked lazily.

'Toast and omelette,' he said.

'Not again!' moaned Manu. 'That dry stuff that sticks into the throat?' The smell of kerosene and this toast together was too much for him. Back home he had never seen eggs or such like. It was forbidden at home. If they came to know, they would skin him alive. Neither was bread something they usually had, although there was no taboo about it 'The easiest thing to make in the world, eh!' Manu quipped.

'Then make yourself something better!' shot back Thomas. In a while the three settled down to enjoying a cup of hot tea and the crisp toast and the omelette that was waiting on the plate. Though dry, the toast was done crisp and tasty, and the omelette too was good. Definitely the days of burnt toast and food were behind them. In between taking bites of the toast and taking a sip of the tea, Thomas then turned to Manu. 'Eh, Manu, we are planning to go to Punnar Dam. Coming along?'

Manu looked up and said, 'It's good,' but didn't show any specific enthusiasm.

But Thomas couldn't resist poking fun at him. 'So it's that circus girl, eh?'

Manu flushed crimson. 'Oh, nothing of that sort!' he said, a trifle irritated at how he had betrayed himself.

'Well then, both of you wait till I return back from the church, and then we move on.'

The three friends roamed around the dam, in the gardens, admiring the verdant environs of the dam, but Manu's thought(s) wandered time and again to the circus and Pawana. The gardens were all splendid, and beautiful yet somehow felt incomplete. All the while during this sojourn, his mind was constantly wandering back to the circus. It was night by the time they returned, so Manu had to altogether give a miss to the circus that Sunday. Manu was on pins and needles the whole of Monday, eagerly waiting to finish his day's work to get to his circus.

In the evening as he stepped into the circus arena, the eyebrows of several of those he knew went up, and so did their hands in gestures that indicated the question 'Where were you?'. By now the circus guys were used to his almost daily presence that his absence began to be seen as some kind of aberration. Seating himself by the side of the arena, well beyond the innermost circle, he watched the jugglers and trapeze artist practise swinging, juggling, balancing, changing course mid-air, with their lives as well. On one side along a rope was his favourite funambulist testing, sharpening her skills.

He got up, still keenly watching this circus for life, and walked closer towards Pawana's corner. There he stood, with upturned head, watching her, as she balanced on the rope fiercely focusing all her attention on the rope and the pole she carried. Step by step she progressed cautiously. Pawana was already a quarter of the way across the rope when the pole in her hand tipped a wee bit to a side. Her body caught off balance, swayed, and shook her feet. As all her body swayed from side to side, looking to balance the dipping of the pole, this further amplified the oscillation of the pole from side to side, caught in a vicious cycle, getting more and more violent in no time. The least hint of trouble to Pawana sent Manu scurrying towards the arena. But in a moment the heavy pole was prised out of her hand and fell heavily on the rope and bounced off even as she tumbled out, off balance, crashing to the ground. Despite the rope not being that high and even with her trained instincts, Pawana fell fast and hard and awkwardly on the floor, with no trampoline to break the fall. The damage was done before anyone could act. She cried out in pain, clutching at her foot, sitting on the floor, as Manu and others bent around her, anxiously enquiring and examining as to what transpired while she doubled up in agony, pointing out to her ankle before groaning, passing out. Manu and others quickly carried her over to a corner of the arena. The chief of the circus and her father also came in there quickly, hearing of the commotion. Some cold water was brought and splashed on her face, and she was brought around. But her face was a picture of pain, and despite efforts, she was unable to stand on her feet. Soon it was decided that she should be taken to a hospital, where she was bundled off to in an autorickshaw.

The doctors decided that for the next two months Pawana's foot had to be in splints. Naturally, she would be out of action. But what's more, they said it may take a couple of months more before she would make a complete recovery. Manu now spent most of his time outside of the factory by her side, helping, comforting her, and keeping company and came to be expected by those in the circus that Manu would be by her side. Most days he would pick up some fruit or snack for her as he visited in the evening. Till the show started at matinee, she would be helped by others in the circus to sit by and watch others perform or practise. But when the show was on, she was left all alone, quite bored. By evening she would be impatiently waiting for Manu. As soon as he saw him, her lips would break into a welcoming smile. He would then help her to sit on her cot while he pulled up a stool or a chair lying by. And then they would go on and on, chit-chatting till it was broken by the entry of somebody into the tent, usually at the end of the evening show. Only then, becoming conscious of his own room and friends, would Manu seek to depart, reminded of the factory on the morrow, and reluctantly bid Pawana good-bye. For once Pawana felt quite low. 'How I wish I was out of this stupid cast sooner! There is so much that I miss,' she grumbled.

But for Manu, it was a bit mixed. It was a golden opportunity for him to get closer to her and know her better. 'But if this didn't happen, we wouldn't be sitting close to each other,' said Manu.

'Ah, that's there,' replied Pawana. It was during these days he came to know the mysteries around her. She recounted the strange events surrounding her tribe and her own birth that seemed like some fable. As per the soothsayers of her tribe, the circumstances and the timing attending her birth were so unique that they denied her very existence. According to them, she was no human but a divine spirit having a human form, coming into this world for a purpose. She said that they were the descendants of the wind god. One of her great-grandmothers was worshipped as a living saint. She had great healing powers. Anybody coming with illness or sorrow touched and blessed by her found the illness and sorrow soon disappearing. In the centuries and decades before her appearance, there was constant strife in the lands the tribe were roaming around. But soon after her birth there was a miraculous turnaround. Slowly the kings and the denizens in these lands realised the futility of war and strife; one by one the lands that she stepped into decided to abjure war and embrace peace. As a little girl, she saw an old woman struggling to even get up. Like all small children, she ran to that old lady, smiled at her, and touched her. That old lady embraced the little child. Within days and weeks, the old one was found to have a real change in her condition. She found her strength returning to her little by little, and within a few weeks found herself walking on her own two feet. That old lady recounted to all and sundry that cared to listen how that embrace of that little girl changed her condition. Soon people from all walks of life, with all kinds of ailments, came to seek the healing touch of this little child. As she grew up, so did the numbers go up, till she began to be worshipped as a living saint. In the time after her death, temples and churches began coming up in those lands. Even now her family, in fact, the entire circus, paid an annual visit to that ancestral church, the original one where the saint had been first deified. Pawana's family legend has it that once a rival king of another land, as did the inhabitants, behaved ill with her ancestors as they passed through that land for a certain pilgrimage. 'Within days of that, there were raging storms and ceaseless rain. It rained and rained destruction till at last the people realised their wrongs and came to my great great-grandparents to seek their forgiveness. It is then the storms stopped and everything turned to normal.'

Pawana recounted her father and grandma tell her that in the few months before her birth, the sun was blazing, with hot and dry winds blowing about. Fears loomed around of a drought, with drying ponds and rivers threatening famine and devastation. People had given up hope that the year would see decent rain or any rain. And then she was born. It rained and rained like there was no end. In the months that followed, there was nothing but surplus of crops, overflowing granaries in the entire neighbourhood they were in. She said with some pride and happiness that everywhere their circus landed, people welcomed them, as the circus always brought on them only happiness and well-being.

Two months after the accident the plaster cast was removed, rather much earlier than the doctors had originally envisaged. But she was far from ready for resuming her circus routines. It would take still many more weeks of gradually increased walking to bring her feet to normal. Every day she would eagerly wait for Manu to come, and together they undertook long walks to rehabilitate step by step her feet to normalcy. Initially their walks were confined within the circus. But later they began venturing outside the circus too. On some days they took a leisurely walk along the main shopping bazaar of that town, with shops of all kinds lined up on either side and taking a peek at them. On more than one occasion they had been to the cinemas, stealing some privacy in the process. How he wished at times that they were left alone, marooned somewhere on an island. Many times they walked along the remnants of the walls of the old fort that enveloped the town.

One day they decided to walk west towards an old Shiva temple there. They walked alongside rows of old homes set on individual plots of land, with walls along the street, entrances with gabled and tiled roofing with two-part wooden doors, one set opening below the centre and the other pair above, which gave a view of the house to those outside and a view of the street to those inside the homes and the porch. These homes had gabled, tiled roofs, with very wide porches, with a large open courtyard with plants and surrounded by tall coconut palms and mango and jackfruit trees all reminiscent of his Puzhakkara. Towards the end of the line of grand mansions came a vast expanse of fields. As they walked along the street, they looked up at the sky that was slowly turning crimson against the backdrop of a setting sun even as a crescent moon appeared a little above the horizon. 'Wonderful sandhya (twilight)!' exclaimed Manu even as Pawana was left gazing intently at the sky.

'Yes, see that crescent moon and the evening star. How beautiful!'

Suddenly Manu remembered. 'It must be the time for the evening deeparadhana (or worship by lights), let's hurry,' he said aloud to Pawana. In the distance they could see the massive walls of the sprawling temple complex enclosing them, set amidst the fields.

Manu and Pawana approached the temple now with some sense of urgency. They hurried along and reached close to the entrance, where, leaving behind their footwear, they entered the temple barefoot, hurrying towards the sanctum sanctorum. Even as they reached the sanctum sanctorum, bells began ringing, signalling the start of the rituals at dusk. There before them they saw the deity illuminated from behind by a circular mirror made of angled mirror pieces fused and spread out like a Japanese fan, with its multiple reflections of the oil lamps. The priest, standing a little bent, moved a multi-leaved bronze lamp deftly with the roll of his wrists and arms, weaving beautiful arcs and ovals before the god. There was hardly any crowd at all in there. Pawana and Manu stood in prayer for a while then partook of the flowers and a pinch of ash offered as prasad, or blessings, of the lord, before perambulating around the sanctorum around the deity. Then they came out into the outer peripheral cobbled stone path to have another round. The sky had turned further red, with the trees and foliage showing up as dark silhouettes as a picturesque backdrop against an illuminated sky with streaks of clouds here and there. They finished their rounds, keenly watching the twilight sky, observing the stars one by one brightening in the darkening night sky, divining their destinies. Thus watching, they sat down by the huge square platform built around a peepal tree, gazing long and hard at the sky, their thoughts far gone into those twinkling, ever-brightening stars in the ever-darkening sky.

In the descending silence of the night, a breeze gently wafted past, slightly rustling the leaves of the trees. Distracted, Manu threw a casual glance by his side across Pawana. His blood froze. 'Put up your feet!' screamed Manu, and Pawana obeyed instantaneously, reflexively. And in a flash he gathered her in his arms, fiercely pulling her over to his side just in time to see with bated breath a cobra slithering down the burrow beneath at the foot of the platform on which they sat. 'Phew! That was close,' he said aloud. 'Thank God!' he added again in relief and stepped down and forward quickly with one hand held around Pawana's waist, nearly lifting her off the ground and quickly dragging her towards him, getting both as far away from the tree as possible. Walking over quickly, they came close to the huge entrance of the massive walls of the temple compound and stopped.

The sense of urgency now having gone, they proceeded at a more leisurely pace. 'Sighting a snake means a lot of wealth and prosperity, they say,' observed Pawana, breaking the silence. 'By God's grace, nothing happened to us. A snake adorns Shiva as a necklace. Maybe we should once visit the temples dedicated to snake worship.' They strolled along the earthen road alongside the long walls of the temple on one side and interspersed by small shrubs and boughs and lined by trees, along with bamboo fencing, on the other. Intermittently they could see small paddy fields and vegetable patches by the side of the road. The trees swaying in the gentle breeze made dilating shadowy silhouettes against the dark sky and sinking crescent moon.

Pointing to the fields, Manu broke the silence. 'You know, Pawana, my grandma used to tell me how, on full-moon nights, she had seen as a child white bulls or bullocks roam around such fields, which, she would say, were actually men practicing black magic, turned into these animals by tying magical amulets or inserting a pinch of enchanted ash along the ears by the side of the earlobes. They lay in wait, sometimes even turn into ash gourds, to beguile poor farmers in their huts or guarding their crops from raised bamboo watchtower to take their lives. But alert farmers could distinguish them and had them hacked down, which by mornings turned into the real men, dead. It was said pious and good men could easily make out these evil beings.'

'Do you believe in them?' Pawana asked him, her large orbs turning on his face, seriously searching his face for an answer.

Manu sighed, taking a deep breath, shrugging his shoulders, and replied, 'I don't know really, sometimes the night and the shadows, the thick green cover, everything around there back home appeared so magical anything could happen. Maybe it's true.' He shrugged his shoulders again rather sceptically.

But Pawana shook her head vigorously in disagreement. 'No, no, the stories are true!' she protested. 'I have heard such stories from my grandpa and other wise old elders. I felt I even saw a couple of them while camping around the jungles.' There was silence as both walked down the road.

The crescent moon was now dirty yellow, barely visible, being close to horizon.

At the first opportunity in the following week, Manu asked her out to the nearby Punnar Dam and the garden surrounding it, which he had visited some months back. Away they went, hand in hand among the bushes, flowers, and trees and along the sides of the reservoirs, slipping into the by-lanes around the lonely wooded spots around the reservoir. There they unburdened their hearts in ways they never could at the circus or in their long walks. It just gushed and gurgled out of their eager hearts, pit-a-pat. 'Did you ever imagine that you, a circus girl, could ever be so involved with someone outside the circus?'

'I never thought anyone outside would be even interested in us, in our nomadic existence, always on the move, never sticking to a place,' shot back Pawana.

'But that's what makes you and your life even more interesting. You are tied to nothing, always free. Tell me, how many places have you been to till now, all these years?' asked Manu to Pawana.

She thought for a while, counting on her fingers, and then said, 'Twelve that I remember, but my mother tells me that we have been to over twenty places since I was born.'

'Well then, have you enjoyed being in these places?'

'Oh yes, very much! Each place is different from the other, so excitingly different, from near deserts to mountainous terrain, the people, the dress, their habits, the cuisine, everything is so refreshingly different! People variously call me as Pawana, my father calls me Ruhani or Rukhsana, Roxain or Esther by some. At one place I was called Athar!'

'How about the circus?'

'I just love it, just love the excitement of each day's preparation, performance, the experimentation and execution, the high and lows, that sense of oneness. We are just one big family, so close to each other! What about you?'

'My parents wanted me to be an engineer, and so I have become one and am working in a factory.'

'We have somebody in the circus who puts up all the lights, sets them right, looks after all that is electrical.'

'Besides, I can play the guitar too. That means I can be useful in your circus!'

It was already dark and the stars shone in the sky above as Manu and Pawana prepared to leave the dam and the park. They first returned to the circus, and then Manu departed to his room. As Manu entered the lodgings . . .

'So we have all become extras, eh?' exclaimed Thomas.

'Ah! It just got a little late, that's all.'

'Is that all? What about our dinner? It was your turn, do you remember? So should we all be going to bed hungry today, eh?' queried Thomas a little sternly.

'Oh, I am terribly sorry, just forgot!' stammered Manu.

'Forgotten, have you?' said Thomas with a frown, exchanging a furtive glance with Raju, and a hint of a smile was breaking out at the corners of his mouth.

'I will take you out to dinner,' sputtered Manu.

Booming laughter broke out between Raju and Thomas. 'OK, OK, Lover Boy, we have already prepared the dinner. We know how lovelorn you are these days, poor chap,' said Thomas with a touch of mock sympathy. For the next hour it was a free-for-all leg-pulling at its best. That night, Manu lay in bed, thinking about Pawana, about the entire day in that park and dam, recalling every moment of that intense, passionate, and happy time spent together. His eyelids were slowly drooping heavily with sleep as these images crossed his mind. He could see them going hand in hand, winding along past the hills, riding over great sand dunes into splendid cities that seemed to emerge out of nowhere amidst those oceans of sand. In these cities appeared colourful people living in this city with magnificent spires, majestic buildings, and beautiful gardens and fountains. There were tall, gaunt bronzed men in colourful headgears and curvaceous moustaches, and dusky-hued women in flowing ankle-length sequinned and embroidered skirts and covered from shoulders to wrists in huge silver bracelets and silver nose- and earrings. The people seemed tough yet friendly. There, amidst the heat and dust, they found a vocation by the day and bliss by the night under the starlit sky. Some toiled in the fields while other weaved, dyed, and stitched clothes, fashioned pots, utensils. Smiths and craftsmen made tools, weapons, or jewellery; herdsmen tended to huge flocks of sheep in a land of dunes punctuated by briars, hemps, and cacti. There were then people carting water or moving things around on camels, found aplenty in these parts. For months they stopped there, entertaining as conjurors or jugglers, revelling in the lives of the people over there, sharing their laughter and tears. But yonder beckoned, and off they went, on and on, till they came upon the foothills of a mighty range of mountains. There amongst glens, trees, and flowers and meadows, they found an abode, most wondrous amidst these enchanting environs, the mesmerising sky, trees, and foliage. They built a small cottage. There they gathered honey, berries, and fruits; foraged for roots, savoured the fragrance, freshness of nature, of the soil, of the water, of the air; marvelled at the grandeur of the mountain peaks. The endless expanse of mountain slopes covered in deodars, pines suddenly opening into clearings of meadows and brooks or thick forests and steep valleys seemed to hold countless mysteries in its embrace. The more they explored, the more they appeared, it seemed, to hold countless mysteries in its embrace, drawing them further into them. It enticed them further and farther and beyond the distant ranges of mountains. And then while atop a mountain, while he stood gazing, lost in contemplation of the magnificent scene before them, a raging storm and blizzard took them by sheer surprise and fear. It howled and hummed for hours on end, when Manu and Pawana were huddled crouching behind a rock. But the howling winds so froze him that he was barely conscious when it stopped. He did not quite know when the storm stopped. But when he came to, his eyes and hands searched for Pawana. Where was she? Was she not by his side? She was very much in his embrace, or so he thought. Where was she? All he could see around was a vast expanse of snow, a sheet of snow. When Manu woke up from his slumber, it was another work day; the mountains and the meadows had all melted. There were just his room-mates, all sleeping around in curious postures, making a curious pattern, and a room largely in disarray. Then he looked up at the clock. It was already very late, and a busy day lay ahead. He called out to his mates even as he got up and rushed to the toilet, tugging away at the towel that hung from a line in the corner of the room. Today there was time only for the toast and milk, nothing else for breakfast. None of them quite enjoyed this dry toasted piece of bread or 'modern bread' from the market. For Manu, even bread was a novelty, and the modern bread was at least better, more 'modern' than the bread that used to be available in the local bakery, a version of over-fermented sour loaves that gave off that sour smell from afar, which was sometimes derisively referred to as that vile stuff in his native home. These days, after three years and more experimenting, usually they had settled down to rasam and rice or uppuma on weekdays. Bread was always a standby, readily available, even if least preferred. On weekends, if they could muster the time and patience, they could make more elaborate preparations. After finishing their toast and milk, they hurriedly dressed up and left for the factory.

The day's work over, Manu, as was his wont these days, went across to the circus. Pawana was watching, not being yet quite fit for performance of the routine that others in her group were putting up. As soon as she sighted him, her eyes lit up. Together they quietly repaired to a tent a little afar. 'So . . . ?' she began.

'Well?' he responded, moving over with her hand, reaching up to hold her. For a minute they looked at each other, deep into each other's eyes. 'I saw a dream yesterday night,' began Manu softly.

'What was that?' she enquired anxiously.

'I saw that we both were travelling on a boat over the seas, rough and stormy, sailing by night under the stars and clouds and rain and on days under the sun or through storms, going across oceans to distant lands of immense prosperity and wisdom, over barren deserts, dusty and hot, yet housing splendid cities and populated by colourful and hospitable and peaceful people'.

'And then?'

'We went on and on till we came to a vast, tall stretch of mountains, so vast and great that it seemed endless, its peak lost in the clouds and rarely visible. Amidst the splendour of nature we settled into a small cottage, where we lived for a while. Then there was a snowstorm and then you . . . vanished!'

'It's wacky.'

'I just keep imagining things maybe,' he said with a wry smile. Manu, for all his bravado, was indeed ill at ease. Both he and Pawana had by now realised, though never put in words, how much they were becoming inseparable, loathed parting company. But Pawana did not laugh. Her eyes were full of anxious concern; she looked at him and shook her head.

'We must pray to a goddess.' Her voice sounded so earnest, even a little urgent, that in spite of himself he involuntarily reacted.

'There is a place of worship, a divine mother, nearby in the hills.' There was a long silence. It was tacitly agreed that they would go there at the earliest opportunity. Manu managed a double shift on Friday and an extra day off on Saturday for his sojourn. That, of course, did not go unnoticed.

As Pawana and Manu set off early morning for the journey in a public bus, their minds were in contemplation of the shrine that they were to visit. On normal days it was around four hours' journey which ended in a hillock in another nearby town. Manu nearly dozed off after a while, but Pawana seemed vigilant as ever, gazing at the countryside scene that was presented before her as the bus rolled at a leisurely pace. Three hours into the journey, the bus came to a halt with a jolt. Manu awoke with a start and found out that the bus had developed a flat tyre. Most of the men were asked to disembark to lighten the load and have the problem fixed with a spare pair of tyres.

In about an hour they again set forth. Pawana was strangely silent and grave looking. She didn't seem happy with the way things went. The bus had run for nearly an hour along the road as the hillocks that they were to have climbed came into sight. Even as the bus was approaching those hillocks before them, they saw an agitated crowd waving sticks and throwing stones, shouting slogans, and waving flags on the way. They saw a few of the vehicles ahead of them and by the side of the road subjected to their fury. The driver brought the bus to a dead halt. Turning around, he said, 'It's dangerous to get ahead. We should turn back.' Apparently, it was the supporters of a party one of whose leaders was just convicted for some crime. They could never accept that their leader could ever be guilty. As though on cue, the crowds were advancing towards the bus as they espied it. The driver made a rapid turn and somehow managed to turn it back along the highway.

Alas, just as they were getting close to their destination, they had to turn back only because of this mob. Somebody who had a transistor in his hand called out and said to all the passengers in the bus that a serious law-and-order problem had broken out around the places here and in Mayapuram as well. The driver, driving back, stopped the bus at a roadside restaurant an hour-and-a-half later. It was already well past noon, and everyone hungry, it was decided that they should have their lunch here. Pawana and Manu ate their lunch in deep contemplation as to the next step in this unexpected mess they found themselves in. The radio that was blaring songs suddenly interrupted for the news at 2 p.m. It said that there were disturbances throughout the state on account of the arrest of the said leader, and the situation was particularly grave near Mayapuram. The bus passengers slowly ate their meal, discussing the situation. One said, 'If that leader has done such a crime, how could he claim to be leader? Then the law should take its course.'

'What a terrible situation! My plan to reach my nephew's house for a betrothal ceremony has been put paid to. I do not know what will happen to that ceremony. My brother too had to reach there. I do not know what will happen. What do we do now? How will we reach back our homes?'

The passengers were preparing to depart.

Just then a wailing child distracted their attention. The hungry infant needed milk, and the group decided to stay back. Unfortunately, the restaurant had run out of milk. As it would take a while for the afternoon supply of fresh milk to arrive from the next village, one of the passengers went around the few rows of houses behind the restaurant to see if any of them had some milk in these households, having many cattle in their backyards. Finally some milk was managed. It was boiled and sugared, before being cooled and fed to the infant by the mother by teaspoonfuls before the baby became quiet. 'How I wish to teach these politicians a lesson. It's my grandson's first birthday. We had to reach there by today for the ceremony tomorrow. What will we tell our daughters-in-law and their family!' said another middle-aged lady.

It was not very long before the futility of waiting in this small village dawned on all and, in particular, the bus driver. He had a job to do and that was to get the bus back to its depot safely. The bus began its return journey in right earnest within three hours; at dusk, it reached the outskirts of Mayapuram. Even from afar outside the town, it was evident that things were really grave here. From a distance, two ambassador cars and a public bus were seen in various stages of combustion. There were burning heaps of tyres set as blockades to the highway. Then there were various groups of people armed with cycle chains and long sticks, menacingly milling around. The bus was now plodding on at a cautious pace and traversing through what appeared as a deserted stretch of open fields on either side when a sudden hail of stones greeted them. Though most of them crashed at the sides of the bus, he suddenly accelerated and sped through that stretch and took a diversion by what appeared to be a small street, entering a residential area of houses, where the fields ended. 'This should be safer,' the driver said quite aloud so that everybody may hear. By the highway the Azad Maidan was two kilometres away. But the route the bus had taken was actually skirting the centre of the town and circling around it in a manner that though they were in the heart of the town, radially it was not any closer to the maidan but in another part of the town. But a kilometre-and-a-half into it, the bus found there were further groups of people milling around menacingly. The driver stopped, knowing it would be foolhardy to proceed without damage. He accordingly told every passenger to get out before all hell broke loose. Pawana and Manu got out, and Manu led her, gripping her by her arm to the by-lanes of these homes that he had become all too familiar with in the while that he had spent in this town. Manu and Pawana went hand in hand, winding through these back lanes and by-lanes. All shops and establishments had long shut shop, anticipating this trouble, and there were few that had borne the brunt of it, and there was much evidence of destruction left on the streets. Anxious and desperate, Manu and Pawana went on slithering through the darkening streets where even the street lamps had not been spared the fury of these marauding bunches of men.

It was well into the night before they managed to reach Manu's home. His friends were waiting quite anxiously as he reached there with Pawana. The news having spread like wildfire by afternoon, the friends had left the factory as soon as it was lunchtime. Things from then on went from bad to worse, explained Thomas. The news bulletins in the radios painted a grimmer picture of the situation than what Manu and Pawana saw in the streets. All of them knew that it would be infeasible to go to the maidan and get to the circus, at least for today. It was clear that Pawana had to stay there for the night. A lady in the midst of so many guys was unthinkable, normally. But in these circumstances, nobody had the time to even care who was where. Every home in the neighbourhood was shut tight with even their windows bolted fast. Of course, that did not mean that nobody would have got wind of this lady in this room, but at least for the moment nobody would trouble them, and later on, it could be explained maybe as some relative or a cousin and so on. But then, how Pawana could be accommodated today in this one room and kitchen was a question bothering everyone's mind.

The boys hesitantly offered Pawana the things that Manu and the friends usually had for supper. Usually any leftover rice was actually immersed in some quantity of water which the next day served as a nice appetiser with buttermilk and a pinch of salt, as the slightly fermented rice had some fizz. But today, thanks to Pawana, there would be none. There was some rasam* to go with the rice besides some fried okras. The radio in the meanwhile was their constant companion. The curfew was on for at least twenty-four hours, the radio said. That meant the maidan was out of bounds at least till tomorrow evening. How will the people in the circus know that she was here safe and sound? There was nothing that could be done. But in the meanwhile, the dinner having been finished, the big question was where they were to sleep. The friends conferred amongst themselves and decided that Pawana would sleep in the one room they had while all others would adjust themselves in the kitchen.

The next morning was a bit of a different scene. In anything that was to be done, Pawana had the first right of refusal. Going outside being out of the question, there was no milk in stock, and so all had only black tea for beverage. But when it came to preparing lunch, Pawana volunteered and stepped into the kitchen. Manu guided her as to what was where. There were a few vegetables there, a piece of pumpkin, some onions, potatoes, and green chillies. But in a while these were chopped, the rice washed, pots and pans lain on the stove,

---

* A soup of lentils and tamarind cooked and flavoured with asafoetida and spiced with salt, red pepper, and turmeric.

and so on. In half an hour the enticing smell of spices were emanating from the kitchen and wafted through the entire room, the kind of which they had never before smelled. Something very unique and different and tasty was cooking, they surmised. It would be more than an hour-and-a-half before the cooking stopped and at least another half an hour before it was ready for dinner.

The friends ate in great silence, as if not to disturb their single-minded concentration on the enjoyment of this great event. For one they had grown tired of the unchanged couple of dishes that they had been cooking over and over. They did not know the name of the dish they ate, but it tasted so wonderful, so unlike anything that they had eaten before, that words failed them in expressing what they wanted to say. Meal over, the friends again huddled together around the radio. To them, such an experience as they were having the last two days in this town was indeed most uncommon. Nobody had witnessed such a violent commotion before. It was beyond anybody's comprehension that anything like that would break out here. Nothing of this kind ever happened here. Whether it was political rallies or show of support for their *thalaivar*, or leader, it was always a lavish show of affection by long festoons, greeting their chosen leaders with huge garlands of flowers. There were huge cut-outs or posters of their leaders lining many nooks and corners. But none here ever had to face a situation of having to see their leaders convicted for some criminal offence for the simple reason that this was getting to become a more recent phenomena. Secondly, rarely did such politicians get convicted, whatever the rumour mills might say or the general populace believe. This was a real first. But the violent reaction was certainly a bigger first. After hours of huddling around the hourly news bulletin, it was only by evening that it came to be known that the curfew would be relaxed a couple of hours for people to transact business to fulfil their urgent daily needs.

The three friends decided that they should make the best of this opportunity to safely guide Pawana to her circus brethren. The three friends and Pawana hurried across the streets and into the main road before coming to the main road leading to the maidan. Here and there they saw people in a similar rush, darting across, some with bags, hurrying to get whatever provisions they could lay their hands on. There were others like Pawana, stranded in some or other place overnight and just wanted to get going to wherever they were heading. They saw stray groups of policemen with lathis and canes in riot gear and a few armed with the vintage Lee–Enfield rifles. It was a good half hour and more, after careful and yet rather hurried walking, that they finally managed to reach the Azad Maidan. Around the maidan and even around the bus stands, they found heavy police pickets standing guard, watching carefully and surveying the scene ahead. All around, the friends could see the vestiges of the anger vented by the supporters of their beloved leader: burnt tyres, half- and fully burnt vehicles, broken glasses strewn across, and so on. So there was a real air of relief when the friends finally reached the circus.

All there in the circus were quite tense and on edge these two days. Although they knew Pawana had not gone alone, they had feared the worst. Her father and cousins all were in a state of deep anxiety. But the moment they heard her voice, a cheer went up, and everyone rushed up to meet her. Everyone was anxious to know what befell them and how they managed to outwit the marauding crowds, how she managed the night. They had a long and animated interaction when Thomas suddenly remembered that the relaxation in the curfew would end soon. He gently reminded all present there that the curfew was to end in a few minutes from now and that they must really hurry if they had to make it in time. And so Manu and his friends hurried back across the maidan and to their abode, making some urgent purchases of some vegetables and milk on the way.

The curfew was lifted for twelve hours the next day from dawn to dusk. That enabled Manu to get back to work to his factory. But it didn't allow sufficient time for spending at the circus. The circus also did not resume until the next day, when the authorities had totally lifted the curfew.

In a month's time, the Circus would complete a year. The patriarch, Pawana, and company were planning how best to celebrate this occasion. Manu also was privy to what went on. They were sitting and plotting as to how new routines and novel items of tricks would give people here a pleasant surprise. They set about their task with careful planning and began their practice of the new items with zeal. As these went on, the town became gripped by expectations of another kind. There was a sudden announcement of elections to the municipal council and the mayor. A frisson of expectancy ran through the town. It was nearly two decades since elections were announced, by which time a whole new generation was born and had grown up to become adolescents never knowing what a municipal election was. Nobody knew whether there was a councillor in their ward and, if so, who they were and what they did and if at all there was a mayor and what he was doing. While for the old it was hope that there was promise of change, an opportunity of excising their franchise which they could utilise to change, for the young it was sheer curiosity, a sign of adulthood and new-found thrill of power. While there were many influential individuals who were expected to enter the race, it was a foregone conclusion that the fight was primarily between established political parties. It didn't take them long for these parties and the politicians to get into the act. A sudden fit of frenzied activity overpowered them. Endless rounds of digging, sprucing up this road and that road commenced. In a while, a few metres of roads here and there, drains, and kerbs emerged as did any number of new foundation stones or old ones refurbished for bridges or roads, parks, or hospitals, all announcing the pious intentions of bankrupt politicians. This set the stage for vacuous claims of fulfilled promises and a request for a further term in office for fulfilling the ones just started.

The campaigning began in right earnest, and rallies began to be held. But there was one problem, the maidan. It wasn't entirely free. The parties that were till now making small rallies in other parts of the town now coveted this open space much and cited how the circus was preventing them from holding their rallies. Suddenly there were demands that this circus thing had gone on for too long and should be wound up. But that galvanised the populace that was watching the whole exercise more from the sidelines. The denizens of the town suddenly realised that their last refuge and their only true reliever from their daily miseries and humiliations was going to be consigned to the waste bin of history. This charged them with an energy like never before. They had never shown any kind of energy, an inclination to dispute anything, and was never suspected to have a mind or initiative of their own. They had always been expected loyally to vote either for X party or for Y party, wholly accepting the promises of one of these as gospel truth. The municipal committee met and decided that in view of the few weeks left for the elections and in view of the time required for the circus to vacate, it would be better if the circus was asked to suspend its activities for a while and yield at least a part of their space for their assembly or, if not, make the circus arena itself as their stage for their rallies.

There were protests, but to no avail. They were ordered either to submit to this arrangement or to vacate forthwith. There was nothing much the circus could have done. They meekly decided to accommodate the request of the municipal authorities to let the politicians address the rallies from inside the arena itself, and this went on for nearly a month. But the citizens did not sit quiet. When the time came for the nominations to be filed for the post of mayor and that of a councillor, quietly by private initiative, the circus buffoon was fielded for the post of mayor and a dozen of the artistes were running to be councillor, albeit by a lot of persuasion. But it wasn't so simple. These were simple people who only knew how to entertain, how to focus on their chosen profession with love, care, and dedication. It's not that they were oblivious to the world around them. Most of them knew the alphabets and kept themselves abreast of things happening around them. Some, like Pawana, were far more than just lettered. But all had a nice clear head with lots of native wisdom. But it is just that they never saw themselves in these roles or never imagined anything like this in their wildest dreams.

The parties deemed the whole thing a joke, dismissing them derisively as a real circus. They were so filled with mirth at the sight of the circus fighting an election that nobody even cared to challenge their nominations. But no stone was left unturned by the people in the town. They had all been given proper addresses, proposed by the requisite numbers, and so on. In time the election pitch was getting shrill and the rallies more biting, with the circus being mentioned derisively only now and then. Essentially, it was all primarily about the opposing political party and how they failed or as to how they were about to usher in a revolution just as though they were certain to be voted to power. But they failed to sense the disgust that the town's people had begun to feel at the boorish behaviour of these big daddies. They had not yet forgotten the recent display of petulant behaviour, triggering the spate of violence and curfew on the arrest of a politician on being indicted for his criminal act, which marred the peaceful existence of this town. Nevertheless, the elections were held even while the notice of vacation still dangled over the head of the circus.

And surprise, and to the utter surprise of these worthies, the buffoon was elected the mayor of the town, and his colleagues in the circus were among the councillors. All known names and bigwigs, including the influential names, were soundly beaten at the hustings. The people saw themselves in the circus, men and women simple and straight, striving to give them all the very best they had, and in the political class a set of scheming conspirators to snatch and wipe them off. Both the political and apolitical elite were aghast. 'What? Will we be ruled by a circus?' they thundered. But so it was, at least till the next elections! But looking at the changed mood of the electorate, these honourable men had to eat the humble pie and accept the verdict and their new masters. The people had just one simple argument; nothing had given them so much joy and purpose in life as this circus. Besides, ever since the circus had arrived, they felt their lives had taken a sudden change for the good. For one, there was plentiful rain, followed by bountiful crops and so much money in the hands of both the farmer and even the worker. There was for the first time a year had gone by in that area without a strike or an industrial dispute. All this, they said, was with the advent of this circus. And this one oasis of peace, a simple piece of hope and cheer in their mundane drudgery of life, was sought to be snatched from them by this band of vain pomposity, with their vacuous claims, and this the townspeople wouldn't allow.

With the elections over and the looming threat of vacation clearing up from over their heads, the circus now prepared for their annual celebrations, notwithstanding that the mayor and the councillors now had other responsibilities. While for the clown the elections itself became the subject of novel items specially developed for the anniversary celebrations, for the other performers, there were other items lined up. The team meticulously planned and practised these items over and over again till they perfected them. But the one real notable thing about it all was the return of Pawana after her fall. She had slowly resumed practise under the watchful eyes of the ringmasters and the specialists. They did not want to push her all on a sudden into the rigorous routines that defined her schedules before her fall but only take light workouts that, though weren't that tough, added to the value of spectacle to the item performed. She had to not only regain the dexterity and the physical strength to perform these acts but also win back her confidence that she could do it without any anxiety weighing on her. As there was a month and more for the celebrations, there was scope for gradual and graded scaling up in both the complexity and the requisite skill levels required for the performance. Pawana was regularly practising her routines, with Manu in regular attendance, in the evening and on holidays. With the appointed day of celebrations approaching fast, there was an all-around nervousness gaining ground. The anniversary celebrations finally arrived and they were a grand success. People thronged the circus like never before. For three days there were three shows, each of which were not only sold out but had to accommodate at least one-fourth more spectators.

With the unexpected success at the elections and the anniversary celebrations over, it appeared that the circus was entering a period of bliss. While the mayor and his colleagues were getting ever busier, still there was just no let-up on their circus performances. They were essentially simple people who could fathom the simplest needs of every man and woman and child in that town. The circus's own experiences with Pawana's accident convinced them that this town needed at least one more hospital, neat and clean, with enough beds. It didn't take them long to go to the public with their intent and the circus serving as their propagating platform. They said that the entire town, particularly the wealthier denizens, must contribute generously while the circus itself promised to set aside a share of their earnings towards this noble effort. Slowly and steadily the campaign caught the imagination of the public. Manu and his friends, both at the factory and his room-mates, were caught in this energy and became a part of the vigorous campaign that even went beyond the town. They even went to the nearby villages and towns, farther and wider, with their mission to have a hospital.

In a matter of six months, they had managed a tidy sum, but the crowning glory came when a wealthy farmer a few kilometres from the town, moved by the dedication of this movement from that town, promised to donate two acres of his land to this great cause. The mayor promptly announced that the town would soon construct a small hospital, both with the accumulated contributions and the annual budgetary allocations. True to his word, the work for building the hospital commenced in right earnest. At any given day and time, a part of the town was found there, not just eager to watch the proceedings but even willing to help out by contributing their mite in whichever way they could. Such was the pitch that this project raised that even the contractors and suppliers undertook to cut down their margins, while the common folk were just more than willing to give this a helping hand. Manu and company, being engineers, weren't far behind. It became now their new pilgrimage site. They volunteered to help in completing the wiring at the hospital and other electrical works and so on.

Often Pawana was in tow in this endeavour. Manu hadn't experienced anything of this kind in this town or elsewhere before. It was inexplicable, almost like a fairy tale, that this motley group of people with the most unremarkable backgrounds just came together to fashion something of such monumental importance to the people. Manu, in fact, took leave from the factory during the while he was helping out at the making of the hospital. After taking turns during the day, he often spent the nights at the circus and even the weekends. Lying on his back in a cot by one of those tents on one night, Manu watched the stars in the sky. The show was long over, and though there was a rare blackout in that town, the standby diesel-powered generators in the circus were idling. As he watched the stars in pitch darkness, life appeared to him blissful. He softly said, 'Those stars, how brightly they shine!' Pawana crept up beside him stealthily and suddenly cupped his eyes with the fingers of her hands. For a moment Manu was a bit startled. Then quickly regaining his composure, he grabbed Pawana by the waist and pulled her down to himself on the cot. In a trice, they tightly held on to each other. They did not know when their lips met, thirsting for and drinking deep into love when their passions gushed over, when their heart deceived them and what their bodies did. It was all love, tight and embracing, warm and wet, smooth and velvety, inside and outside, inside out, feverish and fervent, mumbling, fumbling, tumbling, grappling, groping and fumbling, trembling and touching, searching and finding, wanting and getting, asking and giving for more and more. There was more and more till they were two no more but one, just one with the universe, gliding into the endless, boundless, and seamless expanse of time and feeling.

When his eyes opened, it was still quite dark, and everything around had become very still and quiet. It was well past midnight. Pawana was fast asleep beside him with an arm around him. Gently he lifted her arm, slipping it past his shoulders and neck, and got up from the cot and moved to another in another corner close to the tent.

The work of the hospital did not cease with erecting just a building in place, which anyway happened in six months. Soon advertisements were placed for recruiting doctors and staff. The campaigning having spread far and wide, a couple of young doctors hailing from this very town took on the challenge, roping in their own friends from elsewhere to set up practice. It was only a small hospital with just a half-a-dozen doctors befitting such a small town which already had one hospital that appeared overwhelmed by the demands placed on it, with even those from the hinterland coming to get the hospital's care. With this new facility in place, the townspeople heaved a sigh of relief. It appeared that their long-standing prayers were finally heard. Things appeared to be running quite smoothly. The mayor and his circus colleagues had many more projects lined up.

Over a year had passed by since the circus clown and his colleagues won the elections and when finally the hospital had been built and dedicated to the townsfolk. Manu and Pawana had been so caught up in this whirlwind of activity and energy that they did not quite notice the passage of time. But the politicians were far from being happy. They were still smarting under the blow of being beaten by a bunch of circus buffoons and recovering from the shock. But the politicians, who lay low till now, were getting restless and listless. They knew if they did not act in time to dislodge the growing stature of the mayor and the circus, they could soon become history.

A few among them, recovering from the shock, gathered their wits about themselves and began scheming ways of ousting them. They began a campaign that the circus was dirtying the maidan, what with their animals etc. This they said was likely to bring diseases, even plague. They demanded that the place be subject to inspections and be disinfected and eventually dislodged. A posse of sanitary officials soon descended on the spot. After every fair and every exhibition, the mounds of split peanut shells, toffee wrappers, crumpled paper bags were ubiquitous at the maidan. Yes, in this town as in the country, people had true freedom; there was freedom for people to be and the freedom to pee wherever they wanted and to do much as they pleased. The human dung was not uncommon in the many open spaces of the town either. But this was not so at the circus. To their utter surprise, the inspectors found the circus and its precincts clean and much cleaner than elsewhere in the town! What was more, the dung of the animals found ready buyers as compost material, and so there was nothing left behind here. No matter how hard they tried, the officials found the place clean and tidy. The politicians had to beat a hasty retreat, at least for now.

But the persistence and the perseverance of politicians when they put their mind to things can be remarkable. After a while they began to drum up another tune. They said these circuses corrupted people, even stole children. But the people just laughed these off. In the end, one of them filed a petition before a court, saying that the Azad Maidan belonged to all and that it could not be monopolised by just the circus and forever be its occupant. As they needed it for other uses, they prayed to the court to set it free.

Amidst these, Pawana and Manu wanted to break out of all these rather hectic and tumultuous times that they had been experiencing since the astonishing turn of events commencing with the election of the circus clown and other of their circus colleagues and take some time out for themselves. A whole party was attempted to be assembled. Pawana persuaded her circus brethren to accompany her and Manu on a trip to the sea front and a beach some fifteen kilometres away the coming Monday, when it was off for the circus. Manu took a day off from work. But in the end, it was only Pawana and Manu who went. Early in the morning, they boarded a bus for the journey. They went past tarred, metalled roads, winding past tiled homes set in dense coconut palm groves, up and down over small hillocks and steep gradients sloping down, finally emerging into a vast curved beachhead.

On one side of this descent was a plateau of coconut palms that ended abruptly at a steep rocky cliff, with the sea waves lashing it at its foot, with just a narrow band of sand separating it from the waters. On the other side of this descent was a plain curved beachhead sloping down into the sea from a curved wall of coconut trees stretching far into the distance along the coast away from them as far as the eye could see. They got off the bus and walked towards the scimitar-shaped beach, edging slowly towards the water. There at the beach they saw simple fishing folk scattered around their long wooden boats and catamarans, well away from the water and the waves. There they could see children of fishermen frolicking in the water, diving and playing far out into the sea with shallow waters. Pawana and Manu slowly made their way into a beach untrammelled by the tourist influx as it was, at that point of time, still waiting to be discovered.

It was, in short, a secluded beach, still shielded from prying eyes and baying crowds. The sun was up, but still low and mild, as it lighted up the waters. Far out in the sea one could see as specks slightly oscillating black spots up and down the waves, while closer to the horizon were the white bright sails, visible, with the black bobs standing still. The black spots were catamarans, while the white ones the sail boats. There they sat, enraptured by the sea, hands clasped in each other, as wave after wave slowly, steadily, gently, sequentially washed ashore, for the sea here was hardly rough. The brief stretch of beach in this part was so shallow that people could wade into ankle deep or little more of water for as far as fifty meters or even further into the sea.

There as he sat, he could visualise himself as a merchant in the very distant past, as part of an entourage of merchants travelling in a ship to distant shores to distant lands, visiting exotic destinations, trading in spices, wandering to discover fabulous cities and towns of these distant shores in South-East Asia, from Kamboja (the medieval Cambodia) to Suvarna Dwipa (Indonesia), savouring the best of these cultures, wandering through the streets of these distant and dazzling cities, their marvellous bazaars, past shops laden with goods that were ordinary or curious or precious and even the most exotic. There were jugglers, magicians, mendicant beggars, and thieves as well. And there in his wanderings he encountered lissom lasses, and then someone caught his eye. Somewhere in that crowd, he could place a fabulous face, then again some other time peeping out of a window in a busy street, and then again on a balcony in the street leading up to the palace. It would then become his pastime to follow her around, to discover that she was the merchant's daughter dealing in dry fruits and sultanas. Their gradual familiarity turned into an acquaintance and then into friendship. After having won her confidence, affection, and heart, he won her hand too and embarked to sail back with the entourage with her in tow. But it wouldn't be that simple.

There were pirates, far too many, in these seas. Even as they had to battle pirates attacking the ship for their survival, in the meanwhile, there gathered a powerful storm, with darkening skies, with black clouds, ferocious winds, towering waves converging on the ship. There ensued a battle royale amidst confusion and mayhem; while the battle with the pirates appeared to be won, the storms did them in. The ship was on the verge of sinking, while Manu and Pawana were left floating on debris, clinging on to it for dear life.

That was the moment he was jolted out of his reverie by the tug of Pawana and the heavy winds breezing across and indeed the heavy dark clouds galloping from the horizon towards them onto the seashore out of nowhere! It was a storm building up right here. That's how storms built up near the seashore there; one moment it would be so calm, quiet, sunny with clear skies, and at another moment out of nowhere would blow strong winds, and there would appear clouds, stark and black, leaping and rumbling like some ferocious beast.

Together, they hurried to the nearest hutment which in fact was a small eating joint out there. They had long wooden benches as seats and equally long but taller benches that served as tables. Claps of thunder rent the air, rolling across the sky, reverberating all around, with streaks and webs of lightning flashing across the dark clouds in the sky. Rains began lashing down, while winds blew wildly, spraying the water even into the hutment, falling on part of the benches and wetting those customers seated at the edge close to the wide open-ended part of the hutment. Most of them moved into the room adjacent to the hall, and Pawana and Manu did the same, avoiding sitting by the window. Together, face to face, half drenched, smilingly holding hands, they enjoyed a hot cup of coffee in stainless-steel tumblers and a hot plate of puttu and kadala* served up to them. The rain and storm were so furious, engaging the attention of those around that they were virtually oblivious of the couple.

'How long will it last?' queried Pawana.

'Who knows?' replied Manu.

'It has rained a lot this year' remarked Pawana.

'What are we doing sitting inside here? We came to enjoy the sea,' said Manu.

'Well, let's now enjoy the storm! Let's get outside,' replied Pawana.

'It's too windy. Let it calm down,' said Manu. By the time they had finished their breakfast, the winds had calmed down, but it still rained. Together they set out again slowly towards the sandy beaches, arm around waists and shoulders, locked tightly, feeling the rain pattering on their faces and on their bodies, the smooth sand caressingly rolling against and at times sticking to the soles of their feet. Leisurely they walked down the beach to the waters even as the rain suddenly withdrew. From somewhere wafted the smell of fish frying. Manu crinkled his nose in disgust.

There in the middle of the waters they waded in, feeling its ebb and tide. They bathed, sat, and frolicked around, rolled in the sandy bed for hours on end till the clouds slowly parted to show the rays of a setting sun. Even after the sun had set, long into nightfall they still sat by the sea, engrossed in the starry sky and then at the rising moon, listening to the relentless lashing and gurgling of the waves in the darkness. Finally they got up reluctantly, slowly returning from the waves with languid weariness, trudging to the bus stop, wishing that this sojourn had never ended. But it had to!

---

*   Steamed ground rice and fresh grated coconut dumplings with whole chickpea in spiced ground coconut gravy.

It was that time of the year when the governments began their annual exercise of budgeting for their expenses next year to be presented to the legislature. The previous year the budget was about taxing the rich by increasing taxes on cigarettes, labelled and branded bottled alcohol, even toothpastes, but reducing taxes on items such as fans or razor blades and country liquor; beedis* count, apparently, as concessions for the poor. As the budget session began, a steep hike was proposed by the government to the prevailing rates of entertainment tax. Apparently, people had to pay a price for having fun and enjoyment, and a heavy price at that. Fun was not to be had for free, and certainly not without paying anything to the government. In fact, fun was such a luxury in a socialist state. And then the bus fares also had been raised. Even as Manu and Pawana were returning by the bus, they heard this hush discussion about increase in this and decrease in that. When finally Manu returned to his den, Thomas greeted him with 'Did you know that watching movies is going to cost us a bomb?'. Manu shook his head. Thomas then explained to him that the government had increased certain taxes and among them was the entertainment tax.

But it was not until a considerable lapse of time did the townsfolk, the circus, and Manu realise that they would have to pay hell for this single pleasure of watching movies or a circus. The cinema owners and then circus were served with notices with demands for nearly double of the normal tax they were to pay, which effectively required a hefty increase in the price to be paid for the tickets. The circus was in an awful bind. While they did not want to increase the ticket prices, they knew that they would be bankrupted if they did not increase their ticket rates. In two weeks' time the finances of the circus took a great hit. The whole town, the circus, and the cinemas was still reeling under this blow, trying to figure their way out of this, when they found that the courts issued a summons to the circus for appearance on the matter of continued occupation of the Azad Maidan! It was then that the patriarch, Pawana's father, blew his top. Fed up and disillusioned, he burst out, 'This is it. Let's pack up and leave,' he said. 'Our circus never stayed at one place so long. It's time we moved on.' The townsfolk were aghast. The only thing that was sure to bring a smile in anybody's face anytime in that town was now being hounded out. Everyone pleaded with the old man. But he was firm, though

---

* A thin small rolled country cigar.

sad. 'It's our tradition to move and not stay too long. Besides, we are circus people, entertainers meant to make people happy, not to rule them. We had no business getting into these elections. I think we have overstayed our welcome.' So it was curtains for the circus in this town.

Manu and Pawana were left speechless. It was a bolt out of the blue for Manu and Pawana. As soon as Manu learnt of this, he made for the circus. Two feet weren't enough to carry him as fast as his mind leaped to his beloved. Manu, harried and hurried, went swiftly over to the maidan, past the gates into this tent, out of it, and into that tent, asking after her, panting, running across till he reached her, who was standing outside one of these tents, helping to light a fire. His eyes met hers. He could read in it that she knew it already. But words wouldn't issue forth.

Not a word could he utter, nor could she. With a jerk, she swirled around, diving into the nearest tent, ducking under the flap. Manu followed, and in a moment they faced each other. Their eyes searched anxiously each other's. In a jiffy they leapt into each other's arms, holding each other tight in embrace. Tears flowed freely from both their eyes; nothing could have stopped them, and nothing could have indeed. They clung to each other for dear life for what seemed eons, when her voice pierced the stillness. 'I am afraid, so afraid,' said she, unwilling to let go of him. But both knew one of them would have to if they had to be together. But still words wouldn't come.

Manu wrenched himself away and quickly left the circus. He hurried to his room, where his friends Thomas and Raju waited. Together they spent a long time in a huddle. 'You must immediately go back home to your native place and convince your parents about this,' said Thomas.

'Yes, yes, you should go,' joined Raju.

'Maybe we too can accompany you, if it helps,' joined both together. Together Raju and Thomas urged Manu for urgent action. But for Manu, the question was far too serious. He had an absolute dread facing his family, especially his father. He knew how tough it could be. How strict and rigid the views they had of such things. They took great pride on questions of their hoary traditions, lineage, ancestry, and the perceived culture and were quite obstinate about it. When it came to tradition, ancestry, they never seemed ever willing to give up on these.

Seated in a bus heading towards Puzhakkara, his mind was wandering back and forth to the circus and his native home and the choice he had to make.

As the bus moved, images of *pulikali* hovered in his eyes. He felt he was one among those dressed-up tigers being endlessly stalked by a hunter, in eternal fear of something, someone somewhere lurking. The journey seemed almost an endless crawl, the stoppages needless. Time, it appeared, was stretching itself like an elastic band, taking a malicious delight in delaying his destination. In his heart of hearts, there was tumult and confusion, in his mind a great upheaval. He had long known this deep inside but had always postponed the inevitable, keeping it away for some other time. But the day of reckoning had arrived, and there was nothing he could do about it.

Manu's sudden unscheduled appearance came as a complete surprise to his family. Nevertheless, they were happy to have him in their midst, what with his suitcase laden with goodies overflowing, catering to one and all. He had been very careful to select them. A brand-new pair of dhoti, shirt, and a pair of leather sandals for his father, a sari-and-blouse piece for his mother, dresses for his siblings. 'Oh, Amma, look what Brother has brought home!' cried his sister, just coming back from school, excited at the sight of Manu.

'Ah! Well, no letter, telegram, or intimation eh?' asked his mother as she rushed out from the kitchen to greet him.

'Hmm . . . It was all so sudden,' he mumbled. And then hesitantly he queried, 'Where is Father?'

'Just a few minutes back he left for the market to get somebody to pluck the coconuts. You see, they have ripened, and some have dried out and are even falling down. One doesn't even know when it falls and who picks it away. One hears a thud now and then. But who can be running about each time to fetch it? It's so difficult, you see. You are not here any longer, and your brother is yet to return from school and tuitions.' And she sighed and then, with motherly concern, queried, 'You must be quite hungry, there is dough for dosa, and what will you like to drink? Tea? Coffee?'

But Manu, with his mind busy elsewhere, only half heard, replying, 'Anything, Mother!' (Even the fact that his brother was getting tuitions without having to pay attention to the farm duties, which luxury he didn't have, did not seem to quite register in his mind.) His ten-hour bus journey was more exhausting mentally for the tense anxiety that he found himself in than the physical discomfort he experienced. He was constantly preparing himself to face his family, especially his father, and the anxiety weighed so heavily on his mind, making it taut as a trampoline net. He decided to have a bath, more out of a force of habit than conscious effort, as usually they did after a long travel. Maybe it would serve to lighten him up. He picked up a piece of soap cake and his towel and pushed off to the riverside, slowly making his way through the estate, the coconut palms. He noticed there were hardly any banana plants left. Many of the coconut tree beds were overgrown with grass and other weeds. That they were largely left unattended he could see. In general, there was an air of neglect about the patch of land around the house.

He took his own time to complete his bath, but his mind all the while remained preoccupied by the anxiety of facing the unknown. Back into the house, after towelling himself as he changed into fresh clothes, his mother called out to him, 'The dosas are hot. Come on, have them.' He quietly went into the kitchen, sat on the stool beside the edge of the stove, and took from his mother a plate with the hot dosa. With his head turned towards the window, gazing distractedly out at the estate, he was slowly munching pieces of dosa that he languidly tore out. His mother noticed the furrowed brows and forehead and languid and glum demeanour on his face. 'Too tired, eh, have this, and then you can have a nap.'

But just then his sister came in excitedly, asking, 'Come on, Brother, where is the present you promised me?' A little startled with embarrassment, he said, 'Dumb of me that I forgot to give you. It is there in that suitcase.'

'Where is it? Tell me!' cried out his sister in excitement.

'Can't you wait till he finishes his tiffin?' admonished his mother. 'Poor boy, he looks so tired, and you won't leave him alone, will you? You are grown up and still behave like a child! When will you learn?' And so she went hammer and tongs at her daughter. But Manu interceded.

'That's OK, Amma.' It had, however, little effect on his sister, who scampered off, giggling.

Soon after his meal, Manu picked up a sleeping mat, a pillow, and a sheet. He spread the mat and the sheet over it, with the pillow at its head, and lay down to sleep. It was late in the evening, nearing twilight, as he slipped into a tired and fretful sleep.

He was travelling in a long caravan, in a young group, with a girl alongside him, her hands clasped in his. The whole group were boisterously singing and clapping, interspersed with storytelling and anecdotes filled with humour, wistful and inspirational. As the sun went down and twilight crept in with the advancing night, the party called for a halt. The tired but happy group unpacked, pitched tents, lit a cracking bonfire, and set the food cooking. Soon after the singing, clapping and dancing began. Mugs of hot beverage were passed around as wistful sighs escaped him and his partner as they gazed at the twinkling stars in the charged night. A sweet feminine voice arose and a sonorous male voice followed. Together it caught on like wildfire as one by one all voices there joined, the voices rising feverishly, as the feet followed tapping and hands clapping, rising in an ever-spiralling crescendo, dancing and swaying around the bonfire all night. It was long gone into night before the embers died down, the people and their passions wound down to sleep all around the place. Manu too dozed off. When he opened his eyes, he struggled with six men bearing down on him and Pawana beside him. These men with large turbans and mouths covered by scarves were holding him down as one of them gagged his mouth as well. But from the corner of his eye he espied the swiftly descending glint of a blade. A sudden scream arose in his throat but remained buried in the gag.

Manu awoke with a start and sweat on his forehead. He found himself right inside his home in broad daylight. After having his tea, he folded up his bedding and placed them in the designated corner of the room before proceeding to the bathroom. He did not somehow feel like setting out to the riverside. Finishing off his bath in the bathroom, he went off to the prayer room, sat down, going into deep meditation and prayer. But all his mind would do was go round and round the circus and Pawana. After a while he got up, stripped off his wet towel, and changed into fresh clothes. Meanwhile, his father emerged from his room and came into the dining hall and sat down on his wooden seat on the floor to have his breakfast. 'Manu, breakfast is being served, come. Your father is waiting for you here already.' Thus his mother called out to him. Manu hurried in and sat down next to his father.

'Oh, what a surprise!' exclaimed his father. 'What's up?'

'I just felt like it,' replied Manu a little anxiously, as he saw *sevai*, the rice noodles, being ladled into his plate and with dollops of coconut chutney* by its side. His mind was anxious from the burden of the thought of the task ahead of him. It was then he noticed the absence of both his brother and his sister. That's when he asked after them.

---

* A pasty sauce made of ground fresh coconut, green chillies, roasted chickpea, a bit of tamarind, and salt.

'Do you think they will be waiting for you if you get up so late? Your sister is already left for school, and your brother left for college,' replied his father. His mother watched smilingly as father and son slowly drank the tumblers of tea that she had set down. In a while, father and son, having finished their breakfasts, repaired to the drawing room. 'So how many days of leave do you have?' enquired his father.

'Three days.'

'So short?'

'Father, I wished to say something—about my marriage,' he blurted out.

'Did you hear, Manu's Mother, Manu wants to get married, well, well!' said his father in utter astonishment. 'Yes, we too will be looking towards it, but don't you think you should wait for your sister to get married?' shot back his father. But this time his mother too had joined them.

'What I wanted to say was something different,' said Manu. With great effort he mustered all his courage and blurted out, 'I am in love in with a girl and I want to marry her.'

'What "in love with a girl"? What do you mean?' His father's astonishment grew wider as did disgust well up in his tone.

'Shiva, Shiva, oh God,' exclaimed his mother, with the fingers and the palm of her right hand closing over her mouth in a gesture of shock. Love for such as these conservatives was synonymous with licentious behaviour, and marriage by love a scandal in these parts. Falling in love and elopement were a daring act, an act of rebellion, a sign of insubordination and waywardness. It was certainly a bombshell for his parents. But there was more to come.

'She is a gypsy girl in a circus.' This was the fireball and the thunder ball together.

Anger surged through the whole being of his father as he quaked into an explosion. 'What a rascal have I brought up who romances nameless and homeless vagabonds, dragging the family name into the mud?' The whole house reverberated with his roar. 'How dare you do anything so unmindful! What will happen to your sister and the rest of us? Can any one of us face the world after this? Who will want to marry into this family? What expectations we have had from you after all that we did for you, and now this is what we get!' The more Manu listened to this tirade, the more he felt like that lovingly fattened goat ungratefully desperate to escape from the abattoir of his beloved master just at that moment when it was ripe for him to reap the benefits of his labours.

Silence and shock had enveloped the house, as his parents and he each retired to their far corners, unwilling to do anything except to brood and scowl at their destinies, forgetting even their hunger and thirst. In the evening, his brother and sister came to a silent and forlorn home. Both rushed to the kitchen, finding neither their mother nor anything to eat or drink except water. Even milk had not been set to boil. Together they set about boiling milk and making tea. In a while they learnt that something was amiss, though not the details, and Manu as the cause of it. In a way, the whole family turned against him. He had soon turned the traitor from being the saviour.

The passage of another day did not serve to mitigate the gulf between him and his parents. When he again broached the subject to his mother, she threatened 'over my dead body'. There was now little to choose between the hostile stares of his family or the love of his life. There was no doubt about what he wanted. He wanted to leave with the circus. Yet his mind was heavy and taut. He had to rush back if he were to join the circus. It was certain that Pawana and her folk would move out in a short time, and he was actually taking a risk in having come here. As he lay outside on the mat in the verandah that night, he again heard the favourite guitar piece that Thomas used to often play. It must have been Brandhan Murali. Manu got up from the mat and swiftly made for the riverside. Sitting alone on a heap of sand, Murali was strumming his guitar, immersed in it. But the slight rustle of leaves as Manu tried getting on to the riverbank broke his reverie, prompting him to turn back, looking over his shoulder. Spotting him approach, Murali, in a tone of surprise and even irritation, said 'Ah! You should be actually with your circus, with your beloved. You should be in that caravan.' Manu was breathless with surprise. How did he know? 'My friend, you should be beside her than be reasoning with these idiots. For them love is bigger sin than theft and murder! How could you believe that they will ever agree to such a thing? Nothing can replace what you are about to lose. You are as yet unfamiliar with the pain of loss, my friend! I lost some of my best friends to war, my beloved to such prejudice, my siblings to avarice, and my parents to caprice of destiny. If only we had taken care when we could, all these miseries could have been avoided!' He didn't elaborate but motioned him back with a vigorous wave of his hand.

He rushed back without much ceremony to the bus stand, taking the earliest bus available back to Mayapuram, wearily taking his seat in a bus back to his city of fortune. If coming to his native home was torture, the few hours of journey travelling back were pure agony for him. The scene of hostile stares of his siblings and his parents against the vision of Pawana departing along with the circus was getting to be too much for him. He wanted desperately to be reunited with Pawana the soonest the bus could take him there. He was determined to be with her and leave with the circus, if need be. The journey was too slow, too ponderous, as it appeared, to a desperate mind. Hours later, after a fitful sleep, he arrived at his city, greeted by yet another dawn. Slugging his luggage on his shoulder, head bent, he hurried to his destination at the maidan. It took quite some time treading on foot to reach the place. As he made past a few corrugated-iron sheet barricades and a thick line of trees, he lifted his head up, looking ahead, past the trees to where the circus tents were pitched. His jaw dropped, his face became ashen pale, and he was in a moment breathless, his eyes closing. Fortune and miracles had left the town.

He was with Pawana somewhere on a wonderful mountainside going on and on and away, gliding on a beautiful wide glen. It appeared so beautifully an endless glide, hours and hours on end, on a glen that appeared endless till they came upon its abrupt end, all of a sudden at the edge of a precipice. Pawana just slipped over the edge but managed to cling on to the edge and called out desperately to Manu. Manu managed to cling on to her desperately, with Pawana suspended seemingly endlessly, time barely tickling by, drip by drip, bit by bit, little by little, pit-a-pat, atom by atom, particle by particle, bead by bead, when suddenly she broke free. It was hideously silent and endlessly soundless.

Chapter IV

When Manu came out of his delirium, he found himself amidst his friends and room-mates. He saw them anxiously waiting by his bedside when he came to.

Anxiously he enquired and learnt that Pawana had wanted to know where he was, desperately seeking to meet him before she left. But where the circus went was not quite clear. They recounted how the whole town had turned up to bid adieu to their beloved circus. His friends said that they heard certain towns being spoken about, but whether they would just be stopovers or the next camping site for their shows were not clear. From them he learnt of his delirium and unconsciousness for five days, till he had come around now. His friends had informed the factory where he worked of his condition and requested a leave of absence for at least a week more. By the morrow, his condition appeared stable, and the friends decided that they too needed to go back to their work, leaving him to himself, of course with food and medicine and things he needed.

He sat there, brooding at his new circumstance. Maybe it was time for him to forget this as a mirage, a nightmare, and get on. His right hand clasped, vice like, the arm of his chair as his resolve hardened. Nothing would change this, he was certain. 'Yes, that is it,' he said to himself. Turning towards the window, his gaze focused afar, his lips pursed up as in a hiss, but then . . .

In a flash it appeared like an apparition, even as his eyes took it in and his mind registered it and words issued forth slowly, parting his lips, 'Ah, what a beautiful ankle,' and trailed off. And then a face, copperish brown, arose as in a vision, in a dream, framing a beautiful wan smile, like a withered flower floating across, arrested in time and space, and then vanished, forever.

Instantaneously, in a massive burst of torrential energy, like some primeval force unleashed by an unseen power, surging out of his chair, he rushed out, like on some giant wave of the sea, even as a scream welled up in his lungs, rending the air, raging as a hurricane. 'Oh no!'

He bolted past the door, the window, into the yard, past the gate, into the street, turned to the right, and ran. He huffed and puffed, slowed down, walked, and walked. Neither here nor there, nowhere was she! *She must be somewhere here, somewhere in these lanes. She will come, must come. Yes, she must.* Palpitating and dragging his tired body, disillusioned, he hobbled back and slumped into this chair. There he was, sitting by the window, sitting, sitting, sitting, sitting, and sitting, mumbling, 'Will come . . . must come.' Lips moving slowly, the sound tapering off, with only the lips moving as his mind swirled, eyelids drooping.

Now he walked down the moonlit path, past the magnificent palace, set on a wooded estate, trees whose dark silhouettes made some breathtakingly beautiful patterns against the moonlight sky, swaying gently this way and that in the gentle breeze as if conferring amongst themselves expectantly, as if sensing some mysteriously delightful and delicious occurrence, which sent his nerves tingling.

It was the third time that he had gone by that street recently, but only now had the mansion attracted his attention. The grandeur, style, and abundance of the beautiful vegetation lain out magnificently made it a very unusual, if not an alien, edifice in those parts. Yet it had not occurred to him so, nor had it caught his attention till then.

As he went just past the gates, taking in the alluring contours of the mansion and the estates, still wondering about its residents, the clear tinkles of anklets filled his ears, which turned him around. There was before him the most wonderful damsel, the image of the most beautiful girl his eyes had ever set on, standing there, smiling!

Eyes met; hands clasped. In a trice they went past the gates, which opened on their own. Into and into the garden they went, hand in hand, drinking in the heady magic potion of the moon, its light, the night, and the lake. There beside the lake they watched the moon from the heavens throw fistfuls of silver dust into the water below, and the cool breeze spread them as silver spangles.

Moments rolled by in seconds, seconds into minutes, minutes into hours as hands clasped tight, minds lost in each other, in deep feverish conversation, as though it were the last day in time. Fervent confessions of gurgling admiration and passionate promises of eternal love and everlasting company gushed forth into each other, mingling one into another till no barriers, secrets, or mysteries existed betwixt them and when all their beings became one.

Yet not a word escaped their lips, as they needed none, for they conversed in that language of love that only hearts in love, with loving hearts, silently speak to one another in the silence of love. Certain things occur just once in a lifetime. You know it is the person of your life, and this the moment to seize it. No questions asked or answers given. This was that moment.

And then the trance broke, and she led him along, back from the lake, away from the trees, out of the groves and orchards, up and up the flight of steps, into and into the grand palace. There stepping in, he gazed at the interiors of the great halls, taking in the dazzling chandeliers, the ornate cushioned furniture, the chequered chess boards, fruit-laden silver plates, nut-filled bowls, goblets of wine and beverage placed on inviting tables as though ready only for serving him. As she led him quickly away past this regal splendour, it did not occur to him to ask who she was or where belonged to, where her family was. For a man in love, nothing except his object of love matters.

He was led past the huge dazzlingly lit dancing hall into the dining room. A vast richly carved table was laid out, covered in a magnificent embroidered tablecloth in the midst of equally ornate chairs. Dishes in polished, shining metal and ornate enamel, bowls in gold and silver were all as were the plates expectantly arrayed. Gently she conveyed to him to the head of the table and with loving care and bubbling joy helped him to a scrumptious repast while partaking of it herself. Who actually was she? An Abyssinian princess or the queen of Sheba herself? But she was so much in the image of Pawana. Hunger of the body satiated, thirst quenched, but their hearts still hungry and thirsty, they stumbled into the moonlit night that appeared as though a mysteriously dark and beautiful maiden, a benign enchantress, and the moon shone like some fairy godmother fondly watching her beloved godchildren. A cool zephyr gently breezed past as though whispering 'love, love' into the ears of these lovers, feeding their hearts.

Their eyes met and their hearts swelled, swimming together in the heady wine of love.

All was silence and stillness for a moment. And then hands searched for company, body clasping each other, feverishly tightly, lips meeting ecstatically, drinking deep the elixir of love. The world around and all their beings were filled with the fragrance of love. And then there was love, feverish, titillating, tantalising, starry and mysterious, moony and maddening, love in and love out, love inside out, exhausting, surrendering, wondrously velvety smooth, tender, clasping. Then sleep, the sweet, alluringly beautiful sister of death, overtook them. They slept, warm and cosy in each other's arms, as the children of the moon and the earth.

And then searing heat spread across his back! He opened his eyes, only to see some strange-smelling vapours and fumes floating thick all around and to hear screams and wailing of hundreds of people from great distances. He quickly turned on his side and looked around. In a flash he could see many hundreds of men and women, with and without children in tow, running helter-skelter, panting, some falling and lying still, others getting up and running, and still others writhing in death. In no time he tried dragging the princess out of her slumber and was off and away. But then he lost her. Where? Nowhere! As they fled, they stumbled on bodies lying scattered here and there, barely picked themselves up, and ran for their lives. There were the old and the infirm, unable to walk a step, wailing, unable to get away from these evil and poisonous fumes. And there were a few carriages here and there willing to take in people if they paid in gold and diamonds. That was the price of purchase for their lives. Manu and Pawana ran on till they collapsed of exhaustion and saw the fumes from which they strove to flee envelope them. Dying, he saw, in the faint glimmer of morning, all around sand, sand, and sand, a mountain of sand with bodies piled on one edge with a vast expanse, an ocean of sand stretching into eternity as far as his eyes could see, right up to the edge of the horizon at the other. He was marooned in a desert of sand with only bodies piled around. The garden, the palace, the princess, the moon, and the night were all gone, vaporised into thin air.

Manu was sweating as his body convulsed, jerking him into consciousness. He had fallen into a fitful sleep, weakened by the continuous delirium, while seated in his chair right by the window. Slowly reaching for the towel by his side, he wiped the sweat off his face. A sigh escaped him. He could not help his mind wandering into the past into his carefree childhood days, peaceful. There were no visions, dreams, or nightmares in all these years—that is, till he met Pawana. But now that he had them, he could not quite make out what they meant really.

There he sat, brooding and brooding on Pawana and the circus, on the maidan and his madness. Why did he at all go to his hometown when there was little hope? Bhrandhan Murali was right! Why did he leave the side of Pawana and circus? He had to find her from somewhere. Ah! But where could he search out for her? Where indeed? And in his present condition, how could he do it? Maybe he could put out an ad in the newspapers. But in which newspaper, in which language, and which all languages? But who is going to tell her? Maybe somebody in the circus, if not Pawana, would read and tell her. Certainly the old man, he hoped, read the papers regularly. But where exactly was Pawana? His head went spinning from the conflicting emotions and thoughts welling up in him. There were no answers, only prayers and hopes. Desperate to do something, he inserted an ad in one newspaper after another, even in the papers in the languages of the neighbouring states. He wrote to these offices, requesting for information on one grand circus. He was back to work, but his mind despondently focused only on his Pawana. As he waited, a few weeks after his nightmare came the horrendous news of a tragedy in a city north of India. A poisonous gas had leaked in the dead of night, leaving hundreds and thousands dead. It was then Manu realised that what he saw that day in his nightmare was no passing fantasy; it was a warning of an impending disaster. Overnight that city was reduced to a ghost city, a funerary mound. There were just the dead and the dying and those living who wished they were dead. The estimates of casualties varied. The world would never know who those were and if they ever really existed and if their existence were a mere figment of imagination.

Manu sighed. If only had he paid attention to such visions before, could he have saved himself from his eternal loss? Maybe! He had heard his mother at times speak of something that the astrologer had said about him, something that made her feel that there was some vague but special visionary gift. Was it, then, this? If only he could find Pawana!

Every day he wearily made his way to the maidan in the evening. He would silently stare at the holes left behind by the uprooted poles of the circus tents and the vacant spaces where the circus tents stood, recounting the moments that he spent there. Over there had stood the animal stables, and over here the circus arena, and then nearby had stood the practise area, and there behind it a little farther away was Pawana's tent, where they had all the world to themselves. Every day he repeated this futile ritual till one day hope came floating by a post card to him, which informed of a circus in a town nearby.

There was just the name of the town and no other details. This enlivened his drooping spirits, infusing him with a restless energy.

That Friday weekend he packed his bags and set out eager and expectant. He was already out on the road, in a bus. Yet he was fidgety, nervous, and wide awake through the journey that took him a few hours to reach his destination. He was journeying through roads along verdant mountainsides that were not so tall. Winding and turning, climbing and twisting, dipping and gliding went the roads, through thickly wooded and beautifully landscaped environs, a sight that would have gladdened any heart, soothed sore eyes, healed broken hearts. But it drew only sighs, heightened further his longing, whetting his impatience. As the evening sun lovingly showed its colours, playing hide-and-seek through the verdant surroundings, it only aggravated his thoughts on how better it would have been with her by his side. How her loving glances, her loving touch, and caressing voice would have lighted up the sorceress in the atmosphere. Without her, everything seemed desolately empty and painfully forlorn. Thus it dragged on till the bus entered the town in the dead of the night. Somewhere he would have to put up for the night, as he had hoped to arrive much earlier than they actually did. On their way, at a stretch of a road, they had met up with a long convoy from the opposite direction, which had to be allowed to pass. What usually would have taken half an hour took three-hours-and-a-half, for that stretch of road was not just narrow but in bad condition from much rains and landslides and was yet to be set right. That put paid to his plans of commencing immediately on reaching here, the task that he had set out for, from Mayapuram.

On arriving at the bus terminus, his anxiety for finding suitable lodging was heightened by his inability to understand or communicate in the language of the place. Only those shops and establishments with signboards in the local language interspersed with lines or words written in English helped him in this endeavour. But there were other problems. There were a few touts and a couple of taxis milling around him, offering to lead him to the best of hostels, promising colourful nights. He took the hint but did not respond. In the end he chose to step into one of those lodges of his own choosing, not much far from the bus stop. He stepped into a rather old building, with musty old rooms, rickety bed and furniture, with barely clean bedding. Placing his bag on the rickety table, he sat down wearily.

One part of him wanted to bolt out and run in search of the circus and Pawana, while the other wanted to rest after a tiring journey gone so late into the night. After a change of clothes, he went to bed. He tossed around quite a while before sleep overcame him. Travelling in the bus, he could have sworn he felt Pawana beside him, somewhere close by. It was so strong, the feeling of her presence, that he could sense her in his every pulse beat, in the cooing of the cuckoo from deep in the woods and high in the trees. He could not resist that deep and persistent call from deep in the woods. He got out from the bus and followed the trail of the bird's call that appeared so very urgent as the summons of Pawana. And he was drawn away from the bus and the waiting traffic deeper and deeper into the woods till nothing but tall dense woods were around him, yet the call was getting more and more persistent, more desperate, and his journey longer and longer, deeper and deeper into and into, further and further . . . till when he opened his eyes, he found it was already the crack of dawn.

Yes, when he had heard the cuckoo while he was seated in the bus, he inexplicably felt the longing to flee the bus and run to the call but just didn't. Not wishing any longer to prolong his agonising suspense, in a futile attempt to catch up with more sleep, he got out of his bed, brushed his teeth, did his toilet, and thereafter followed it up with a refreshing bath. Having said his prayers in his still-dripping towel, he put it out on a line to dry as soon as he had finished his prayers, changed into a fresh set of clothes, locked his room, and climbed down the stairs. At the reception he found a still-sleepy-looking receptionist having his morning cup of tea. He looked up at Manu and smiled as he saw Manu come up to him. Manu enquired from him about the grand circus. The man at the reception, after reflecting for a while, nodded his head and explained to him in mix of English, Kannada, and Hindi that there indeed was a circus recently arrived but couldn't quite recall the name but said it was at least a couple of kilometres from this spot. That sent Manu's spirits soaring. At least in the grand circus there used to be no performance before noon, although on weekends and holidays there were matinees before the evening shows and on Sundays even morning shows. But so long as it was the grand circus, it just didn't matter whether there was any show or not. But before he could proceed he had to have a quick breakfast. But where could he have one? Well down the lane, it was explained that there was a small but nice restaurant that opened up quite early in the morning as was usual in these parts of southern India. Thus informed, Manu stepped out of his lodgings down the lane, heading towards the restaurant he had been told about. Head bent, his mind whirled in thoughts about the circus, of where, if, how, and what, and so on when soon he came upon the eating joint. Quietly he stepped in and sat down by a vacant table. Soon a waiter took his order of a glass of coffee and a plate of steaming pongal (a dish of cooked rice and lentils spiced with black pepper and with a sprinkling of clarified butter). When his food arrived, he quickly finished it and set out on his sojourn.

The receptionist at the counter had told him to get to the northern outskirts of the town, where the road leading to the National Highway Number 4 commenced. A little further down the road, he had said, would be visible a huge open area to the right, where the circus could be seen to have pitched their tents. After much enquiry at the bus stand, he was finally shown a bus that was leaving the town by that road to places farther beyond. The conductor of the bus was constantly yelling, 'Para, para, para,' the final destination of its journey, constantly soliciting passengers. Although the wait lasted for just about five minutes, it appeared to Manu that the bus would remain immobile forever. And that twenty minutes of slow but steady bus journey seemed so excruciatingly slow to be almost never-ending. He was squirming impatiently as the conductor was calling out at the top of his voice the names of each stop as the bus approached the same, facilitating those wishing to disembark and taking in those boarding to go further. In a while the conductor called out the name of the same stop from where, the hotel receptionist had said, he could get to the open field hosting the circus. That jerked him out of his seat, and he moved with alacrity to the door, ready to alight. As soon as the stop came up, he got down swiftly. Without even waiting for the bus to move away, he got down from the back door and briskly turned around the corner behind the bus and, after checking for any oncoming vehicle, dashed across the road to the other side in a moment. He anxiously scanned the scene before him, which showed a vast expanse of area stretching up to the horizon, dotted with huts grouped into clumps of settlements surrounded by trees, probably a village, interspersed by long stretches of fields, and there towards the left, a little farther, he could see a bigger distinct set of tents with some flag appearing amidst them, which he instantly recognised as being those similar to his beloved circus.

At last, indeed at last, there was the circus! He couldn't contain himself, just couldn't wait anymore. Walking, running, stumbling, and puffing, he advanced rapidly and in a while entered the village. Then steadily going past a wide road that winded through the village, he came upon, on one side of it, a huge gateway. Strangely, it didn't indicate any specific name. But he went ahead and moved towards the ticket counter. But he didn't find the familiar faces manning the counter. He asked for Anil and Gangoo and then for Munna and, after a pause, for Robert, but nobody seemed to be aware of anyone by those names there. He thought it was funny and again persisted in his questioning, asking for Pawana and her old man. He was puzzled as to why it felt so strange here. Irritated by this persistent questioning that the man at the counter felt was interrupting his work, he motioned to someone manning the corner gates. 'He's come in search of someone, please help him' he said.

After much explaining and convincing, the guard decided that this visitor needed someone more knowledgeable than he and took Manu inside. Someone met him there, and soon he realised these were neither the people nor the circus that he was looking for. This was just a very different circus, completely different one. For him all circuses were one in which Pawana was there. For someone whose mind space was taken up by Pawana and her circus, it just didn't seem to register in his mind that there could well be other circuses around. Somehow it did not occur to him till that moment when that reality struck him hard. He felt as though something rammed into his solar plexus, sucking the air out of him. Disappointed and dejected, he made his way out. He wearily and reluctantly made his way back to the hotel and by noontime packed up and left the lodge. After having his lunch in a restaurant, he trudged back wearily to the bus stop and, after waiting a while, on the arrival of the bus going towards Mayapuram, boarded it.

Manu had a recurrence of nightmares. In the vision, he could see vividly a place of worship with a gleaming temple where a large number of men and women had congregated, amidst whom men heavily armed with swords and all barged in, taking cover and positions among them even as shouts emanated for surrender from the king's men. There was utter commotion and chaos, although Manu escaped from it all in the end. On another day, he found himself in a medieval fort in a grand city ruled by an empress, and then he got to see the empress in person till one day she was attacked right before his eyes by her treacherous minister, who, of course, was overpowered by her loyal guards and later executed. Who was it? Raziya? Her beloved subjects mourned her.

As weeks went by, the agony of false alarms and tantalising hopes intensified. Even as his friends and room-mates, Thomas and Raju, tried to console him, urging him to forget Pawana and get on with life, every corner of Mayapuram reminded him of his beloved Pawana and the circus. After months it came to his mind that in this town the memories of Pawana would haunt him forever. There was little he could do to get away from it here except maybe by leaving this town. Even while he was trying to get to terms with the loss of Pawana, a new threat loomed in the horizon of a strike in the factory where he was working. In fact, the entire industrial town was in a state of dissatisfaction. The workers union in and around Mayapuram announced a unanimous joint action against the companies there for going on an indefinite strike. For long they had been negotiating a wage hike, considering the exponential increase, in their living costs, but to no avail. Exploitation of workers had gone on for too long, they felt. There was an imminent threat of a lockout now, and how long the stalemate would last, no one could say. There was nothing but loss of wages for prolonged periods, even loss of their jobs, and a most uncertain life that stared at them all.

Meanwhile, Thomas was planning ahead. He disclosed to his room-mates that there were some of his relations in the Gulf, and he had a standing invitation to get there. Maybe he would move there if things got worse. His other room-mate was also making efforts to move elsewhere. He was exploring a possible opening in some Bombay-based firm and maybe he could make a move at an appropriate time. And then simultaneously for Manu hope floated in as an idea! Maybe he could go somewhere much farther, say, to the north of India, and perhaps somewhere locate her. Yes, it was a distinct possibility that he could locate her more easily from there. She did say her ancestral land and their family deity was somewhere in the north or north-east or north-west, thereabouts. He had never quite asked the exact details and locations. He never imagined such a day as this, completely separated, lost and away from her, would ever come. By simply sitting here, it was clear that he was never going to find her. He was now going through advertisements seeking for all kinds of engineers and applied for positions for the public works department in Delhi. Later he appeared in the public selection exam for the positions.

Meanwhile, the situation in the city of fortunes was getting from bad to worse. Old-timers saw something sinister in it. Nothing like this happened before, they bemoaned. For them, bad days had befallen the town the moment the circus was driven out. The years that the circus remained in the town were the best that town had witnessed. But for Manu, there was no choice but to wait it out. It was a torrid time for Manu and his room-mates. After a protracted battle of wits, a lockout was declared, as they feared, in the run-up to which Manu, Thomas, and Raju prepared carefully their war chest, even moonshining, trying to save that extra penny lest they should be left in want and penury. It was not just Manu, Thomas, or Raju who were desperate but their families too were getting even more desperate, and so were their landlords. Despite all the efforts the threesome made to keep the regular flow of money orders to their families and hide the ugly reality, the newspapers sooner or later did them in. The landlords, surviving on the rentals, were equally desperate and worried about this regular flow of income that they had so taken for granted coming to an abrupt end.

A few weeks into this Industrial action, Manu was called up to Delhi for an interview for the exam he had written. He had to book his tickets and prepared to leave for Delhi. When the train pulled up at the station and he managed to alight, he emerged into a sea of humanity on a scale he had never experienced before. It was like a fifth of Mayapuram had converged into that one single railway station. It was thick with people all around and everywhere. Puzzled and a little lost, in the end he managed to find an autorickshaw. On the train to Delhi he had been advised by passengers about affordable and convenient lodgings close to the station. The autorickshaw proceeded from the railway station to a lodge quite close by, in Pahar Ganj. He found travelling even a distance of a kilometre was only at a snail's pace, twisting and turning and avoiding a tonga (a horse carriage) here, a pushcart there, some pedestrians now, a cow later, or cycle rickshaws, cycles everywhere. Getting through the hustle and bustle amidst a sea of passengers bound to or from the railway station with bag and baggage, with the way lined with shops and eateries, with patrons queuing up, all jostling side by side on these roads, amidst the smoke-spewing automobiles was a lesson in existence. There were any number of eatery carts on four-cycle wheels with iron dixies on kerosene pressure stoves containing heated oil and flat white pancakes being deftly broiled in the oil into hot and crispy fluffy ovals or roundels as puris or *bhatura*. Close to another corner was a filthy semi-open urinal. The air all around was a heady mix of smells of automobile exhaust, acrid burning oil, and stench of urine, which made him giddy. That's how he was welcomed to Delhi. But it gave him more hope, for it seemed so much in sync with what Pawana and her circus were. A lot in his dreams and nightmares and that which Pawana described bore much resemblance to many things here. He became now confident of finding her.

Moving across in the autorickshaw to the central verge of the city into the Connaught Circus, he gazed around in amazement at this colonnaded centrepiece of Delhi, of the stately architecture housing a series of shops that was once the principal marketplace in the early history of New Delhi. But he did not know that it was only the beginning till the auto passed by the many imposing buildings, the roundel-like structure housing the parliament, the various ministries, and then the ultimate, stately President's Bungalow, called the Rashtrapathi Bhavan, flanked on either side by gargantuan red sandstone blocks of buildings called the North and South Blocks, standing like sentinels, one on the north side and the other on the southern side, as the names suggested. It was a grand and imposing ensemble set in stone, more inclined to awe. It was a grand and bewildering change from the chaos and earthiness of Pahar Ganj to the centre of Delhi. It appeared as some journey through a time wrap, in a way, but it filled him with hope. Maybe here lay his destiny to find Pawana again. But in a while he reached his place of interview.

The interview took him now through a journey of myriad and inane questions, from names of obscure presidents and lands and things from the morning's papers. He returned to Mayapuram, awaiting further developments. But things at Mayapuram were getting nowhere, with the lockout limping on, although there were signs that the end could be nearing rather positively, with everyone's patience wearing out. Like Manu, Thomas and Raju too were making their moves. It was only a matter of time before the three friends departed, albeit one by one.

Meanwhile, for over a year in the north-western state of Punjab, things had been getting out of hand. There were killings and armed men milling about in places of worship. Mayapuram and Manu woke up one day to learn from the newspapers of the action by the government of the day as the army cleared these places of worship of armed men. Manu took a long breath and sighed. Armed men in a temple, and this! This wasn't good augury. Was this, then, what he saw in his visions?

Life was ticking by in Mayapuram, with Manu going around as usual with his routine. At around tea time, he and his factory colleagues assembled to have their scheduled tea break. Thomas sometimes played the radio in a low volume in the tiffin room as some sweet film music would flit in. Today too he flipped the switches of the radio with everyone enjoying their cup of tea, the music wafting in slowly from the set. But at times it only reminded him of Pawana and just served to heighten the pain of her loss. Many of these melodies were ones which they enjoyed hearing together. Meanwhile, Thomas queried one of his factory colleagues, an active member of the factory workers' union, 'What about the bonus this year? Is the management ready for it?'

'Yes, I think so,' replied the man. Abruptly the radio broadcast of film songs stopped, and after a brief pause, the radio was playing a bland melancholy tune, as though of mourning. This sudden change was inexplicable. A short announcement followed. Something grave had befallen the prime minister of the country. Only in the evening it was broadcast that she was assassinated by her own guards. It reminded Manu of his visions. Was it a true portent? What was becoming of him! Till the arrival of Pawana in Mayapuram, he saw no dreams or nightmares. It was all his farm, his parents, and work. And then it all began.

Events that followed in the days to come in the national capital were horrifying. Events of rioting, arson, killing of innocents in a fit of anger, piled on one another, which left hundreds of families tattered, bereaved, mourning their dear ones killed. Young ones were orphaned, girls widowed, the country shocked into tears, the capital gripped in fears. Man was adept at inventing miseries. In Mayapuram, these developments were met with incomprehension and fear.

Just then the news of the job offer that Manu was desperately seeking came in. Now more than two years after Pawana and the circus had left Mayapuram, Manu prepared to leave his town of fortune as well as misfortune. If Mayapuram without the circus was agony for him, then life without Mayapuram was a pain. He had to wrench himself from Thomas and Raju, with tears welling up in their eyes. Yet his spirits soared purely on the hope that he was, he believed, closer now to his quest of finding Pawana. In this sojourn, his family had almost no hand. But once informed that he was leaving for Delhi on a government appointment, the family welcomed it with cheer, yet apprehensively. Delhi, if not remote and unknown, appeared now more intimidating and grim. Yet to his family, government service was a matter of social pride that their family member obtained a position of authority and financial security. It was a statement of their arrival in society! But Delhi was so distant, two-and-a-half-thousand kilometres far, that there was none around who had actually been there except Manu. People around here only read about it, a news item to be read from papers or heard about it over the radios. The recent happenings there were certainly so scary.

When Manu arrived this time in Delhi, it was October and getting close to winter. But between the Delhi before and now, there was a sea of change. Coming to his lodge at Pahar Ganj from the railway station, moving through the Connaught Circus, and going to his place of reporting, he encountered any number of yellow-painted iron-framed movable wheeled barricades and police checkpoints closely watching every vehicle passing by as it slowly wound its way through the narrow opening between the barricades. Police presence was ubiquitous. There were cubicles or police watch stations with a wall of sandbags stacked before them. The plush bungalows of dignitaries in the Lutyens Zone had police watchtowers with mounted machine guns. Anoop had told him that this was part of the DIZ area, and Manu had rather innocently asked, a bit probingly, 'Denizens in zoo?'

Anoop was amused. 'Oh no, it is the Delhi Imperial Zone!'

'Who live here?'

'Oh, top officials of the government, Armed Forces personnel, MPs, ministers, etc. Here, you see, there is never any problem with water, electricity . . .'

And of course he could notice these were grand mansions laid out in sprawling lawns. The empire had long ended and the emperor is dead; long live the new emperors! While the proletariat and socialism was banished to the realities of Pahar Ganji, the old Delhi, in dilapidation and beyond the eastern banks into squalor, the new masters were quietly ensconced in the manicured lawns of their departed masters, in a dreamland far from the madding crowd, in wistful memoriam of the grandeur of a bygone era. Manu had an overwhelming feeling of being in a fortress, almost a war zone. Where had he come to? Was it the same place that he had been to a few months back? The very buildings of parliament, the ministries, President's Bungalow, the North and South Blocks that were stately and grand had become fear inspiring, a grand fortress. He felt besieged, like in a large prison from which escape was impossible. It had become a grand and imposing ensemble set in stone, more frightening than majestic, designed to subdue the viewer than invite. It was an inexplicable change bordering on insanity. Delhi was never going to be the same. When he finally reached his destination, he felt more relieved than anything else.

As he entered the office building, a guard who stood there stopped him and enquired about him and his business. On showing his papers and credentials, he was shown to a reception where a bored clerk looked up, scanning him from head to foot, and then took the papers from the extended hand of Manu. Presently he made out a pass and handed it over to Manu after he had appended his signature on a register. Manu then stepped into the building and took the lift to the first floor. Inside there he walked along the corridors, searching for the administration section to report.

Entering the section, he found it to be a grand room with several desks, big teak-wood ones, with green Rexine-covered squares at the centre of the wooden tops. These desks were all lined up opposite the wall facing the door from where Manu entered and opened into the room. The desk at the centre of this row along the wall was the biggest desk, behind which was seated an elderly man. It was flanked on either side by smaller desks turned at right angles, occupied by similar functionaries sitting behind these desks that were lined up from the farther end right up close to the door. That central desk, he concluded, must have belonged to the most important person in that room, the one in charge, whose nameplate hung outside. Around the rectangular room on the right and to the left along the walls, Manu saw that there were only steel-slotted angle shelves with piles and piles of dusty files behind the desks and chairs. It was a feeling of one having entered a warehouse of papers, with people in it only just by chance.

He could hear in the background the sound beat of *clickety-clackety*, which he later discovered to be that of a typewriter being furiously worked by a typist. Manu went up to that central desk in that room and stood there, papers in hand at the ready. The elderly official sitting there made no move whatsoever, his nose buried in the opened file before him. It was quite a while before he lifted his head to look at this young man before him. 'Kya hai?' he spoke in Hindi, before realising that this young man before him had come to take up his appointment. 'Naye langroot?' he exclaimed with a half-mocking laugh, again in Hindi, meaning 'a new recruit', or rather, a combination of langoor (a large grey-haired black-faced monkey) and a recruit. He took the papers from the outstretched hand of Manu, quickly read through it, and called out to one of the staff there, asking Manu to go along to him.

There were formalities to be undergone. He made a joining report and was advised to undergo a medical fitness test by appearing before an appropriately constituted medical board. He befriended Anoop among his new colleagues in his office. Although he was still waiting for his posting, his immediate and first concern was a proper accommodation. It was too expensive to stay on there, even in that rickety hotel. His mind thus engaged, on an impulse he confided in Anoop about his predicament. 'I have just arrived in Delhi today and am putting up in a hotel in Pahar Ganj, near the railway station.'

'Ah! You need an accommodation? Is that what you mean?' interrupted Anoop.

'Yes,' replied Manu.

'We three of us are putting up in Munirka, near R. K. Puram, sharing a rented flat. You are welcome. By the way, what about winter clothing? Have you any?' queried Anoop.

'Well, nothing specific. But what's so special about winters here? Is it so cold?' asked Manu.

'Ah, cold? You will shortly discover in a couple of months! So we must be doing some serious shopping for sweaters, razai, and so on.'

'What's a razai?' asked Manu rather quizzically.

'It's a quilt that you cover yourself with while sleeping in winters.'

'Oh!'

'Do you have enough money with you?'

'Ah, yes!'

'Oh, now you must actually be opening a new bank account. Come on, let's go to that State Bank branch over here.' Anoop led and Manu followed him.

Briskly, they finished the business of opening a new account. While Manu was anxious to know if they would be found missing at the office, Anoop told Manu that he had his bosses' permission, and anyway, Manu should not worry till he formally got his posting. Then they went around the state cottage emporiums, viz. those selling handloom textiles, cotton or woollen, including sweaters, metallic or wooden wares, and the like, set up by the various state or regional governments as representing the best on offer from their respective regions. Soon they wound up their purchases when it was nearly past lunchtime. They headed towards an eating joint, or dhaba in the local lingo, actually a Punjabi term. There he saw in operation a tandoor, or charcoal-fired oven—in fact, a steel drum walled and pasted with thick clay and wide mouthed at the top, with a small opening at the side at the foot of the barrel that kept the supply of oxygen steady into the oven whenever opened from time to time. It was shut off for most of the time to prevent excess of air, fuelling flaring flames, endangering both the baker and the bread. Manu observed the man first quickly placing a little ball of dough on the centre of his palms and swiftly switching sides in a cross-palmed clap action, once tilting to the right, with the right palm below and the left above, and the next moment keeping the left palm below and the right palm above, and repeated the motion till the ball of dough was worked swiftly into thick roundels. Manu then saw the man placing these roundels of doughs on an orb of thickly knotted cotton fabric flattened into a convex surface to hold the dough placed on it and gripping a convenient 'handle' of knotted cone of cloth on the reverse side. With a swift move the baker assiduously thrust the cotton orbs with the roundels of dough thus placed into the hot oven, or tandoor, sticking it onto the hot mud-lined insides and equally swiftly retrieving his hand back. Manu admired the mastery of the man on the job. He then watched with fascination the equally swift and deft retrieval, with a pair of long iron rod hooks, of the roundels of freshly baked unleavened bread, or tandoori rotis, out of this oven, being passed on through the waiter to the waiting hungry customers, who wolfed them down as quickly as they came. It was like watching a smooth production line in a factory!

But much as he admired the skill and artistry of the bread maker, he couldn't help but notice the sweat from the forehead of the baker dripping onto the bread and how he wiped them with a swift move of his fingers across his forehead while resuming to knead the dough in the same motion of his fingers. Truly he was now eating the sweat of the baker's brows! With hunger gnawing at him, he could barely tarry any longer. He would have to eat that hot piece of bread with or without the sweat. Slowly as he ate the hot tandoori bread accompanied by the spiced vegetables and a plate of sliced onions with a squeeze of lemon and a pinch of salt sprinkled over, along with a wiry piece of green chilli, he had to admit it tasted good. It was for the first time he experienced this strange and different but uniquely satisfying cuisine.

Manu took up residence with his new-found office friend, Anoop, along with another bachelor room-mate, Ramesh. All the three of them shared a two-room kitchen, toilet, bathroom government quarter in a residential area consisting of government quarters built for government servants. It was sublet, albeit surreptitiously, to these bachelors by the one to whom it was originally allotted, for a tidy sum. Anoop and Ramesh had arrived in Delhi only a few months back, at the end of the last winter. Being from the neighbouring states with a similar climate and having experienced Delhi winter, they were better prepared for it. Like any other set of bachelors, they were absolutely irreverent about household chores but ready to explore everything else around and got along like a house on fire.

As Manu slowly attempted to settle down, he discovered new problems. Every morning, they had to get up early, at the least by five thirty, to be able to fill up their buckets with water for bathing, washing, and so on, as the supply stopped by seven. Should they fail to rise up in time and fill the buckets, they would all be left high and dry. The evenings of many a day were spent wandering around that ended in a nearby shack in the edge of an ill-kept park. It was a place for them to have their dinner when they got tired of the chore of cooking, the kerosene fumes, and the food itself. But a careful scrutiny of the shack was a revelation for him. What passed for a roof of the shanty were gunny bags and plastic sheets spread overlapping on each other across bamboo strips in a framework supported by intermittently placed poles. Thick cobwebs or strips of gunny bags covered in ample soot emanating from the coal-fired tandoor in which the unleavened bread was baked hung from above here and there. The plates which were set before them were wiped clean with a cloth blackened with grease, by boys or men who were themselves clothed virtually in rags or soiled attire. He was reminded of a story in *Mahabharata*, when Guru Drona took a test of the archery prowess of his prince pupils. As he pointed to a tree with a bird perched on its branch, asking each prince what they saw, one replied he saw a tree, the other a tree branch, yet another a bird, but only Arjuna saw nothing else other than the birds eye. Such was his focus and so his success. So did Manu sigh; he was allowed only to focus on the vegetables, the bread, and his hunger and on nothing else. But if he had to escape this and the kerosene fumes, something would have to be done.

Even as Manu became aware that except the enticing aroma of the onions and finely chopped tomatoes being fried in oil to garnish their plate of vegetables

or lentils and the hot roundels of bread, there was precious little else inviting in
that joint to focus upon. He was reminded that he had come thus far thousands
of miles across, only in search of his beloved Pawana. Nothing else should
matter except Pawana. But then where was she? He was only fuelled by sheer
hope and hunches but knew not in the least where she was. There was just a gut
feeling that she was here somewhere around. But then *where* was the question.

There he sat brooding, lost in deep thought, mulling his next course of
action. Suddenly there appeared along a posse of policemen, each one of whom
were gripping the long straps of a long narrow rectangular box in dull green
with a long thin collapsible steel antenna, hanging down from one shoulder,
while a Sten gun, or a self-loading rifle, hung from the other shoulder. A
couple of them approached the hutment; the stall 'owner' and a couple of
boys obsequiously went up to them, greeting them smilingly and went about
inviting the cops to be seated on a *charpai* (a wooden cot covered by cotton
tapes, like a trampoline) laid just outside the shack, by the side of the lane.

The cops accepted their invitation with a grimace and set down that box on
the cot by their side, sat down on the cot, legs splayed and the weapon dangling
by their side and resting on the cot. Sporadically a commanding human voice
emanated from these boxes, streaming instructions or commanding someone
to do this or that. It was then Manu realised that this contraption was a
portable wireless set. He saw this unwieldy walkie-talkie for the first time, a
contraption that he saw was ubiquitous with policemen in Fortress Delhi, as
was the Maruti Gypsy, a vehicle that served both as a moving control room and
as impromptu roadblocks that appeared out of nowhere pronto to divert traffic!

One day, alighting from a bus, coming back from his office, he and Anoop
were strolling by the road, trudging the way to their residence, when they
were shooed away by some policemen. Looking up, they found a long posse
of policemen placed every ten meters or so along the wide road leading to
the airport, stretching perhaps up to fifteen kilometres. 'It's some damn VIP
again!' said Anoop.

'Who is, by the way, a VIP?' asked Manu. 'A very idiotic person?'.

'Oh, oh,' tittered Anoop. 'Here usually it is some minister. Everyone here,
especially the Ministers, are so scared after that assassination and subsequent
events they are surrounded by policemen armed to the teeth wherever they go.'

A very old gentleman living close to their quarter recounted with a nostalgic
and wistful look how in the very distant past, as a young boy, he had happened

to witness Mr Nehru go past him at a leisurely pace at almost touching distance on an open vehicle, smiling and waving. That very much reminded Manu of the time when he saw as a child the prime minister of this country going in an open jeep, waving at him and the crowd around him. That seemed like some other era in another planet.

With it being mid October, the Dussehra Festival was picking up pace here, Manu and Anoop eagerly awaiting it. Manu found that people in Delhi celebrated Dussehra as marking Rama's victory over Ravana the demon, which festival was celebrated and observed down south or in the east as Navaratra, or the nine nights of victory of the mother goddess Durga, achieved over another set of villainous demons. But even in these festival celebrations, the presence of policemen were ubiquitous. Even though the fair-like atmosphere prevailed, what with the Ferris wheels, ice cream carts, cotton candies, the vendors of aloo *tikkis*, or spiced potato patties, samosas (mashed potatoes spiced, wrapped in a thin wheat flour pancake folded into a near tetrahedron, and fried in oil), *golgappas* (or small roundels of fried pancake puffed and punctured to form a cup to hold spiced tamarind water), and so on, there were swarms of policemen milling around, checking the entry and exit of people into the maidans or open spaces, even making body searches. Even as Manu was watching in muted, somewhat bewildered, silence, Anoop shook his head, murmuring, 'Nobody at my village ever had seen a Ramlila with so many policemen with guns around. I don't know what madness has come over here!'

What Manu saw in the maidan were tall effigies made of straw and bamboo dominating the arena. They had large heads with exaggerated shapes of eyes, armed with a shield on one hand and sword on the other. The central piece was a ten-headed one. 'This is Ravan,' explained Anoop, pointing to the tallest effigy, the centrepiece in the group. 'And this is Meghnad, his son, and this is Ram.' Manu and Anoop together explored the city to discover that in almost every colony, in and around Delhi, in any open ground or maidan or park, a Ramlila was being enacted with these effigies. They varied in size and artistry and in grandness, depending on the size of the neighbourhood, their financial resources, inclination, and enthusiasm. But the principal celebration was at the one place where the largest gathering could assemble, the Ramlila Maidan, not far from the New Delhi Railway Station.

But with any number of these *leelas* and maidans, the celebrations were spread across the city, creating a security nightmare. Obviously, there were real one-headed villains to complement the mythical ones that the police were seeking to counter. But the prevailing atmosphere was such that people and the police saw only villains everywhere in men and women people with 'suspicious' looks or 'behaviour', whatever that meant, in the things they carried, in the tiffin box in the bag, carelessly placed bags under the seat in the bus, unclaimed luggage. In short, if your looks or movement or the things you carried didn't appeal in the slightest to someone, you were a suspect! In fact, anyone, anything could be a suspect! Such was the fear and tension that gripped the minds of people here. Fortress Delhi was reacting to the assassination of a prime minister!

With every passing day, Manu and Anoop together were exploring and absorbing the life in the city and its experiences. They sought to escape each day from their daily chores of housework, office work, and commuting from office to home. If the evenings were spent loitering around in the markets at their dinner 'stable', it was a total outing on weekends.

On one such weekend, tired of their daily fare and not quite in mind to get to the dhaba routine, Anoop, as usual with his adventurous streak, proposed they should be visiting the 'Tibetan refugee market'. Manu, curious to know what it was about, learnt about how the Tibetan refugees had set up a market in a location close to the ring road along the Yamuna River. Manu liked the idea of going there to have a look at what the market looked like but evinced some doubt about having food there, being told it was all Chinese. Anoop was rather critical. 'All you Madrasis are happy only with rice, with all that sambar and the dahi all!'

'But that's unfair! I have been having flat bread, tandoor roti, ever since I have arrived here.'

'So let's try out this too!' butted Anoop. With this ostensible reason of having food, they spent quite a bit of time in the said market, which Manu found had plenty of clothing, especially winter clothing, jackets, and so on.

In the course of it all, he saw how the Tibetans, since their arrival in India, had established themselves. One ageing pleasant Tibetian gentleman recounted an exciting journey winding through the passes amongst the snow-filled peaks of Himalayas to their perceived freedom, exciting because any journey to freedom was. Though he was happy here, he could not but look back to his beloved Tibet and to a day when he could get back to his mythical homeland arrested in the mist of his mystical memory.

Manu found that the western part of Delhi had Punjabi-speaking refugees from Punjab settling down, forever speaking of their *pind* in Karachi, Lahore, and so on, while the Bengali-speaking ones had settled down in the southern parts of Delhi, in Chittaranjan Park. Chacha, the old man in their neighbourhood whom they had befriended, related to him the tale of how he fled from West Pakistan along with his parents when as a mere boy, leaving everything behind and landing here. In the beginning, his father eked out a living as a hawker. Chacha too assisted his father every day once he returned from school. As he was a bright boy, he did well at school and landed a job in the government as a stenographer and slowly managed to get his siblings schooled and settle them in life. There were a minuscule number in Delhi from Burma as well. Delhi, it appeared, was one big refugee colony! Did he qualify to be one, he wondered!

On another weekend, the friends chose Karol Bagh, or 'crawl as bug', as Anoop quipped, referring to the snail's pace at which traffic and everyone moved around the place crowded with cycles, buses, motorcycles, autos, and shops spilling out onto the pavement, with a surfeit of pavement hawkers, hawkers, handcarts, etc. It was an age-old shopper's paradise of Delhi. It was an excellent way to window-shop, especially during the winters, when even if you bought nothing of note, you could savour the fun of poking around, get to see not just some interesting things but also get some balmy winter, with the sun on one's back, explore some street food, and avoid the boredom of the daily grind of chores and routine they followed. From morning they went around the place, first having their breakfast then going around watching hawkers set up their stalls, the shops open one by one. Manu and Anoop went around, finding some garment or trinket that they could take home to their siblings and family. By noon the place was packed with people jostling around. But the police pickets were also ubiquitous. Late afternoon, the two friends decided to have their repast and then, with nothing much to do, boarded a bus going to the Connaught Circus.

Manu was lost in thoughts about Pawana. For some time now he had not been experiencing any of those recurring nightmares or dreams. He had by this time a feeling that ever since the days of the circus, he always had some kind of forewarning of any impending disaster, near or afar. But apart from his room-mates, Thomas and Raju rarely disclosed or shared his fears. Few, if any, would, even his friends, comfort him, let alone believe in him. He himself never understood it at times, fearing he was going out of his mind, attributing these to his anxieties till he saw how events unfolding had an uncanny resemblance to what he saw in his visions. His visions were replicas not in details of time and space or even in the personae but in substance. It never told him if it was a past event or a future one and, if so, when or where except a vague hint. It was a matter of interpretation. But the moment the vivid details of these got reported, he knew that was what he saw. Maybe with time he might learn to refine and discern it. Mostly the dreams of his distant past had invariably Pawana in it, which he could not quite comprehend. What did those mean? What were they hinting at? If only it could give a clue to where she was, life could be easier!

Kutub Minar, Delhi

The bus had barely filled up with passengers, with the driver taking his seat and the conductor beginning to issue tickets to each passenger and collecting the fares. Just then a posse of policemen stormed in, demanding at first to inspect the bus and then commanding all to leave the bus. Apparently, they had some credible information of some object planted in the bus being a likely explosive. All of them rushed out in a hurry and drew as far away from the bus as possible. The policemen at length found some small metal lunch box tucked beneath a seat, left behind, taking it to be the suspected container of explosive, which was spirited away to a safe distance.

Manu and Anoop returned to their room as quickly as they could manage by another bus. Their day's fun was quite spoilt by this one incident that rather unsettled them.

Amidst these Manu joined an evening course in an engineering degree programme for diploma holders.

In the winter months that followed, the friends embarked on a mission of getting to know the very city they lived in a little better. They went around the ruins of the city, the many forts and the Tower of Kutab, or the Kutab Minar, and a mosque in the complex, which complex, Anoop explained, was built out of the materials of ruins of the very temple located in situ that was destroyed by these very builders. It housed an iron pillar, holding up a symbol of another emperor of ancient India. It appeared to him to be the totem pole of all the misguided ambitions and grandeur of empires that buried all the goodness of simple folks. They loitered around scores of forts, abandoned water tanks, and gardens in the three sub-cities that were built at different times that comprised the current Delhi.

But his dreams began reappearing. He saw himself in the precincts of a grand fort encompassing a very wide walled city. A grand city that was well fortified, its denizens all well provided for. He was a young soldier, curious and energetic, but content till he met this damsel—Jasmine, a lookalike of Pawana, except for her colour—that completely shook him up. Her allure was as overpowering as the fragrance and the colour of jasmine. So delicately chiselled were her oval face, her eyes dark and long as that of a gazelle's, which could put any man into a swoon. Her brows arched like the bow, her bosom full and yet delicately, beautifully shaped, her lips luscious and red like pomegranate, with a smile like that of a flower in bloom. Her flowing jet-black hair could keep him enthralled for hours. From then on she became his sole focus of his life, with the quest of becoming hers. His love interest was equally reciprocated, and the two were fast becoming inseparable. He discovered that she was the daughter of a petty official at a court, though higher in station than himself. Just as it appeared that this would continue and their dreams realised, a palace coup happened. In the battle between the rival princes, while he landed on the side of the victorious prince, his fiancée's father ended up on the losing side. Not that it mattered much to him. But it mattered to the victorious prince, who ordered a massacre of all those loyal to his half-brother. Manu tried hard to protect Jasmine's family till they were forcibly taken away. Her father was executed, as was her mother, while Jasmine was to be taken as a concubine for one of the nobles as reward for the services he rendered to the victorious prince, the king designate.

But Manu was not one of those to remain silent. He schemed, plotted, and planned, and together with Jasmine, escaped from the fort. But soon enough this escape was found out, and troops fanned out in search of the rebellious couple. But they had gone long past the chasing troops into the jungles and yonder. They had set themselves on the path leading outside the realms of this kingdom. They rode in the moonlight along the clear paths, while they hid in caves and thick jungles during the day. Three days and three nights thus, they rode till it appeared that they would finally be out of the reach of the marauding troops following them. But on the fourth and fateful day, luck deserted them. While a single stray arrow accounted for Jasmine, his anger and grief knew no bounds. Single handed, he destroyed a whole company before he was overcome and he saw a sword plunge down his throat, at which point he awoke from his dream-filled sleep.

Much later, when he went along with Anoop around the Chandni Chowk and the Red Fort, it felt strange that the whole of it seemed so familiar till he realised that it was these very settings that he had seen in those dreams of his. But he could never make out how he could have dreamt of something he had never laid his eyes on before, nor could he explain the connection that Pawana had with it. Was he getting to be a crackpot?

One night, as the room-mates had just gone to sleep, they were awakened by a big rattle of drums and fireworks late into the night. Manu actually thought it was part of some nightmare that he was having, only to realise that it was actually emanating from outside the window of their room and had actually awakened his other mates. When he peeped out to investigate what the matter was, he saw a long procession of men and women dressed in finery, with many men with grand headgears or turbans and a young man mounted on a horse, accompanied by those carrying lanterns on either side, while a set of men as in some band led the procession with their drumming and trumpeting. Although the faint resemblance to the tunes of popular Bollywood songs could be made out, it was barely musical. But the sheer cacophony was quite unsettling and unnerving. The procession and the band was a cheap and garrulous imitation of the military bands with their neat uniforms, with their horns and pipes and the drums. Perhaps the practice originated from the British times. With Manu enquiring, a sleepy Anoop replied, 'Some infernal marriage party. It's the groom's procession!'

....

Manu received a letter from Thomas, informing him that he was leaving for the gulf state of Kuwait and enjoined his friend to join him there. His other room-mate, Raju, apparently, had left for Bombay. Good for them, he thought. That meant none of those closest to him would now be in Mayapuram. But his thoughts went back to Mayapuram, the time he spent with the circus and Pawana. It was like another age, a completely different atmosphere and pace of life, something so magically far removed from this madding crowd here. And now his friend was calling him up. But his quest for Pawana had barely begun. He sighed. He would have to put away for the time being any idea of leaving this quest for her midway for distant shores.

Manu was back to his daily grind, wondering about what next and how to proceed, when he saw one day on the way back from his office a familiar banner that sent a wave of excitement. Was the circus here in Delhi? But this had a different name! He knew that having high hopes could disappoint him, as it did before. Nevertheless, it enlivened his slowly drooping spirits. At least it would be worth a try to have a look. Anoop accompanied him and was rather thrilled. He had just been once to a circus while still a kid, and he was anticipating some real fun. But he forgot that it was Delhi. There was a heavy posse of policemen all around, with lots of checking and security. All concerned in the security establishment were wary at any possible incident of bomb attacks. But actually into it, Anoop thoroughly enjoyed the show. As was only to be expected, Manu found no Pawana there, nothing even remotely concerning her except that it was a circus. At least it brought back some of the memories of the precious moments he spent with Pawana, but it also stoked the pain that he had for some time now suppressed.

Nearly a year passed since he had arrived in Delhi. With no movement forward in his quest for Pawana, he was at a loss to know where to begin. But then when he was asked to proceed on an official training to Jaipur, the capital of Rajasthan, suddenly he saw an opportunity come his way. Anoop, his senior colleague, had already undergone it, and now it was his turn. He grabbed the opportunity that came towards him with a greed and eagerness that surprised many around him. Only he knew the desperation within. Maybe this was going to be his chance, the chance! He carefully went over in his mind all that Pawana had told him about her ancestral homeland but could not remember of any pinpointed reference to any location. He knew that they worshipped the mother goddess, but where exactly lay their lost empire and kingdom was left tantalisingly unclear. If they were sufficient hints pointing to one direction or location, then there were equally strong hints pointing in another. It lay north. That much was clear, but how much further north—or was it north-east or north-west?—he wasn't exactly sure.

The journey to Jaipur was just about seven hours by train. But someone told him that going to the dargah at Ajmer was indispensable. Its hoary history, their description of its aura, its benign power to fulfil people's wishes were compelling enough to convince him not just of the possible chance of locating anything related to Pawana or its definite connection to her but also as an opportunity to at least seek all the blessings he needed for his endeavour.

The dargah at Ajmer, though not far from Jaipur, was in a densely populated locality surrounded by people largely poor in their shanties, with petty business around, in dilapidated old dwellings in a state of disrepair since time immemorial. And when it rained, the place was a sight to behold. The haphazard, congested setting, if anything, closely resembled the lanes and by-lanes of old Delhi, in and around the Chandni Chowk or the Darya Ganj, and so on. It was teeming with people, suffused with all imaginable smells, a heady concoction of incense and stench, the divine and the mundane, of filth and purity. But about its power he had absolutely no doubt. The dargah itself was nondescript, with well-worn floors and its not-too-alluring settings, yet there was a feel of power pervading its atmosphere, a soothing calm that was as instantaneous as it was electric that he could not but feel it. Of about so many things that she had said, this certainly looked a place that matched the descriptions of the places among those that she visited. The dargah was the tomb of a pir, or a saint, who had with his divine presence and blessings in his lifetime had wiped many a tear of both the high and the mighty and the low and the lowly. Now dead, his aura had acquired even a greater presence. More than just his divinity, Manu felt Pawana to be somewhere so close by in there yet proving to be so elusive. Thus he headed out of Ajmer to Jaipur in peace and calm, with redoubled energy and vigour, with a conviction that he would get to her certainly eventually. The moment he arrived there, he had the eerie feeling of familiarity. Everything around him kept him enthralled, as anyone setting his sights for the first time on a beautiful medieval city would be. In between his week-long training programme he and other participants got plenty of time to get around, looking up every spot. There were temples in and around Jaipur, each of which he sought to connect either with what she had described or he had seen in visions. Yet nothing precise was located. He waited for his programme to finish to begin his serious quest. As soon as it was over, on the weekend he headed for Udaipur. Sitting by the lakeside and dreamily gazing at the huge white palace on the edge of the lake framed by hills in the background, he watched the golden and silvery sun shine, now hiding among the clouds and now coming forth and playing on the waters in the lake below. He felt so much at home, as though he belonged here since millennia, watching the epic battles, princes and kings, the commoner and the nobility, all leaving their imprint, living through the changing seasons, of nippy air and blazing suns, dripping drizzles, howling storms, still waters, blooming meadows of the Haldighati, through the undulating sands of time and bristling brambles, and always with Pawana by his side. He continued sitting there long after the sun had set, the sky turning crimson and then dark, when the stars shone, the sounds of a hundred crickets emanating. He had no words, no explanations, nothing crossing his mind. He just remained immersed in the moment. He gazed at the stars, at the constellations high in the sky, wondering, *Are those stars still there?* He was told in his physics class that what he saw as stars were actually images of them that were light years away from them, carrying the images of what they were actually billions of years ago, just illusions of what they once were. Like images in a mirror, were they virtual or real? Were they still there? Who knows? Were those that transpired in Mayapuram real, all the feelings, the passion, and the love, or were they just illusions? But it didn't matter. The stars shone brilliantly, with the starry sky looking mysterious and magnificent, and it felt magical. And somewhere, he was sure, Pawana watched these very stars at this very moment, and he was sure she knew that he too watched. It's all that mattered.

A long whistle jolted him from his dreamy meditations to remind him how late it had gotten now. It was a whistle blown by a guard doing his rounds in the stillness of the night much after the crowds of tourists had departed. He got up, dusting his pants, and slowly and steadily trudged back the road a little uphill along the way, winding back, looking for a transport, and found the ubiquitous auto to take him back to his hotel. As the auto meandered through the nearly deserted and poorly lit streets, his gaze fell on a knot of women a little further up moving slowly as a group. They appeared to be villagers in their flowing ghaghra—i.e., ankle-length skirts, big nose rings, bangles covering their hands and arms, thick silver amulets at their ankles—trudging back to their dwellings after their day-long business. These were the kind of costumes that Pawana was found fond of wearing. His eyes picked out a particular lady latched on to a lanky, diminutive figure—was she Pawana? Instantly he thrust out his head from the side of the auto, peering long and hard to catch a glimpse of the half-veiled faces that were not clear in the sodium vapour lamps. In that flash, he felt she appeared to be indeed her, just a glimpse of that nose, the beautiful mouth, the small angular chin.

Impulsively, Manu motioned the auto driver to stop, but the driver, having watched his passenger's moods and actions, simply glanced at him with a suggestive smile. 'Good, eh? Sahib, tell me, I can arrange . . .' he trailed off. It was a while before Manu caught the hint. He could do nothing but gulp in shock and silence, and before he had recovered his composure, they had arrived at the doorstep of his hotel. Yet he had sufficiently gathered his wits about himself at that moment to dismissively gesture in an expression of disgust and in a firm voice, though with some agitation. He quickly paid his fare and alighted from the vehicle and fled into the hotel. He packed his bags and left for the railway station, this time by another auto. He was back in Delhi.

. . . .

Before Manu could drown again in his sorrows, there were urgent summons from home. His father wrote to him, saying that he was urgently needed, as he had begun to seriously consider finding a match for his sister, who was in the final year of her graduation, as it was an appropriate auspicious moment to begin. Meanwhile, his younger brother, he was informed, had got through his schooling quite well and was now preparing to pursue professional studies. But how was he to get home at such a short notice? It always needed a couple of months' advance booking to ensure the train tickets for the 2,400-kilometre-long journey home. But here, his father wanted him back home in less than fifteen days' time! And then the question of managing leave from his bosses. These were no immediate answers. If only maybe he had that divine power of teleportation as easily as the visions he saw, maybe he would be back home in no time. But eventually he managed it somehow.

His return to his parental home nearly a couple of years later after he left Mayapuram was greeted by his father with a 'Have you forgotten you have a home? Did it take a letter from me to bring you here?'. His mother was more than relieved on seeing him. It wasn't exactly the kind of reception the average son would expect. But then their household was no average one. In fact, the family hadn't seen him for quite a while ever since the Pawana episode, and he hadn't visited home when leaving for New Delhi. Now, seated, cross-legged on the bare floor, he was carefully listening to the exposition of his father. 'You see, your sister is now in the final year of graduation, will be twenty in a few months' time. We have been anxious to get her a good match. There are several proposals from various quarters. Your mother has identified the prospective grooms from among them. We would like to discuss this with you before we invite them over here. We would expect you to be here throughout till we conclude fixing up a match.' It was more a command than a request or a mere expression of desire to secure his cooperation and contribution.

After the breakfast, both he and his parents soon repaired to the drawing room to begin considering the proposals at hand. As they went through these proposals, his attention was caught by a particular one of a young diploma engineer like he was, working in a foundry. Manu enquired. His father replied, 'Oh! That boy, his horoscope matches quite well with hers, but you see there are other boys here with better future prospects. They have excellent well-paid jobs or professions. Look at this guy, he is employed in the Gulf, in some oil company. His horoscope is OK. But look at this other proposal, he is a doctor, excellent really, but the astrologer was a bit sceptical, you see. But I persuaded him to reconsider. He said that it can be fixed up by some poojas. They are from a well-to-do family. They have lands and buildings and . . .' he trailed off.

'But she will also need to be dowered well,' observed his mother.

'Yes, yes. But then what are sons here for?' replied his father, nodding at Manu. 'Wait till my son becomes a CA,"* he added, meaning the younger brother of Manu. Ever since the Pawana episode, he was becoming the cynosure of his father's eyes.

---

*   A chartered accountant.

After a while, Manu again spoke up for the young diploma engineer. 'Don't you think this boy will be more suited . . .?' prompted Manu, darting a glance a little sideways at his mother, tacitly seeking her support for his prompt. His mother nodded in agreement. But this prompted only a retort from his father.

'I told you, he doesn't have much prospects. Just look at the others! Don't you understand?' he spat out in irritation. It was obvious where his sympathies lay. His father was not seeking any opinions but was only seeking confirmation of his own opinions. Initially he was not even inclined to invite anyone but his own chosen favourites but eventually was persuaded to give in and invite all those shortlisted. In time, the prospective grooms were invited to visit them by Manu's father. His father was eagerly waiting from the very beginning the doctor's visit. They were the one's actually invited first and cajoled into making a visit as early as possible. They came, they saw, and they conquered—Manu's father, that is. Their dignity, poise, education, and most importantly, their wealth, status, their future appeared so awesome. He was more than prepared to accede to their every demand. 'Anything that you say and that we can' was his motto. The boy appeared nondescript, while Manu's sister was quite undecided. On the trot appeared the Gulf oil rig technician. He looked jaded, tired, a tad old. Though Manu's dad seemed quite satisfied, Manu's sister didn't seem interested.

By the time the turn of the third boy came, the reception from Manu's father turned quite cool. They were categorically told that he was already expecting the first two proposals to materialise, that he was a simple man capable of only a simple marriage. Manu's little sister was more inclined to this match than the others. The boy was handsome and winsome in manner.

A couple of days later, the doctor's family sent in their regrets, assigning no specific reasons, while the oil technician's family expressed their eagerness but, citing the horoscope, said it was unfortunate the proposal couldn't be taken further. 'Arrogance,' thundered Manu's father, 'of these rich and the educated! Oh, those horoscopes, what does it matter?'

'So why not try the third proposal?' was Manu's refrain.

'Oh, that foundry man, well, let them come if they want to!' It pinched Manu a little to hear that!

During his stay at Puzhakkara, Manu met Madman Murali. 'So you are here for the marriage market, eh!' remarked Murali as they met. They sat down to have a long chat. Murali disclosed to him what he never had all these years to anyone here. 'I left the army early despite having a commission and further prospects of advancement. I was witness to the brutal genocides by the enemy on defenceless people while working behind the enemy lines. War was no romance, nothing heroic about those soldiers there. While working behind those enemy lines, I happened to meet a girl. She was a Bengali, and I spoke no Bengali. Mostly we just used signs till I had learnt slowly to speak Bengali. Nevertheless, we fell in love.'

But she was a Muslim. It took some time before he learnt. But somebody didn't like their liaison. In an alien country, things could be difficult. The girl was spirited away, flailing, wailing. 'People cling on to their prejudices and miseries dearly even if it kills them all. They love it more than even their lives. It was so strange that people find war so heroic and killing a great act of valour. The piles of bodies that I had to push around and carry, those of everyone from heroes to the villains and to the innocents, made me sick. But it is stranger still that love is found even more hateful!' When he was back home after being discharged with a pension, he found both his parents on their deathbeds, having contracted serious diseases by the neglect of his brothers. They never completely recovered despite his efforts. When they were gone, it was a battle for their legacy. He left eventually his native home in disgust with whatever he had, settled down here, never to return. 'For others, we are mad! Ah! The circus will come. Atta boy, you be at it. But before that, there will be more pain!' But suddenly he sounded a note of caution. 'These days, so many of the youngsters are all going across the seas to the Gulf. Don't go there. I somehow feel it wouldn't be good for you. Be careful, Manu!'

Manu returned to Delhi without any proposal being concluded, a little unhappy at it all. He was back into the hurly-burly of everyday life, the nine-to-five man listlessly getting by. It was now summer in Delhi and hot in the day and even in the nights! One of those days, as he slept drowsily, drenched in his own sweat, with hot winds breezing over his *charpai* or the four-legged cot on the terrace of their flat, he drifted in and out of a scene where he saw himself seated in a bus among several passengers going somewhere along that looked like some mountainous terrain. As they traversed some distance, the bus suddenly stopped, and he heard some shots fired and shouts ringing all around and suddenly masked men barging in. A sudden gust of hot wind broke his sleep and his visions. It was fairly short, and by the time he woke up the next morning, he vaguely remembered something about some bus travel and dismissing it as something silly.

Manu, having discovered Delhi in winter, was now bearing the brunt of summer. Summer days in Delhi, he realised, could be spent, whether at home or at the office here, only huddled behind 'coolers' that gave them some relief from the scorching heat. Manu saw these coolers, unique to Delhi, for the first time there. These were a contraption comprising a fan and a motor pump fitted into a rectangular metallic box having metallic covers, with ventilating vanes on three sides. The metal cover had pads of wood shavings held in place by a wire mesh. As the motor pumped the water tanked inside the metal box, the water would circulate through a PVC pipe and drop onto the pads from all the three sides and the fan would blow out the cooled air.

For hours Manu and company had to spend night and day in these harsh months huddled behind these coolers in the rooms, listening to the constant sound of water dripping pit-a-pat in the insides and the whirr of the fans, which made afternoons drowsy and dreary despite the cool wind blowing generated by the evaporating water.

One day that hot summer, out of the blue, Anoop suggested to Manu, 'Why don't we got to Kashmir? What do you say?'

Well, he had never really given any thought to it. Then it crossed his mind in a flash—will he find her there? Why not? 'Yes,' he said firmly. A few days of leave combined with the weekend was about enough, by their reckoning. Ramesh excused himself, as he wished to go to his village in Bihar. The two set out at first by an overnight train to Jammu. On the morrow, they set out by bus from there on to Kashmir. In summers, Kashmir was the ultimate that allowed a temporary reprieve from the harsh summers despite there being other hill stations nearby.

The bus slowly and steadily meandered out of the city, heading towards the valley, and both of them slowly were taking in the beauty of nature that was unfolding before them. For Manu, seated by the window, he took in the scene unfolding outside, so eerily familiar as though he had seen it all before. He rummaged the innermost recess of his minds.

He recalled the dreams seen in Mayapuram in which he lost Pawana in a bizarre turn of events. He recollected seeing himself as a shepherd tending to his flock of sheep. Day in and out, he followed them. From early morning till late evenings or even in moonlit nights, he was shooing and shepherding his flock, keeping an occasional eye on the very young ones from wandering and getting lost, sheltering himself under the shades of trees or caves when the sun shone too harshly. He kept playing his flute all the while, by the moonlight, at the sunset, at the sunrise, much as he pleased. The only family he knew were his sheep; the only brothers he had were his sheep. The only friends were they. He wandered from glen to glen, brook to brook, in the woods, wherever there was grass and greens, water, and shelter in plenty. Lying on his back on the soft grass below, he gazed long and hard the at the sky on starlit moonless nights, at the honeycomb of stars that suddenly erupted when the sun went down, wondering what wonders lay amidst and beyond them. Were the heavens truly there somewhere up or somewhere here around?

Thus time passed till he met a young shepherdess, comely and kind, lovely. In one moment he was lost and found. He had lost himself as he never had and found a heaven that he never knew was here. He lost himself so totally in her that he knew neither day nor night, when the sun rose or the moon came or how many days or nights went by. All became one whole existence condensed into a moment revolving around his shepherdess. For him the staff in his hand was his sceptre, the sheep both his subjects and his family, the shepherdess his queen, the glens and woods his realm, the sky the roof of his palace; his heaven was right here itself. It was all so till one day some marauders attacked his herd of sheep, drove them off, and in trying to save them, spirited her also off. Yet he gave them chase till one of them shot an arrow into him.

In Mayapuram, Manu had woken up in his bed in a huff, with his sleep interrupted suddenly. He casually had related it to Pawana, even hinting that it was all maybe the imagination of his overworked senses. But for her it was something profoundly meaningful, no poppycock. She offered him no explanations but was only scared of its portents. Something evil had befallen some people some part of this planet, she said without explaining.

Now, Manu could see how all those glens, brooks, and mountains were right before him. As soon as the sun went down, the sky was a mass of starry spots so crystal clear, only because the whole place was far away from any city lights or any kind of lights at all. All that he saw in that dream seemed straight out of this place. He had never been to this place ever before, yet it was so familiar. As darkness enveloped one and all, with the bus chugging along hours into its journey, his enthusiastic friend dozing by his side, soon Manu also felt sleep overcoming his eyelids. Gently and slowly he slumped with his head resting by the side of the window on its frame of the bus.

It was nearly daybreak when the bus came to an abrupt halt. Manu and Anoop were still fast asleep, blissfully unaware of the world around. He opened his eyes to a great deal of commotion and shouts all round and people rushing out and some people vigorously motioning them to move out. Still groggy and not still comprehending what was happening around them, Manu and Anoop staggered out without any arguments whatsoever. As they alighted, hurried right on the highway flanked by open fields on either side and mountains visible in the distance, they suddenly heard gunshots ringing and some men rushing from a great distance towards them menacingly with what appeared to be weapons. Someone nearby, possibly a fellow passenger, motioned to them, and a couple of others close by literally pushed them in the direction of the fields, where the crops were grown quite tall enough. In that moment, they understood that something was seriously wrong, and running into the fields was a matter of saving themselves.

All the three made for the fields in time amidst the thick growth. They heard the shots ring not too far behind. On and on they went, a little bent as far as they could before they came to a halt. Spent, they stood there for a while, hoping to catch their breaths. Meanwhile the commotions around had died down before they resumed their journey further deeper into the fields till they came upon a small clearing. For the first time, they heard themselves utter something. 'Gayee kya? Are they gone?' asked Anoop in Hindi in near whispers to the man accompanying them, who replied in a heavily Kashmiri-accented Hindi, 'Hann shayad. Maybe.' But he signalled utmost caution.

After a considerable lapse of time, when they must have walked quite far from the highway, sufficiently deep among a wooded location, the man spoke up. 'I am Abdul, and I live not far from here. It was sheer luck that we were warned in time. I had woken up at least an hour before dawn and had seen some disquieting movements, and in the few villages on the way, someone waved and warned about trouble ahead. Thank God we are alive,' he concluded. After a long pause, he explained how he had been to Jammu on some business. The times here had gone from bad to worse, he said. In all his life he never saw anything like this. All their lives had become topsy-turvy. He said as a child and as a teen their lives were hard but beautiful. Despite their Spartan life, life was nevertheless enjoyable. Nature was benign and bountiful here, and one felt fortunate to be here. 'Now it's become living hell,' he said, shaking his head ruefully, his face creased with worry. He showed at a distance an abandoned-looking building which he said was that of some business that shut shop ever since armed men showed up there, abducted a few workers, shot dead one of the family members of the owner, and decamped with whatever they could lay their hands on. The owner fled, according to some to Jammu, according to others to Bombay or elsewhere. Presently they came upon a house amidst these trees and at a corner of a field, almost hidden amongst the vegetation. Abdul motioned them in. Abdul brought them into his house, where an old woman busy with household chores stopped in her wake and turned towards them, smiled, and greeted them. She was his mother. At length they entered the room and put themselves at ease.

Abdul even, as he said to his wife something about food and drink, all sat around in the room, setting down their baggage at a corner. Continuing from where he had left while they were hurrying through the fields, Abdul told them how over the years, through want and at times even penury, they had led a life of quiet tranquillity and calm till this calamity struck them. It was as though people had forgotten to smile. He said the fear here around was so real that it shone in people's eyes and haggard faces. You never knew when anyone here might get a midnight knock. For any resident, if answering the knock was inviting an imminent danger, then ignoring it was doubly so. It could be the marauding gunmen or the suspicious security men. They could displease neither. If they let either of them come anywhere near them, the other wanted to know what had transpired and if they were the other's agent! He didn't know where those good old days went and when at all it might return. He said he rued the decision of his father to turn a plainsman, into a farmer, from being a herdsman in the mountains. Life was tough, he said, there. They could barely survive and rarely afford new clothing. Even the footwear they used had only more stitches than leather on it! Yet it was beautiful, peaceful despite the hardship. As Abdul related wistfully to that distant, almost magical past, as a shepherd up in the mountains as a kid, it was then Manu remembered the short nightmare that he had some weeks ago. Coupled with the vision he had at Mayapuram, he realised that it mirrored just what he had just experienced in this journey and what Abdul had told him. Somebody, marauders, had robbed them of their heaven.

It was very clear that they could not go much further in this journey. After they all partook their breakfast and rested for a while, Abdul told how it was wholly unsafe for them to remain long here. He said he would make sure they were put back in any transport that would take them back to Jammu and back to their homes. He led them, at some risk to himself, to the outskirts of the city, past pickets and guard posts, to put them in a bus getting back to Jammu, then thrust at them a small pack of titbits to serve them during the journey despite their vehement protests. All the way back, the friends hardly slept. The same hills and mountains and the verdant scene seemed mysterious and frightening, as though hiding some venomous villains in its folds, ready to spring a nasty surprise, which appeared so inviting the day before. That they did return at least in one piece seemed a miracle when three days later it was reported that a bus full of passengers in the valley were waylaid by gun-toting men ordering the passengers to come out, segregating them, and singling some out of the many to be lined up and shot.

After their-near disastrous experience, Manu was despondent. He could do nothing. 'Where was she' was the constant question that racked his mind. He had consistently failed in his attempts to find any trace of her. There were tantalising whiffs of her presence in the midst of many a place he went, somewhere he could almost touch her, but nowhere did she materialise. Even as these thoughts were occupying his mind, tidings from home informed him of another disaster, rather for the pride of his family, especially his father.

A few months after those attempts to find a match, his sister eloped with a young carpenter. She then married him. Later she left for the Gulf across the seas to be together with her husband, leaving behind a huge gulf in the pride of her father and the minds of the family as also for their standing in the society. It all happened, at least to the appearance of his family, in a jiffy that nobody had time to react. From now on, at his native town, the family came to be referred to as the family whose daughter eloped with so-and-so. His father, meanwhile, was venting his anger at his ungrateful children, which conveyed itself in the letter. But his faith in his younger son still remained, as was his boasting. 'Wait till he becomes a CA!'

Anoop, seeing the moodiness of Manu, enquired politely what was troubling his friend. When he learnt about what transpired at Manu's home, he pacified him like all young people, saying, 'Why should it bother anyone if she is really happy?' But what Manu dreaded more than just the happening was the urgent summons that his father sent him. With his own mind in confusion about Pawana, he had no more stomach to face his father and family. He went off to the nearest STD booth and rang up his home to tell his tearful mother (luckily, not his father) how terrible it all was but that his job kept him too busy for him to be able to come there and signed off. It was the first time ever that he had, in a manner of speaking, defied his father's command. It would in fact be a long time before he would meet his family again.

It was back to routine, though their minds were not still back to routine. Their experiences were something that wouldn't let them be so. It took some weeks for them to calm down. A few months down the line, Anoop was at it again. As usual, he was finding another way to get himself and his room-mates out of their monotony and his friend's despondency. 'Hey, why don't we get to Shillong or somewhere there?' he proposed. It was possibly the better time of the year for them to make such a foray. It was a picnic to a picturesque spot that was actually driving Manu to this journey. They moved along the plains, across Uttar Pradesh, the vast fields, small towns, and villages and leaving the land of Ganga and approaching the land of Brahmaputra. Even as they reached past a narrow piece of land a few kilometres wide that shared borders with neighbouring countries on the south, north, and even a little in the east, there was trouble awaiting them. When the train stopped at one of those stations, it was already dusk. After its halt, it would not move, even after an hour had passed. They did not know what the matter was. There was small talk among the passengers, all enquiring anxiously as to what the matter was.

'There is some problem,' said one of the gentlemen with an assured shake of his head. Certainly something was not right there.

In a while, they found out that there were physical disruptions to the tracks a few kilometres ahead and it would be hours before it could go ahead. The adventurous young men, who were so enthusiastic on this journey just a while back, were now having furrows of worry on their faces, particularly Anoop. 'Hey, was this idea OK?' Anoop asked Manu.

Manu smiled back. 'No point in worrying. Let's enjoy this adventure,' he replied. Slowly Manu and Anoop began to doze as soon as they had finished their train packed dinner of some watery lentils and stiff half-cooked piece of unleavened bread. Though a little restless and worried by this sudden detention of the train, Manu was soon deep in his slumber. It was still dark when he felt a sudden jolt wake him up. It was actually the sudden pull of the locomotive, as the train had finally got started.

It had taken nearly two days for them to finally reach Guwahati. From the morning newspapers, they learnt that were some armed militant groups that were aiming to disrupt the railway traffic and causing a derailment that had actually removed fishplates from the railway tracks, holding the steel rails in place, which was luckily discovered and an accident averted. 'Would it be again another . . .' was the question beginning to take shape in their minds. For Manu, it never mattered, so long as he could get to Pawana. And strangely he noticed there were no dreams this time. Strange that he was almost wishing for visions, even as these were now beginning to trouble him. Coming out of the railway station, they were besieged by men swarming around, haggling for customers, offering either a taxi or a lodging. But the friends were not in any hurry. They were looking around, taking in the sights and sounds of the place, walking around till they noticed the vast expanse of the Brahmaputra rolling by, the only male river in the country. The sight of the sheer expanse of water was so compelling that they watched it for quite a long while with mouths agape. For Manu, it took him back to the backyard of his native home and, in fact, to so many places there, where such a sight of a muddy, reddish expanse of water amidst the overhangs of verdant banks was usual except that this was such a mighty expanse of water that he would never get to see back there.

As both the friends stood agape, watching the river flow, taking in the verdant landscape, each lost in his own thoughts, a gentle voice snapped them out of their meditative state with a polite poser. 'Sir, don't you need a lodge?'

It was Anoop who actually spoke up. 'Actually, we want to go ahead to Shillong.'

But this guy was not one to take a no. 'Yes, yes, we can certainly take you to Shillong. We provide taxis for local tours and also to Shillong. But at first you need to take rest, freshen yourself up, take breakfast. Besides, there are wonderful things to see here at first!'

'Like what?' asked Anoop.

'The bison, the tiger, and of course, the rhinoceros?' The logic seemed irrefutable and the rates reasonable and the offer irresistible.

The friends repaired to the suggested lodgings to what was rather an old building, an aged bedstead with folded, laundered bed sheet, actually a yellowing, stained sheet passing off as white sheets, and a passably clean toilet. Anoop and Manu hurried through their routine before getting ready for their breakfast and then for their rendezvous. As they began their ride, neither of the room-mates had really any idea as to where they were heading nor about the hazards, although they were told that the ride was a few hours long going further north-east. As they wound up the long road through thick jungles, the escort regaled them with stories of tigers, bison, and rhinoceroses, even boasting about their bravery in dealing occasionally with incidents involving these animals going wild and how they rescued many a tourist narrowly from the fury of these animals.

A couple of hours into this wild journey their van came to a rather sudden halt. The driver and their escorts closely examined from every possible angle the reason for this sudden stoppage. With some sustained efforts, finally the vehicle started off just as mysteriously as it had stopped. Finally after hours of driving through thick jungles and forests, they were approaching their destination. As they were on the outskirts of the protected park for these wild animals, it was thought prudent to proceed at a very leisurely pace, where animals, if any, would be sighted and so as not to disturb them right in the middle of their routine.

Everything was going along fine. Manu and Anoop were gazing at the distant scenes as well as that close by for something lively, interesting, and lo and behold, they espied not one but two rhinoceroses, a big and a small one, possibly a mother-and-child duo, rather at close range. They might as well have missed it because of the screen of trees and bushes hiding them from the view. The van was halted, and they were all attention, gazing at these wild denizens. All were in rapture, most of all the guide, who confessed to them the truth that in so many visits here he had rarely got to see the rhinos, and that too up so close, quite in contrast to the boasting of their heroism in face of such 'close encounter', as claimed earlier. Just for a few moments, their attention distracted, they turned their heads at some slight ruffle on the tall grass and jungle, coming from the other side of road, though nothing appeared. But in another moment a rustle was heard exactly from where the rhinos were there, and they turned their attention back. Their blood froze and each one left nearly motionless as they saw the big one charging at a furious pace. The 'brave' driver and the escort were the first to capitulate from the vehicle, leaving the hapless friends in jeopardy. Presently, they mustered enough courage to immediately abandon their vehicle and take shelter behind a huge tree just close by, by the time the rhino had spent her fury on the vehicle.

But suddenly something else distracted their attention. Gunshots were heard. There was commotion and confusion. The rhinos had disappeared, and so had the driver and the escort. Before they knew it, heavily armed gunmen surrounded them. They had gripped them, motioning them to move. Their hearts leapt up, as one couldn't argue with those with guns. So they moved through that jungle land, now across grassy expanse, and now by the side of trees and bamboo bushes. After seemingly a very long trek on foot, they came upon a clearing where, seated beneath a large tree, were a couple of men again with guns, who looked up. They had an air of authority, both in their demeanour and by the deferential behaviour of those escorting Manu and Anoop to the seated men. Both Manu and Anoop were motioned to sit right down on the grass clearing while the escorts stationed themselves behind and by their side. Neither Anoop nor Manu understood a word spoken among them in a language quite alien to them.

In a while they were offered some water to drink in what appeared to be a piece of bamboo pipe fashioned like a glass for holding water. Both of them drank silently, not yet comprehending what had befallen them and in whose company they were. Who were they? Were they some desperadoes, some poachers, or some extremist group, and what did they want from them? Nothing was clear. In moments, the men got up and asked the friends to stand up, and then all moved along as a group. They must have kept on for at least an hour, sweating in the humid environs, before they came upon a few small huts and were led into it. Inside they were again motioned to sit down. Where they were and how far from the nearest highway or road, they knew not. Hunger was by now gnawing at them, and Manu motioned to indicate thus. It was quite a while before they were offered some cooked rice. Some of the guards were also seen partaking of it, with their weapons held across their knees. A couple of them, however, stood guard with the weapons drawn at the ready. These thatches held inside simple benches or chairs and containers of wood, which appeared like regular dwelling units of tribesmen. There was as yet no hint of who they were nor what they wanted. There were here and there some vestiges of animal remains, a mounted bison head, and what appeared as a few animal skins. Were they tribesmen or poachers or still some others? Not a word was spoken among them, and there was hardly any communication except by gestures. Slowly it was getting dark, and they were tired, and when sleep came over, they just rolled onto the mud floor, watched by the men.

Manu slept only in fits and starts. In the dead of night, all were woken up by a short alarming shriek. A snake fell on one of the men, who was jolted out of his sleep. There was such a frightened commotion, weapons being drawn at the ready. Apparently, a rat snake, in its frenzied scamper along the smooth bamboo pole high up in the cross piece holding the thatch above in chasing a rat, fell down on one of the men sleeping below, thus the commotion. His sleep disturbed thus, Manu woke up thereafter intermittently, only to see someone or the other of these men keeping watch, guns at the ready. It was very late into the night when Manu finally dozed off.

The entire ensemble, barring the couple of guards, woke up quite late in the morning. And then it was time for those two guards to snooze. For Manu it appeared now that these men were some kind of rebels. So Manu surmised that they were apparently destined for captivity for quite some time. Neither its intention nor the purpose was known. For the first time after their capture, Manu enquired from his room-mate, Anoop, how he slept and whether he wasn't feeling hungry, as they had got nothing after the lunch of rice and some lentils. Even as Anoop began to reply, one of those gunmen motioned to him and pointed at Anoop's side. Someone brought in a huge bunch of bananas and placed them before these men. Each had their own pick, and both the friends were motioned to take their own. The thought that came to Anoop was almost instantaneous: that they were monkeying with them.

But it came as a surprise when the seeming leader of the group suddenly addressed Manu, in comprehensible English, as to what exactly they were doing here. While Anoop was quick to say that they were just tourists, Manu paused for a while before he replied about wanting to see a temple somewhere around here dedicated to a saintly princess of a tribesman of a lost empire. For a few moments nothing seemed to have registered on these men, all of whom seemed immobile and became sort of speechless. After what seemed, in that charged atmosphere, to be an eternity, the leader shot back, 'How did you know this?'. Manu slowly related to them about Pawana, how she was variously known as Ruhani, Ruksana, Esther, etc., about Pawana's father, their tribe, and the tribesman, slowly and finally touching upon briefly how he came about them all without quite betraying the love interest he had in the chief's daughter. Did they know anything like that here was Manu's question. He then followed it up with a request for their assistance to get there, if they knew anything about the place of worship. He wished so very much to visit the place. By this time, Anoop was left staring, almost open-mouthed, at this narrative by Manu, which he could barely believe. Was it some fantasy to get them out of here, or was Manu just getting unhinged?

After a considerable pause and seeing that his lengthy recounting of the true purpose of his visit elicited no response, Manu again repeated his request. The 'chief' responded, 'Yes, we will take you there.' But he added, 'Only you!' While Anoop felt even more perturbed and mystified, Manu was not just elated, he was ecstatic.

He couldn't believe his ears. It confirmed at least the location of those related to Pawana's ancestral land and that it was no fiction. So could Pawana be far? His hopes soared. But sounding concerned, he asked, 'What about him?', pointing to his friend, Anoop. A firm 'Don't worry' was the answer.

But it was no easy passage for Manu. He was taken blind-folded for nearly an hour on foot then in some vehicle, possibly a car, for what appeared to be almost two or three hours, on what felt like some hilly terrain from the twists and turns he felt the vehicle was making, the steep gradients that it negotiated, and the knocks it was taking before they arrived at some location. After walking blindfolded for a while, his blindfold was opened for him to behold on a verdant hill side a very old place of worship a little way from a group of dwellings. Slowly entering its hallowed portals, he found slowly, steadily, calm and peace descend on him. He felt slowly filled with some inexplicable hope in his heart that was missing since the time he spent after the circus left Mayapuram. Maybe he could know something about Pawana. He saw an old, a very old man, possibly officiating there as a priest or maybe some mendicant, seated. He approached him and gently enquired. The old man said nothing. Manu wasn't sure the old man understood what he said. He wondered what language he would understand. He just related to two names—that is, of Pawana and her father, the chieftain of the tribe. On the second repetition, the old man merely nodded and said something which meant nothing to Manu. Meanwhile, the guards accompanying him, after observing the blank look on Manu's face, translated what was said by the old man, albeit haltingly, in English. He meant, in effect, that it was long, long ago when the chieftain was a young man and Pawana a baby girl. He hadn't seen them since.

When Manu was back, the chief, so to say, told him how it was unfortunate that they had to meet him as fugitives. They have been like Pawana, been accursed to keep fleeing from one hiding place to another, for ages. This had been a peaceable land, fertile, fecund, and there was much happiness and harmony till it all got disrupted by rivalries. One day, he hoped, their aspirations would be met and things return to as before. For a long, a very long while, even after returning to Delhi, Anoop was groping in the dark, still speechless about what happened. Despite repeated questioning of Manu and straining his mind, he couldn't understand what really special transpired between that militant rebel and Manu that these dangerous-looking men just let them all scot free! But Manu didn't quite let him into Pawana and all. But though he told Anoop that all this were no fiction, he confessed his surprise at this fortuitous coincidence.

It was with a great deal of relief, so to say, even with a sense of light-heartedness, that Manu returned to Delhi. He had this feeling of somehow getting to Pawana ultimately; although he could find her nowhere, he got to see those lands and vestiges, connected to her. But the images of those armed men didn't quite gel with that of the temple of peace and love. After his return, he had a recurrence of nightmares not once but twice, in one of which he saw scenes that certainly belonged to those lands that he had just been to. There were violent conflicts and deaths, where the victims resembled people from some other lands. And then he was reminded of what had happened to the railway tracks on their onward journey. He felt uneasy. Something sinister was brewing there. But the second nightmare showed him levitating all on a sudden in a crowd and getting blanked, by which time he had woken up, with that scene left incomplete. He could make nothing of it.

Days later came the answer to one of those. As he had apprehended, armed men, possibly native rebels, had killed labourers who came from outside these parts for eking out a living, getting death as wages in return. After every such development, Manu and Anoop saw the mood in Fortress Delhi was getting tauter. Almost every day, they were getting stopped on a sudden at least a mile away from a roundabout or crossing through which a VVIP passed. Traffic all around came to a halt a mile away. Police pilot jeeps would zip in, coming around these roundabouts and alert those on duty on these roads. Policemen swung into action, setting up roadblocks. The Gypsy patrolling the area were turned right into the middle of these roads and parked themselves, barring the way across, till the esteemed heavenly bodies with numerous escort vehicles in tow with blaring sirens had passed by. Thereafter, another pilot jeep, with its own siren, signalled the end of the siege.

Advisories and announcements made either in media or even over public-address systems set up in vehicles, usually autorickshaws, plying around the city, warned people to desist from picking up unattended objects anywhere. Carrying bags or even water or tiffin boxes to cinemas were forbidden. It became a routine to have men and women to be patted down whenever they had to come in to watch a film. It was as though the enemy was there everywhere, not in some distant borders. That year, the Dussehra Festivals passed by with some anxiety, as did Diwali, under the watchful eyes of the police. Every nook and cranny, every marketplace and place for congregation were under watch. Meanwhile, there were makings of a scandal brewing for some time now in the purchase of some guns for the Army, and a new government came in with the promise of getting to the bottom of it. But it ended up sinking to the bottom by the detonation of the reservation bomb. Delhi still continued in siege.

Effigy of Demon Ravana & Brother at Dusshehera Celebrations at Delhi

One of those days, on a routine phone call back home, he learnt that his brother had finally cleared his CA exams and had now been offered some position in a firm in Kuwait. Well, his father was a very proud man, and he made this known to Manu. If nothing, his hurt pride after the episode of elopement of his daughter was somewhat assuaged by his second son's success. It was just the icing on the cake that could possibly wipe off the last vestiges of bitterness remnant in his father's heart. But that could anyway put Manu's position in jeopardy! His monthly remittances from his government salary in rupees would pale in comparison. That set Manu thinking. He too was an engineer, now nearing the end of his graduation, with plenty of experience, and the Gulf needed plenty of engineers. His erstwhile room-mate and friend, Thomas, was already there and constantly exhorting him to come over. Manu felt that may be he too should make a move.

He first applied for a passport. Thomas was all eager to help when he learnt of Manu's interest in moving to the Gulf. He asked for Manu's curriculum vitae to be sent over to his company, which had some opening in a branch in

Iraq for their consideration. All this was happening without even his other room-mates or his family knowing about it initially. As he awaited further development, the International Trade Fair come upon New Delhi. Circuses here had inexplicably disappeared. Manu hadn't seen them at all except in the very first year of arrival. But these trade fairs were becoming something of an occasion for picnicking, where the whole of Delhi and around converged despite all the security threats, pat-downs, and hassles.

Anoop and Manu too decided to pass some time there. There were stalls all around in huge halls. Foreign traders came with their wares, the Iranians and Afghans with their dried fruits, the Turks with their glassware, and so on. There were separate pavilions that housed permanent exhibits from each state spruced up for this occasion, with artisans joining in with their wares. Crowds thronged. From the morning, Anoop and Manu strolled around lazily, looking up each of the stalls and wares, including exotic-food stalls giving a selection of the regional cuisine. Like everyone else, they too lined up before these food stalls first to have their breakfast and much later at another stall for lunch. Sauntering around in the balmy winter sun, Anoop struck up a conversation with one of the girls, while Manu was lost in his own world. And then they got into one of the halls exhibiting household wares. With the whole crowd pushing them on, they were moving as though in some conveyor belt, gazing around. Manu and Anoop and indeed the whole crowd around there were so absorbed in gazing around and shopping, oblivious to what was happening around them.

The next moment, Manu felt levitating out of the ground so smoothly, much in the manner that he had visualised in his vision, and he thought, *What the hell?* And then there was a loud, deafening sound, and it was all blank. Nobody knew what was happening. The explosion was so powerful that it ripped and killed scores, with torn limbs and body parts thrown all around, the injured and the bleeding all scattered around. There was utter confusion and mayhem, with thick smoke emanating from there. Nobody knew what exactly happened and where. Those surviving were in a daze. They were still trying to figure out what actually had occurred.

When Manu came to, he saw himself in a strange place hooked to some tubes, with his ears still feeling stuffed and ringing. He drifted off again to sleep to wake up a few hours later. This time he saw images of a woman in a white overcoat and another man in a white overcoat, presumably the doctor, asking how he felt. He was told that it had been over three days since he had lain there, and he had been drugged but otherwise, he should be fine except for the few scratches on him here and there. But they said he needed to be kept in observation for a while. It was becoming clear that he was in a hospital. He asked after Pawana and Anoop, but nobody could say anything about someone of that name. He drifted back again to a dull stupor. It was nearly a week when he regained full consciousness, but still there was a complete blankness about what had happened and why he was there. All he recalled was his going to the trade fair, and nothing beyond. It was then one evening that he saw Anoop trooping in, looking for someone all over the place till he espied Manu looking at him. Anoop almost gave a whoop of joy and rushed to him. Manu and Anoop were relieved that each of them were alive, and at least Anoop appeared to be OK. Anoop came over, literally shouting, 'Are you OK? I have been hopping mad, looking for you.'

And Manu replied calmly and rather a bit feebly, 'Yes, but I too was asking after you. But nobody knew anything about you!'

'How could anybody have known anything about me in that big crowd? I had completely lost you. I was busy striking up a conversation with that girl you saw there, you see! We were so busy talking that we were very slow walking up to that hall and stopped at the very entrance of the hall you entered. Meanwhile, I did not notice that you had disappeared inside. It all happened while I was still at the entrance, talking to that girl. The force of the explosion was immense, and so was the sound. I was just so lucky to be quite away from it. In the confusion that followed, none of us knew what to do or where you were. Just then many firemen and armed policemen streamed in, along with medical staff. We were all asked to get clear of the place.'

In a while, the doctors treating them all came on their rounds. Seeing that there was finally some visitor for Manu, they nodded at him, telling him that he was doing well and could be discharged soon in a couple of days. Manu, just in the passing, asked how and who had discovered him and brought him here. Was it the policemen? The doctor faintly recollected rather a young woman with a small boy in tow helping a couple of attendants bring him in from an ambulance to this hospital. But who was she? How could he have known? He replied it was by sheer chance that he was at the entrance to the building, and in that prevailing chaos, it was some miracle that he could even recollect this much. 'It's true!' seconded Anoop, further telling Manu that for days after, there were alerts all around the capital, and hoax calls and rumours floated around. These were hogging the headlines in all the newspapers as well creating an atmosphere of fear and anxiety.

Well after his coming back to work, Manu required regular visits to the doctor to help him cope with the sleep disturbances, nightmares, and hearing issues that he faced. The doctors said these were post-traumatic events that might take a while in subsiding. A few months later, it hit him again. Manu had a stark, clear, and horrifying nightmare. He saw clearly some kind of gathering where a rather prominent gentleman in appearance, like some leader, making his way to what appeared to be the stage, to address the huge gathering. Even while that man was on his way, Manu saw in his nightmare a woman with a pleasing appearance and grace approach him with folded hands and a smile and get very close to him before everything went up in a flash. In a moment, the place was transformed into a funeral pyre.

In another one of his visions, he saw a massive sea of people, literally thousands, spread over a vast area like a square, punctuated by pagodas, like multi-tier temples, rather a grand assemblage of temples. From somewhere out of the skies appeared a monstrous dragon-like figure breathing fire, swooping down, setting down, trampling over the hapless assembly, transforming them into a mangled heap of torn limbs, smashed bodies, and gore, like in some legend of a bygone era!

For days these images troubled him to no end before he decided to confide in Anoop, something he had never done before. Only Pawana and Thomas, to an extent, were privy to his dreams and nightmares, although he often tended to be dismissive about them then. Now after having seen how many of the nightmares he saw had something to do with things actually happening around or about to occur, he felt the urge to share it with Anoop. Anoop heard it and then just dismissed it. 'There are so many bombs going off and so many dying these days! Hey, you are a crystal gazer, the radar man!' Anoop joked at Manu. But Manu was insistent that this appeared to be something involving some significant somebody, perhaps a political person, that could be even catastrophic. In a few weeks this topic for discussion was forgotten.

Manu had soon after finally graduated as an engineer.

Meanwhile Manu got his passport. Anoop was a little curious, puzzled, and even miffed in turn about this hush-hush approach of Manu. 'Boss, we are all friends wishing you the best!'

Manu became defensive. 'I was not sure what exactly I wanted. Even my family doesn't know. Some of my friends are there across the Gulf. Now there is my brother up there, and I feel at times claustrophobic, in this fortress here and . . .'

'Maybe we should all be going on a trip to a foreign country like some tourist and maybe relax'.

'I think you too can come over there. You are an engineer, and I am sure there will be appropriate positions for you. Should I ask my friend Thomas there?'

'Who wants to leave this government job? It carries a lot of prestige back home, and it's secure. But it has lots of scope,' he said, winking at Manu rather mischievously, meaning the sleaze and the greasy palms that the government was so famous for. 'I am not sure if my family would want it. Let me see,' replied Anoop. But the real reason that Manu found out soon was something else. Anoop confessed shyly, 'I am actually involved with a girl in my village.'

Manu saw no problem in it. 'Tell your parents, persuade them, and get married,' he counselled Anoop as though it was the easiest thing in this part of the world to do, forgetting his own experience.

Anoop winced at this suggestion. 'Oh, that's my misfortune. She is a Muslim. If we got married, the whole village will be after us. We could get killed or driven out. Even our families may have to abandon their home, land, possessions.' Manu was somewhat taken aback. There was little he could suggest. He was agonising after his Pawana, paying dearly for his miss, and here Anoop was still persisting. Soon Manu learnt of the offer for a position in Iraq from his friend Thomas. Manu got busy with his preparations for his imminent departure. He had quite forgotten all that Madman Murali cautioned him.

CHAPTER V

Manu had known that Iraq was the Mesopotamia where his grandfather had served in the British Indian Army and often referred to by him rather fondly, sometimes proudly, recalling the hardships they faced, the toughness and bravery they displayed, and at times with despair the terrifying conditions they faced, of the high temperatures, sandstorms, disease, and sickness, and so on. The Ottomans had long departed, and so had the Brits. It was an independent country now. Having ended the war that it had waged with its neighbour in the recent past, there were construction projects going on at a furious pace there that was contributing to their general economic boom. Manu, when he arrived here, saw a desert locale setting which at once was familiar and strange. Though less sparsely populated, the dry and dusty climate, the bazaars, the busy streets, the hot temperatures in summer weren't much unlike what he saw and experienced in Delhi, or rather a combination of the old and new Delhi. It was in many ways tantalisingly similar, yet much distant and different. People here wore a mix of Western and native clothes just as he was used to back home. In many of the buildings in these suburban districts, he saw murals of huge portraits of the current ruler in military fatigues, a hero for many not only here but even in all of the Middle East, much like the huge cut-outs of political leaders he got to see often back home at Mayapuram. And in fact, he saw that the current ruler was housed in a grand palace reminiscent of the monarchs of Mesopotamia in the ancient past and reminded Manu of Delhi's many bhavans. In place of coconut palms in Mayapuram and at his native home, there were date palms here, given that it was terribly dry and dusty in summers, even much more than Delhi. It was used to fierce dust storms. But much more, the many images that he saw in one of his dreams with Pawana were replete with the many ancient and medieval edifices he saw there. In his dreams, there were gigantic pyramidal structures, huge mountain and cliff sides with bas-reliefs that he now recognised were ziggurats, and other edifices that the ancient Sumerians built. There were locations of busy markets and by-lanes, buildings that looked so much like the many medieval mosques he saw here. Some of these scenes appeared straight out of the *Arabian Nights*. He couldn't make anything of the connection. Among his new colleagues, he saw so many from India, some not far from his own native home. Slowly they were gravitating into a social circle to meet and spend time together, reliving, recreating the sounds, the fragrances and cuisines, the functions and celebrations, the experiences that they were familiar with. There were communal feasts, weekend meetings, festive get-togethers, and so on. Occasionally one or the other members of the group went back to India for some or other functions in the family and returned with tales about their home, laden with home-made titbits, seeking to reinforce the collective nostalgia, homesickness, the longing in the group for everything that they were so desperate to leave behind.

Back home, Manu's parents were rather miffed at his sudden departure to the Gulf without due notice. Neither were they aware of his accident in Delhi or his pursuit and completion of graduation. But on the other hand, they were rather relieved that not only was another of their sons would relocate to the Gulf but that he was moving away from an 'unsafe' place. But there were more surprises in store for his parents, especially his father, though Manu's remittances were still punctually reaching them. Meanwhile, Manu had received a letter from his brother on how he was infatuated with a Christian girl nurse in Kuwait hailing from near their native hometown. He had decided to marry her and, before anybody could react, had indeed married her. *Shattered* was rather a modest term to describe what his parents, especially his father, felt. But for Manu, his own woes of the heart continued. While the money here was good and the small but tightly knit Indian community, especially from his native home, was quite welcome, his quest for Pawana had become just a dream. He wasn't even sure why he even came here. Just only to flee from Fortress Delhi, or something else? If he had not met Pawana in Mayapuram, he could well have mistaken her for a Bedouin, searching for her in these deserts, for she seemed to belong to such free-spirited nomads.

His intermittent sleep disturbances and splitting headaches reappeared, and as did Pawana in his dreams. He was feeling now a compelling need to seek medical advice, having discontinued some of the medications he was taking till he left Delhi. His fellow Indian acquaintances referred him to some hospital, where he was told that some Indians were also at hand to help him in the hospital, if need be. But he was not quite ready for what was in store. Getting inside the hospital, he awaited his turn to register himself. As he listlessly shuffled on his feet, waiting, he felt he found a familiar face among the hospital staff. Who was it? It was Rema! It was one moment rolling by into another and then all of those moments rolling into seconds and then into a couple of minutes as each stood, transfixed, before Rema reacted to him. 'Oh, Manu!' That's all she could say. Soon they pulled themselves aside from the crowd, and Rema led him into her nurse's chamber. They fell into recollecting everything and everyone, every event. It was clear that for Rema, Manu was not just an acquaintance. He commanded a place in her heart of hearts that none had yet managed to displace. Manu warned Rema that it would be a long story that she would have to listen to, if she chose to, and wondered if it was quite the time for it. But she said she had all the time in the world for him, and if not now, certainly after her shift got finished, which was due to end in an hour's time anyway.

Manu wasn't quite sure where to begin, what to say, and how much. But once he began, it poured out pit-a-pat. There was no holding back. She listened to him patiently, even a little adoringly, like she did when he was a school student, the consummate master of everything he surveyed, discussing with or teaching her brother the nuances of maths or the sciences. She came to know about who Pawana was and what she meant to him, his parents' intransigence, his fatal error in delay, and everything since, his going to Delhi, his extensive search for her, the blast in Delhi, his narrow escape, and then his decision to come here on his friend's initiative. They had so much to catch up with to make up for the lost time that separated them.

'Where is Rajan, and how is he?'

'He is in Bombay working in the port. He has been continuing in Bombay for quite some time, I guess. When I came back home once from Mayapuram, only you were there, and I was told he had left for Bombay.'

'Didn't he want to come over here?'

'He may have. But he is happier being there, being able to visit home quite frequently. You know how homesick he gets!' It was virtually an overnight journey for him to reach their hometown from Bombay. 'He was here for a week here last time, and I was actually wanting to go to Bombay and then to home! It's terribly lonely here, and what with being a girl. Thanks for the many lady friends here with me who hail from near from our hometown, I feel better. It has some exotic feel at times, like you are part of the *Arabian Nights*, so mystical. At other times, it's so alien. Now that you are here, it feels so good.' She stopped short of telling him how truly elated she felt. It was a long time since Manu had met either Rajan or Rema, especially after his departure from Mayapuram. And then he told her about the visions he was having. He told her that it was something he had been having since his time at Mayapuram, ever since he laid his eyes on Pawana the first time. He related to her how it had distinct patterns, one a series of dreams, the other a series of nightmares. The dreams had invariably Pawana in it, in fantastic landscapes and lands that he had never been to, maybe in times and periods belonging to some very distant past, although each time he saw in them their separation, somehow, she eluded his grasp. The dreams actually puzzled him more at times than the nightmares, as they involved Pawana. Most nightmares had not much to do with Pawana, especially the recent ones. But at times it was difficult to say whether something was a dream or a nightmare, especially when a wonderful dream abruptly ended with Pawana vanishing or getting lost in the end. He related to Rema how at first he dismissed them as silly though Pawana took them seriously. It was only of late he had begun understanding his nightmares as being in some ways related to happenings in the future or in the past. When the first mysterious dreams with Pawana appeared to him, in almost every one of them, it showed him losing her in every such instance. He told her that these were premonitions that he had not cared to pay attention to. Only gradually had he learnt to discern from them the contours of the events and the locations; though thus far in relation to current events, it's been almost always only after it took place. But of his dreams he understood, as yet, little. While at Mayapuram the dreams and nightmares never actually bothered him. It only intrigued and enriched his inner world, which was at once puzzling and enjoyable till Pawana left. After she left, every dream left pining for her almost turned into a nightmare. But after the bomb attack, the frequent headaches and sleep disturbances was rendering him quite exhausted and shaken. Rema gently told him that much as he needs medical attention, it might not be necessary for the doctors to know all, as they would believe none of these. She always knew that there was something special about Manu. If there was something inexplicable about him, at least for her it was only natural, as he was someone special for her. But how special a someone was he for her, how dear, she could never muster the courage to tell him. On examining Manu, the doctors told him that what happened to him were traumatic events. In addition, hard physical knocks to the head resulting in concussion, from falling down or in bomb blasts, could result in such conditions. It was but natural to have these terrifying nightmares. They advised him to continue his medications without fail. It was, simply put, post-traumatic stress. Rema recalled the incident when he had fallen from the jackfruit tree. Possibly that was the first trigger and the subsequent events and anxieties relating to the circus as the possible events that triggered these.

Every day it was now becoming almost a habit for Manu to spend his evenings with Rema. Among his various work colleagues, one was Abdul Aziz, from Palestine, another Ahmed, from Egypt, with whom he often spent time watching Hindi movies, like *Awara*, in theatres. These were so popular. This story of a tramp, Awara, so enamoured them. 'Look, such beautiful songs and soulful music! Some of those scenes are so fantastic.' To them these films were like a journey through a dream, of realising human hopes, a release from the drudgery of their daily lives. It enabled attaining through cinematic fantasy that they could barely get in real life.

Abdul would recall, 'I would be sick from childhood into my teens with this constant bombardment over our heads. It's such a relief these days to get away from it all. In a way, a dream come true.' But they quickly noted how Manu was disappearing quickly in the evenings without even some notice. 'Some girl I guess, eh?'

'So it's your Laila, eh.'

'Why, don't you have any?' countered Manu. And then came the shy confessions of both. They disclosed how they were trying hard to save enough money so that they could get married and set up a family.

'I have to save enough for the mahr for my girl,' said Ahmed. He had to satisfy the rather demanding prospective father-in-law back in Egypt to get married to his beloved daughter.

But Aziz had other problems. Initially he was not that forthcoming but later reluctantly admitted, 'I am in love with a Jewish girl.' This was a secret, a discreet relationship between them. None of their families had got wind of it as yet, although the families knew each other, being in the neighbourhood. Even the rendezvous between them were a stealthy affair. He didn't know how to go about it. 'I guess we will have to go elsewhere,' muttered Aziz, rather worried.

And then there was Hussein, a middle-aged father of three, a local. He often teased Manu for his sudden disappearance every evening for his 'Taj Mahal'. He actually meant Noorjahan, the empress for whose love, Shah Jahan, the emperor, built Taj Mahal, the monument of love. For Hussein the Taj was shorthand for love, something feminine and relating to India. But Hussein was always worrying about the future of his family and his country, Iraq. He fondly recalled the years he grew up in relative calm and quiet. It excited him to describe how as a child he would celebrate Id with his cousins, uncles, aunts, brothers, and sisters, frolicking around. It was *jannat* for him then. But later he lost his siblings, many of his uncles, and others to the brutal war between his and the neighbouring country. He was often referred to as the sad Hussein, who reminded Manu of the mamu, Salman, a cheerful man in contrast, working in his office in Delhi.

For Mamu, celebrating Diwali and Ram Navami was as important as id. He spoke about his neighbours with affection and how they celebrated these festivals together. It was a truly fun time amidst friends and family. Every time there was a festival, without fail he disappeared to his home in Faizabad near Ayodhya, his hands laden with presents, clothes, and mithais (sweets) for his wife, children, and relatives. 'Kya farak padtha hai sahib, bachhe khus ho jainge. Bure ke upar ache hamesha jeetha hai.' That is to say, for him it didn't matter what the name of the festival was so long as it was meant to celebrate the good over evil and it made children glad. He used to always cite his relations living in far off Calcutta, some of whom made clay idols for the Durga Puja every year, on how they used every opportunity to celebrate. Even in times of crises, he recalled, how they would come together to help each other. Once, Mamu recalled how when his neighbour fell ill, he took turns along with the family of the neighbour to keep watch, ferrying food and medicines, and how another of his Hindu neighbours were helping his children with their lessons.

Manu now had time only for Rema these days. Cinemas with his work colleagues were now passé for the moment. For Rema, that Pawana was his dream companion never quite mattered, for she was getting to be secure in the knowledge that she was the prosaic while Pawana a mere fantasy, a phantom ghost. She was the real one beside Manu, who could keep fantasising about Pawana in his dreams. That held no fears for her. As Manu became closer with Rama in reality, Pawana receded along with his dreams into the background for now. So did the nightmares, apparently, for the time being.

For quite some weeks, time seemed to roll by sweetly. With Rema by his side, nothing could have gone wrong. As it was, one day he learnt of the terrible news of the assassination of a former Indian prime minister in a bomb blast along with policemen and scores of his party colleagues down south of India. Each of his visions, apparently, were becoming a disturbing reality. Manu confided in Rema. He recalled to her another one of his nightmares he had just before his departure for Iraq and feared something similar was about to occur. 'Don't worry yourself. There is nothing one can do about it. You seem to have some peculiar powers to look into the future. Maybe something good may come out of it.'

Weeks later the world got to see what happened in Beijing. Rema was getting to be convinced now that Manu had indeed some unusual powers that most people didn't understand and which to the medical world was some kind of a mental disorder. It convinced her that his dreams had really nothing to do with any illness.

Amidst these, Thomas wrote to Manu, inviting him for a visit to Kuwait. He said he could well make it a business trip and maybe even move things to attempt and get a position there in Kuwait itself. Manu related these to Rema, who was rather alarmed! To lose Manu again was not a prospect she would ever dream of. But Manu quickly dispelled her fears. 'I really want to meet him badly. I miss him so much ever since the days we spent together in Mayapuram. More than money, the sole reason to actually come here to take up this job was actually owing to the prospect of being with Thomas, my ex-room-mate and dear buddy and also my brother, in Kuwait. He was the reason why I am here. Initially there was no opening in Kuwait, and so I came here and have been thinking of moving to Kuwait whenever the chance presents. But now having discovered you here, I do not want to leave! But I do want to meet him.'

Rema felt finally she had got the affirmation she had awaited for so long from Manu.

• •

Thomas was in very good spirits as both the friends met. 'Did you ever imagine that we would be travelling in these aeroplanes and live in these plush apartments?'

Manu smiled as he settled down in the plush cushions in Thomas's apartments, recollecting the summertimes he spent just a few months back behind those water-filled coolers and wet bed sheets hung out to form a cool curtain inside the room in Delhi, in the blazing heat of the summer. 'If life here is luxury, Mayapuram was magical,' he said with a sigh, and Thomas quickly nodded. And Manu added, 'I couldn't care for all these.'

Thomas placed his hand on Manu 'Yes, it was just wonderful. Those days aren't coming back.'

Manu spoke about his life in Delhi, then his futile search for Pawana and sighed. 'But I see everywhere violent upheaval. People are fleeing, cowering, seeking refuge. We all have become one big set of Awaras.' And then he spoke about his life in Baghdad, how he was fascinated by it all, both the exotic and the familiar. But the moment he spoke about Rema, his face seemed to glow; a certain joy seemed to light up his face, which Thomas noticed.

'Rema, your schoolmate Rajan's sister?'

'Yes!' replied Manu. Thomas could see how his friend had now regained some of his old spark at the mention of Rema. He sensed that Rema was maybe the healing touch they were all waiting for to happen to Manu. His ostensible reason for inviting Manu here was actually to get him to shift to Kuwait and make way for it. But now he wasn't sure whether at all he should even broach that anymore. 'Let's play some music,' said Thomas, reaching for the synthesiser and fiddling with the keys. That was enough hint for Manu, who espied a guitar at the corner of the room and jumped at it. Together the friends were playing their heart out after a long, long time. It was a day spent in an absolutely memorable reunion.

And it hit him again. Manu saw fire raining down all around Thomas, in the very locales that he was in now, terrible sounds like explosions, smoke enveloping all around, walls, whole buildings coming crashing down, people fleeing helter-skelter. When he woke up it was the wee hours, and he found himself right beside his friend. He didn't know how to interpret these. Certainly people here around were in some kind of danger. He confided in Thomas about the series of nightmares and dreams he had been having, recalling how he had been ignoring them since the time at Mayapuram but only realising recently that it often presaged the terrible things to follow. He disclosed that he had been on medication since the explosion that had befallen him, which got interrupted for a while, only to resume it after Rema and his doctors had persuaded him to resume it. 'I think you must consider leaving this place,' he told Thomas.

Thomas was rather bemused. He knew his friend had been on treatment and was privy to the happenings while at Mayapuram, how they all were desperately attempting to calm down Manu in the aftermath of Pawana's departure. But Manu sounded so serious. Thomas tried to pacify Manu, sounding a touch unconcerned, 'My friend don't worry, it's just that we have met up after a long while and maybe it's your anxiety and concern for me that's showing up.'

But Manu was not so convinced 'I wish it were so, a mere nightmare, but I fear otherwise. The signs here are not so good.' On the weekend, after meeting his 'little' brother and his wife, Manu returned.

In only a couple of weeks Manu had it again; this time he saw the same trail of destruction coming down like an avalanche right beside himself and Rema. He saw onion-domed palaces violently swaying as in some wild storms in some distant exotic lands, many people being blown away by these very winds, and many clinging on to anything to prevent it. There were inexplicable scenes of huge crowds gathering around in a large square before everything calmed down. And somewhere amidst those, he saw a flash of Pawana as though fleeing the scene. Rema persuaded Manu to continue his medications, which she herself had suggested to be stopped, no longer wishing to see him suffer. 'You know that often what I see becomes true,' proffered Manu defensively.

'Maybe, but I do not wish to see you suffer so. We cannot always prevent what happens everywhere, but why torture ourselves with these thoughts?'

But Manu continued seeing things. He saw that he and Pawana were fleeing from a very ancient city that had been invaded by a king, a brutal, ferocious-looking man with a long curly beard. Not only was the city waylaid, the king deposed, the young and old disembowelled, many captured as slaves, and women taken as concubines. In his dream, all he saw was that they barely escaped this madman. He couldn't tell whether it was a dream or a nightmare. If his successful escape along with Pawana was looked at, it was a dream, but if the horror of the destruction of their city was considered, it was a terrible nightmare. Was that madman Ashurnasirpal laying siege to Judea? He had seen so many of the bar reliefs of such bearded men in the mountains in the outskirts of Baghdad. *Maybe.* Manu sighed.

Firdus Mosque at Bhagdad

CHAPTER VI

Back in India, Anoop was going full tilt chasing his fiancée. He and his fiancée planned and executed an elopement, getting married on the sly. But trouble was not far. Police complaints were filed about abduction by the girl's family. It turned into a riot-like situation in Anoop's village. There were serious threats to the life of his family members, with a further threat of social boycott. Anoop's family ultimately disowned Anoop for this 'terrible' violation. So did his fiancée's folks disown their daughter!

In Puzhakkara, Manu's father had grand plans for renovating the family home. They had just managed to get a telephone connection after four years of waiting post application. With both sons in the Gulf, there was nothing stopping him now. He had dismantled a couple of rooms having tiled roofing, converting them to a concrete, albeit sloped, rain-proofed roofing. While the renovation or rather rebuilding came to a conclusion, he drew up further plans to get the other parts of the house rebuilt. With both his sons in the Gulf, he had to show the folks around how the family had arrived to gain their 'true' place in society! This was also the trend in these parts of those with the Gulf connection.

Not long after, Iraq had invaded Kuwait. Bombs and shells rained on Kuwait. The Hammurabi Armoured Division and the Nebuchadnezzar Motorised Infantry were deployed by Saddam Hussain. The joy and pride of having their son in the Gulf was turning into a concern and then despair for Manu's parents. What would happen to their younger son in Kuwait? There were frantic efforts to establish contact and calls made, asking him to come back. They learnt that the Indian embassy was making efforts for evacuation of Indians in Kuwait. Manu's nightmare came to haunt him. He was more worried about his dear friend Thomas, who seemed so nonchalant towards

Manu's forewarnings post his nightmare during their time together in Kuwait. He learnt that Thomas was still reluctant to leave Kuwait, even after Manu's own brother had managed to leave for India. Thomas was far more fatalistic. 'If God wants me to remain on this planet, I will be alive no matter what.' But Thomas also knew that he was the sole hope for his family back in India. He had his brothers and sisters pursuing their education. His aged parents were there. They had all just managed to have a refurbished new home with a decent sum of money parked in the banks.

A month later, along with the many, Thomas was bombed out of life exactly the way Manu had visualised. The tarrying cost him his life. Manu was aghast and devastated that despite his warnings and his best efforts, he could not save his friend. With Pawana a mirage, Thomas now history, who was next was troubling his mind. And recollecting his other nightmares troubled him further. He was constantly confiding and conferring with Rema and his colleagues about his growing disquiet over the frightening developments in these parts. Rema was as usual pacifying him through these events, while his other colleagues had yet to betray any nervousness on this. They had been used to it for a while now and to these kind of things intermittently all their lives. It didn't seem as yet such an impending disaster.

It was early in January when his worst fears seemed to come true. Suddenly war clouds were right over them. All ultimatums had been ignored by the invading country, and it seemed determined to bring destruction upon itself. Everyone had a prayer on his or her lips, some to Allah, some to Jesus Christ, and others to the various other gods they could think of. But the gods wouldn't relent on the destruction man wrought upon himself. It was only a matter of days when bombs began raining on them. It was in the dead of night when the first bombs fell, and the explosions awoke them. His first thoughts went to Rema, whom he quickly called up. She too was awake and assured him she was safe. But such instances were repeated so often. Hussein was indeed so sad and angry that things in his country had come to such a pass. 'It is a conspiracy of our enemies!' he spat out. There was none like Harun al-Rashid to stop the madness all around, he lamented. He was worried as hell as to what might happen to his family. For Manu and Rema, there was no choice but to flee, and they had Aziz and Ahmed. Among their friends and colleagues, Hussein prayed harder than others for their safe passage. It was a miraculous escape in a borrowed car for the foursome. But along the way there were explosions, bullets, and shrapnel flying around when their car also was hit, shattering the side and back window panes. Yet the damage wasn't serious enough to stop their advance to Jordan, where Manu and Rema were to get to the Indian Embassy at Amman to make their way back through to India. His other friends, Aziz and Ahmed, were to drop them there and then proceed further to Egypt and Palestine. It was a little like the biblical exodus, except those fleeing were leaving a little reluctantly and with some support and help of all, including the gods.

Those few months saw mass exodus of refugees and camps. People were refugees even in their own countries. As a child, whenever Manu read or heard news items like 'Beirut bombed, refugees streaming' or these being read and discussed by his father, his grandfather, or other elders, he wondered then as he did now why these had to happen. But the happenings in a distant land were like a story. The immediacy and the misery could never be so graphic and touching as he experienced now. As Manu alighted from the car, he found Rema not responding to his call. When he shook her up, she slumped to a side. He searched all over her thoroughly, without quite knowing what happened. There was only the slightest of a lesion on the side of her head, just a hint of scratch. They rushed to the nearest possible hospital. The doctor examined her thoroughly and pronounced her dead. 'Shrapnel,' he said and shrugged his shoulders.

It was late in the night when he landed with Rema's body at Bombay. Rajan was there, and both moved on together, speechless. Neither had the courage to say anything, nor had they the courage to face Rajan's parents. Per chance, they were there right at Bombay. Everyone's beloved was now up in fire and smoke, reduced to ashes. From one myth to another, Manu had made his journey.

Along with Rema and Manu, there were thousands of Indians who were back all of a sudden. The mass exodus from the Gulf had its indelible impact on India. With the balance of payments in doldrums, a few months later, the licence raj in India ended, and Indian economy was opened up for foreign investment.

CHAPTER VII

It was early morning in Bangalore as Manu and Rajan woke up. They quickly finished their bath before moving to the hall to join the guru with other yoga practitioners in the ashram. It had been a week since they had arrived to the mild wintry and pleasant weather of this southern Indian city of Bangalore, situated on the Deccan Plateau at a height of nearly a thousand meters above sea level, which bestowed it the year-round pleasant weather. Slowly the friends were attempting to deal with their current state. Manu had no inclination for anything. Rather than go to his parents at his native home, he chose to come here. That things after the Gulf War looked bleak, even in his native town added to it. There was a whole crowd of those in his native place who had returned from the Gulf with little else belonging to them than the palatial homes they had built. Should there be a cash flow crunch on their prolonged absence from their jobs, some would be forced to sell these homes.

Manu was tired, extremely exhausted, living this dual life of nightmares and dreams and this terrible reality of his physical existence without Pawana. He didn't want to look ahead even think of anything about the past or future that anyway looked bleak. His spiritual guide urged him just to focus on the moment just as he did as a child. He felt hollowed out, just an empty nothing. And then his guru told him, 'What you have been seeing as dreams were your past, the distant, the very distant past, those that passed centuries before. But you could not recognise or understand them. And what you see as nightmares are portents of the future. Most normal beings cannot cope with knowledge of the past and the future. It will overwhelm them. Most struggle to cope up with even the present. That's why only rare people have the gift to actually see both into his past and into the future, and you are among them. But you need to train to handle it.' For Manu it was merely information, not a realisation about himself. It was not yet the moment for that. He knew many things from

151

the past and the future but was yet to realise that he was part of those events or recognise himself in them. There was only silence and prayers and practice for now.

It was weeks after they had arrived here that Manu and Rajan felt for the first time the desire to venture a little beyond the precincts of the ashram. Together they wandered, rather aimlessly, into the city. Briefly they came upon the Cubbon Park, listlessly wandering among the flowerbeds, shrubs, and trees. Manu felt the sudden descent of a heavy hand on his shoulders and a strong familiar voice calling him out.

It was Anoop. 'I am so glad you are here. When we learnt of the Gulf War, my first thoughts were with you,' said Anoop. Manu painfully recounted his final days there. Together the friends made their way over the grass and sat down. Anoop told him how he was now married to his sweetheart, and as staying at Delhi was becoming untenable, given the constant threats and the bad blood between him, his wife, and their families, it was then he resigned his position in Delhi and relocated to Bangalore, deciding to enrol himself in a computer programming course, and now he was in an IT firm. 'Manu, it should be an excellent choice for you, given your engineering background. The opportunities are fantastic.' It took some weeks before Manu decided that he too would join a course in programming. Rajan by now had returned to Bombay to his vocation.

It was close to the end of monsoons in these parts when the world learnt that the Soviet Union had collapsed and a grand coup against the democratic forces had failed, transforming Manu's visions into reality. A new era began. A few months later, Manu finished his computer programming course and joined a company. But his visions didn't quite end there. He saw huge crowds almost maniacally dancing and chanting, going round and round a huge mound like in some kind of a ritual. The swarm of people grew and grew till it formed an ocean-like expanse, engulfing the mound, the whole of the surroundings, till the mound itself was overwhelmed and disappeared. Only the crowds dancing and chanting were visible, as in some kind of dance of death. And then there was utter chaos, some attacking, a few people screaming and wailing in death. The scene rapidly shifted to some large city, with explosions and smoke, with bodies strewn around, severed limbs covered in gore and blood, and then his vision was broken. This set him thinking. Only sometime back he dreamt that he and Pawana were gaily going about their lives in the vicinity of some place like where the mound appeared but with the centrepiece as a temple. It was a scene from a bygone era, long past, when that town was sparsely populated, in beautiful idyllic settings, with people living in harmonious times. And there was the surprising and sudden assault on that city by a marauding group of horsemen with muskets, even cannons. He saw the city violated, the temple disintegrate in the onslaught, the laughter of people reduced to wails and mourns, frightened and subjugated. Both he and Pawana had fled forever. Manu confided in his friend Anoop, who quipped and consoled him 'The radar is back, eh! Have you any clue on what's going to happen and where? What's the point? Are we so powerful to stop things from happening?' Something real bad was going to happen somewhere.

Still learning his ropes in code writing, Manu was now getting a hang of his new job, slowly a grip on it. Deadlines and late nights were frequent. Bangalore, the garden city, which was laid back as a pensioner's paradise only a few years back, was now bustling with activity. It had become a refuge and haven to those who sought a retirement nest and now played host to a different crowd. First it played host to the professional institutions and now unobtrusively into a hub for IT companies. Yet it was a garden city, retaining its charms, its languid meditative quality with mind over matter. Maybe that's what calmed Manu, even made him disinclined from visiting his native town despite its proximity. But his banking remittances continued, as did the occasional phone call. He learnt that his brother had again left for Kuwait. In leisure, with Anoop and his wife often for company, life was getting to be tolerable.

It was approaching winter and the weather was getting balmy in Bangalore. For a while, things seemed so pleasant, slowly soothing and healing for Manu. But in that December, exactly eight years and three days after that day when thousands of people were gassed to death, there were more victims today. Some madness possessed people. While an old mausoleum was demolished after a war dance, more graves were dug for people who became its victims. It stirred Manu from his reverie, reminding him that his nightmares were no fiction. Now he feared worse was to follow. He then remembered suddenly about

Mamu, his likeable office colleague whose family resided there. 'What about Mamu?' Manu anxiously asked Anoop. Both looked at each other, silent yet worried

'I hope nothing has happened,' Anoop replied with a shrug of his shoulders. What if things were otherwise? Neither was quite prepared to face that. Eventually, they learnt that, luckily, Mamu was safe.

Manu had a vague feeling of some impending doom. There was some clue of a catastrophe hidden in his nightmares! And then it flashed in his mind. It was a vague connection that became suddenly clear, that forced him to get up abruptly while actually working at a project at his desk. He quickly shut down and hurried to the nearest STD booth to call up Rajan. He got him on phone in the nick of the time late in the evening, when it was closing time for offices, after which it would have been near impossible to call him up. He told him that he wanted him over here immediately on some urgent pretext. Rajan was rather surprised and a bit hesitant. Initially he expressed inability to come over at such a short notice but finally relented at the persistent insistence of Manu. He quickly came over in a couple of days, planning for a week's stay at the most.

But something else supervened. Peaceful demonstrations exploded in Bombay into riots, where hundreds got killed. Even after the situation was said to be under control, Manu wouldn't let Rajan go despite protests from Rajan about his possibly losing his job. But Manu was relentless. He confided about his worst fears to Rajan. He said it was unsafe. Anoop concurred with Manu. 'Listen to the radar. So many things he had said turned true. This one makes sense. Let me see if something can be fixed up here.' Finally Anoop managed to find a position for Rajan right here in Bangalore. Barely a couple of months later, there were a series of bomb explosions in Bombay. The very complex where Rajan used to reside was heavily damaged. Many among his neighbours were dead, some maimed for life.

• •

In the summer of that year, Anoop was allotted a project that was to take him to the USA. For Manu, despite his re-engagement in Bangalore, he was still ill at ease, feeling orphaned, having lost Pawana first, then Thomas, and then Rema, and now Anoop would get away. All those whom he treasured in life were lost. It was only a hope that he would get to Pawana one day that kept him still going, a desperate hope. Maybe, like his father would say, having a roof over one's head and getting his daily bread was blessing enough to be thankful to the Almighty. One shouldn't think or feel beyond. Maybe he too should be thankful for being just alive. Perhaps his imagination was his enemy.

But soon when Manu learnt from his project manager that he was being considered for a project in the USA, his spirits became lighter, quite forgetting Madman Murali's caution!

CHAPTER VIII

Washington was so unlike what he had expected it to be, with plenty of space all around, not the crowded, tall-skyscraper images of cities that one usually went by. It had wide swathes of green, very wide roads, avenues, wide bridges across the Potomac. While Anoop was closer to New York, executing some project there, Manu was placed here. Summers were pretty long here, and he took to having long walks along the mall whenever he had the time after work or sometimes over the weekends. At times he visited the Smithsonian Museum, gazing with equal fascination at the rockets as at the rocks, precious stones, or the dinosaurs or the fossils. Doing these rounds time and again didn't tire him. On other occasions, he would gaze at the paintings at the National Gallery and enjoy the musical gatherings on the weekend evenings at its lawns. Occasionally he himself participated with his guitar.

But many weekends were spent by the friends together. Occasionally he spoke to his parents back home. Wandering along one day, he saw a familiar face with a woman in tow. Was it not Aziz? As he gazed at him intently, their eyes met, and instantly the face of the man lit up with a smile. 'Hey, you, Manu, here? Thank God you are OK! How come you are here?' he exclaimed all at one go. Manu explained calmly how he became a software engineer before being asked to come over here to execute some project. But it was Manu's turn to express his surprise at Aziz being here. At this, Aziz became a little hesitant, even coy, before he introduced the lady by his side. 'This is Jemima! Yes, she is my Laila I used to tell you about! We couldn't continue there for long, not with our affair. They would have killed us. We just managed to come over here.' He recounted how he managed to make passports and papers on the sly for his fiancée. Then he and his fiancée managed first to slip out from their homes, reached the Jordan borders as man and wife, getting past it to the Amman Airport, from where they took a flight to the Americas, citing the possible risk to their lives and the persecution they were likely to face. 'Initially I had managed a position in a project and she worked at a store for over a year, before I enrolled into a course on CAD and got a better position.'

Manu was, meanwhile, getting busy with his projects. He was in the midst of completion of one of these, working continuously, spending several sleepless nights before finishing the same. That night after he had finished it, he slept so soundly that he got up pretty late in the morning, actually surprised that everything around him was intact when he had actually expected debris and ruins. He had seen himself in his sleep in some strange land where everything around him was shaking up furiously, the ground underneath, the trees, the buildings resembling some pagodas of the Far East. Even the mountains around were swaying, and he saw the pagoda crash down when a huge towering mushroom cloud, rising up, growing into a massive envelope of cloud, engulfed all the earth. He had slept so soundly, believing his dreamworld to be real, that when he woke up, he found it difficult to believe what he saw around till he realised that was actually a dream. It was the sixth of August.

In a few months, he returned to Bangalore, having finished his project. By this time, on return to Bangalore, it had become nearly certain that Manu would be working on off/on projects in the US. But It was not until another couple of years that he actually went back. It was in the month of January in the year following his return that the world witnessed a monstrous earthquake in the Far East, in Kobe. Many thousands died anonymously. Who among the future generations would know who lived there and how? Were they myths or for real? Manu just sighed.

• •

It was four years since he had been rather unexpectedly kept way from Anoop and others, feeling rather listless. His attempts at locating Pawana being futile and with his visions continuing intermittently, an air of defeat was creeping on him. On several nights he woke up from disturbing visions coming back to him. He saw a great temple by a seashore tremble and sway like some leaf in a storm, as did the devotees and denizens in and around it, the whole landscape sway and shake and quake, before everything around came down crashing, with collapsing debris all around, wailing people caught in the mounds of stone and masonry. There he saw someone so closely resembling Pawana, something tumbling on her, and then he woke up. Where was she?

'Manu, this is important.' It was Rajan who spoke. He told him that Manu's father was not keeping particularly well these days. His parents desired that Manu should visit them soon. He came to know of it while on a visit to his home. Manu had been out of touch with his family for quite a while, especially with events in his hometown even after his return to Bangalore from the US. With the approaching weekend, one Friday, Manu set off to his native home. In the course of his trip he found a new acquaintance. He found a youth approaching to sit beside him in the bus they had chosen to take. He looked up at him and smiled, noticing that the young man had a slash mark across his left cheek, just below the cheek bone, a reminder of some deep gash or wound that he suffered that left behind its indelible mark. Casually striking up a conversation, he was a bit startled to learn that Karunan and his family nearly lost everything in Lanka, their home, possessions in the conflict there, before his father was detained by the army on suspicion of being a sympathiser, never to return. Not long before, his mother, unable to bear the grief, committed suicide. He, being the eldest son, fled, along with his younger siblings, and took refuge here. He said he knew that the rebels would come after him to get him to enlist him in their cause, leaving his young siblings to the wolves, which he was determined to avoid. Among those he lost was his beloved, killed in a crossfire in a secluded park into which both of them had sought to escape where they had been on a lover's rendezvous when a suicide bomber who had unobtrusively crept into there blew himself up when a passing column of soldiers had stopped by on a routine check. He had managed somehow to get to the sea coast in darkness and stealth and across the seas to India. He related how he had taken up a position as an office boy here while enrolling part time in an undergraduate programme. Despite the many hardships and deprivations that he suffered, he managed to graduate and was now employed as a sales executive. Both his little sister and brother were safe in a small town in the South Indian state of Tamizhnad with their aunt, pursuing their school education, with his regular financing. For now this was his home, his refuge. He had little hope he could ever return to his native homeland.

When Manu reached home, he found a modern concrete mansion replacing the earlier edifice. His father was not particularly ill; he had simply aged, mellowed down, and felt lonely. He had now a grand home, lots of prestige, but no company. The acme of success, apparently, was loneliness. Of course, his uncles and aunts were around and would drop in as they too were likewise lonely, their own children in distant lands in search of fortunes. The cows were long sold off and the entire estate left in a state of neglect, with overgrown grass, weeds, and so on. Milk, anyway, came in packets, and once in a while somebody came to get the coconuts down. At times the entire estate of coconut palms was sold off—the nuts, that is. Some coconut palms, he learnt, had suffered from root wilt disease and had to be burnt.

When Manu met Bhrandhan Murali, now getting gray and older, in his cottage, Murali shook his head with a rueful smile 'How I wish you had been more careful. I warned you to keep away from the Gulf. Poor Rema. Again it slipped you.' He patted him consolingly. 'There is more pain to come for this world. What could you expect from hatred, stupidity, and hubris! Be careful and don't go near the sea,' he warned. It was strange that he should warn thus, Manu thought. Looking at the surprise on Manu's face, Murali smiled a little ruefully and said, 'Ah! I had been for years practising some rituals which an old priest had once taught me. That allows me to interact with spirits that tell me many things. Even during war and thereafter, it helped me avoid bigger disasters. But I couldn't still evade it all.'

When Manu finally got back to working at a project in the US, he was, truth to tell, more at ease. The frequent meetings with Anoop and then Aziz were, in some ways, a solace. It soothed his despondent and drooping spirits, and the visions seemed to recede. But he held on to the hope grimly. Meanwhile, he was back to visiting the various galleries and museums, attending jazz or other musical concerts in the lawns of the National Gallery, with himself occasionally strumming on the guitar. It was in one of those weekends that he met Ahmed. He couldn't at first quite place him. But the Egyptian quickly recognised him. He was thrilled to bits. 'Manu, oh! What a surprise! I am so glad to meet you here!'. By his side was his wife, whom he introduced to Manu. As the friends walked around, he quickly recounted how he managed in the end to get to his Juliet by satisfying his demanding father-in-law. In the course of their walking around, he introduced to him Yusuf, his Somalian friend. It was then Manu told him about Aziz and how he too had finally found refuge in America. Ahmed then recounted to all there the harrowing tale of the escape of the three friends and colleagues, along with Rema from Iraq and her unfortunate demise.

Seated in one of the lawns along the mall, Yusuf had his own grim story to present. How amidst the civil war and disintegration of his nation, he was just lucky to be in one piece reaching here. Growing up as a young man, there was much hope both for himself and his country. Life was Spartan, but happy-go-lucky. They rode the new wave of literacy and education, and he benefited so much from his liking for learning languages, particularly English, though he was studying to be an engineer. 'Who could have predicted the hellhole that we were getting into? I lost much of my family, caught in the civil war. I do not know the whereabouts of many of my kith and kin. I just about managed to reach here alive!' Another refugee of this world!

Just as he was getting to be at ease, it struck him. He saw very tall towers, like the Tower of Babel or a ziggurat, something terrifying and imposing. And something like a flying dragon, a dinosaur with huge wings, like a giant bird, dropping out from the sky and swooping down, crashing into it, turning into a huge ball of fire. Elsewhere, some bearded men were leering, laughing, and dancing around him tied to a stake, being poked around by spiked lances, and the tallest among them, with a long flowing beard and a turban, standing aside, with sadistic eyes, urging them on and on holding on to what appeared like a spear. He saw these men holed up in caves in distant mountains in isolated terrains interspersed by a gigantic figure of an ancient statue carved out on the mountainsides, standing erect in a calm meditative pose, with palms folded in prayer, as though beseeching all of the world to desist from madness. But it was not to be; the prayers weren't about to be answered. In another moment, there was a blitz and blasts, a blaze of fire from some cannons. And then the gigantic figure was gone. But what followed was even more terrifying. There were scenes of sudden and terrifying sounds of great fires, marauding killers emerging from nowhere, people dying in droves, ripped, roasted, maimed. Suddenly huge swarms of people gathered for fleeing like in the great exodus, but with nowhere to go.

Nothing that he attempted now really stemmed this tide of visions. These were getting to be sudden and unpredictable and getting inexplicably more and more violent than ever before. He feared something fantastically sinister that the world had never witnessed so far was about to occur. It was only a matter of time, but when would it be?

One of those weekends, he decided to pay a visit to his buddy Anoop in New York. While Manu felt quite uneasy. Each time he sighted a skyscraper with its dizzying heights, it somehow made him uncomfortable. Anoop, blissfully unaware of what was going on inside Manu, was relating to his friend the latest gossip in the town, even as Manu made a passing reference to his recurring nightmares. Anoop consoled Manu that he should stop worrying but ended up relating to his own nightmare he and his wife lived through, with his wife Aiysha by his side. 'We barely escaped alive.' He shuddered at the thought of what went through their great escape. He and his fiancée had long concealed their relationship. Being childhood acquaintances, their friendship grew over the years through their schooling years, though owing to their differing community backgrounds, they met only on the sly in the immediate neighbourhood. But their relationship eventually blossomed into love. But this was no Bollywood movie of girl meets boy to live happily ever after. Everything remained confidential even after he got into his profession but at some point had to escape secrecy. Once their relationship became known, all hell broke loose.

There was a watch over Aiysha's movements, restrictions, clampdowns, and curfew hours. Anoop had virtually stopped even coming over to his native place. Every means was being used to coerce them into submission. There were explicit and implied threats, physical and otherwise. It was in the winters when Anoop, without notice to anyone except to one of his most trusted friends, arrived at the closest railhead at the city a few kilometres from the village. Through a mutual female friend, Aiysha was told overnight about his arrival next day and that he would leave the same day. On a foggy late winter evening, Aiysha left home on the pretext of going for some household purchase and left for the railway station to the designated rendezvous. She had to ensure that she escaped prying eyes, familiar faces, and known persons beneath a hijab on her tryst with destiny. 'Those hours were the most uncertain and frightful hours of my life, or rather, our lives. Not until we were together in the train could we be certain that we will come together and be away, safe from danger. As soon as we reached our destination, we got ourselves married, with my friends as witnesses. By the time the escape was discovered, it had become a law-and-order issue, a matter of pride and prejudice of communities in my village. There were policemen set after us even so far away. That we were legally married helped. Yet there were charges in the court of abduction, summons, and later threats that had come right to our doorstep. That's when we decided to pack up and come over to Bangalore, and now we are here.'

Anoop had till then not dwelt at such length on what transpired on his heroic elopement. Anoop then quipped, 'Our experience in Assam wasn't any less hair-raising. It was your miraculous fiction that worked wonders upon our captors and saved the day! It was the greatest escape one could have engineered!'

It was Manu's turn now to surprise Anoop. 'It was no fiction!' he countered, to the utter surprise of Anoop. He disclosed his life at Mayapuram, the circus, about Pawana, his entanglement, and the legends associated with her, his constant battle with his visions, and so on. Anoop could not still contain his astonishment.

'Wow, what a story, and you never let us know all these years!' But as if on cue, both the friends had unexpectedly run into a colleague of Anoop on the way. 'This is Abebe, from Ethiopia,' said Anoop to Manu by way of introduction. And to Abebe, he said, 'This is Manu, my close friend and room-mate while we were in Delhi, working in the CPWD.'

'What's a CPWD?'

'It's a Complete Pain-in-the-Arse Works Department. Jokes apart, we were part of a unit looking after buildings, even construct or obstruct them from getting constructed! But it was real pain in the . . . Well, that was no joke, mind you,' said Anoop laughingly to Abebe.

'Oh, I see,' Abebe replied, nodding.

'What's your story then?'

'Well, like many from my continent, I fled this cycle of boom and bust, wars interspersed by ravages of nature. I had learnt dramatics but managed to reach here and worked in a bar while I did a course in communications. Now I am managing the PR here!'

On January 26 that year, the earth shook out the lives of so many in Gujarat in India. In the hours and days following the earthquake, the horror and the misery of the people afflicted was becoming evident. Ancient temples were razed to the ground. Thousands were entombed in their homes, whole villages and settlements erased from memory.

In its aftermath, realisation crept into Manu that the temples and pagodas he saw quaking were a preview of the earthquake that had just then taken place. As for Pawana's image in the vision, well then, was Pawana there? How was he to know? There was nothing apart from his visions to guide him. But in all his attempts to find her, there were many areas that he had not explored. Was it a hint that she was somewhere there? There were just questions. At one point, he had an urge to take the next flight out and go there. But he didn't.

It was another work day when Manu finally reached his office and switched on his computers. As the computer booted in, he plugged into the Internet the first thing. Out sprang the images of the Twin Towers, with smoke billowing out and the replay of a flying plane crashing into it. Simultaneously the news of another plane having hit the Pentagon also flashed on the net across the images of the burning towers, with screaming headlines: 'America is under attack', it said. When the first planes crashed into the Twin Towers of the World Trade Centre, he was still out on the road, getting to his office. But now looking out of the window of his office, he could see some smoke billowing out across the Potomac. Nobody knew what was happening. Everyone there around was in a daze, terrified, instinctively ducking as though expecting something to crash over their heads.

These were the days of the Internet and instantaneous communications, when everybody could talk to one another although none listened to anyone. Instinctively, he reached for his phone to speak across to Anoop. He was frantically trying time and again to get to him. It was a good couple of hours before he finally got through to him, only to know that although safe, Anoop had suffered some minor injuries in the melee that followed as he fled from the scene.

Weeks later Manu learnt that Aziz and Jemima were missing, presumed entombed in that debris only because they had gotten there earlier than others to work and never returned. They could not escape these falling debris and the towering inferno after years of dodging bombs and bullets in Palestine. What the hatred of his and his fiancée's kinsmen did not achieve, fire and falling debris had achieved! Ahmed, who by chance had just then returned from Cairo, was inside, with little chance to escape. The sheer audacity of it, the barbarity of it had shaken them all. No corner of the planet was safe from this madness now!

That's when Manu's nightmares struck even right at his desk. One day he saw the rough sea advancing towards a seaside city, like in a tsunami. He saw a divine figure of a guardian angel of a city seated ashore a little away from the sea with a flute in hand, a headgear with a peacock feather, unconcerned, immersed in blowing his flute disappear in the surge. What followed in his delirium was a long caravan of what appeared to be a group of pilgrims, attacked, looted, even killed and burnt by a marauding mob that came from nowhere and vanished into nowhere. Among those attacked, he saw Pawana and her caravan, which startled him. It was mayhem, with whole towns and townships set aflame, people fighting a pitched battle against each other, not even sparing women, children. The locus appeared somewhere in India. Was it something in the past, or was it in the future? Where was she? Increasingly his images were getting free of time and space. It was becoming difficult to tell the past apart from the future, the present from the past. His mind was a swirl of images from tyrants to leaders, fire and bombs, dragons or temples and pagodas, of wailing and screaming people and flight of the Romas, of the dead and dying, of his father, Pawana, Bhrandhan Murali, his mother. His state was getting out of hand. Alarmed, Anoop and his other friends sought medical help. The diagnosis was a relapse of PTD. He was on the brink of a complete breakdown.

CHAPTER IX

Manu was back to his ashram at Bangalore, broken, exhausted. He spent time meditating, recouping, reflecting on everything, on life, on his Pawana and the circus. *Ruhani, where are you, where?* That was the only thing that was preoccupying his mind now.

Despite the advice against it, he had this urge to visit Mayapuram to rekindle the memories of the circus and Pawana, maybe find clues to her existence from somewhere there, a desperate mind desperately in search for some straws to clutch on. One of those weekends, he set out for Mayapuram. It took quite a while for Manu to actually locate the maidan at Mayapuram, which he had left behind years back. It bore little resemblance to the open arena that it once was, now encroached upon, so overrun by big shops, petty shops, hawkers, making it virtually impossible to identify with the once-vibrant open space for staging protests, independence rallies, with leaders making passionate and fiery speeches, hosting political rallies, fairs, and circuses. The maidan looked sold out! The town had signs of transformation, with new buildings appearing as signs of possible prosperity. So many things had changed. The once leisurely pace and sprawling town centre was congested, crowded, what with innumerable bikes and the ubiquitous small Maruti Suzuki cars replacing the bicycles and the occasional Ambassador or Fiat cars. There were spanking-new buildings with glass façades and show windows with the latest Western apparels displayed on mannequins in place of the textiles shops with cloth bundles. And the mobile was becoming ubiquitous. He went around in search of the cinema theatres that he had once patronised and located the Ragam with some difficulty. It had now been transformed into a multiplex, a glitzy building housing multi-screens, as they called it. And of course the tickets were pricey, reflecting the pelf of the nouveau riche and not to forget the entertainment tax. But many theatres couldn't survive the twin onslaught of the TV and multiplexes and taxes and closed down. He went in search of the Shiva Temple, hoping to catch a glimpse of the deity and the scene of his excursions with Pawana. Although the deity remained undisturbed, his abode was not so untouched. Concrete roofing had replaced the wooden scaffoldings and tiled roofing. The oil wick lamp had given way generally to electrical lighting. Expediency had gained over artistry, the grandeur and serenity of the old. Thankfully, the peepal tree was still there, though with the bricked podium around continuing in the same dilapidated state. He then tried locating the many industries that were running here, among them his own factory. He was told that most of them had shut shop, with many becoming either uncompetitive or unviable. He was told the youngsters these days were interested only in BPOs or had gone overseas to the Gulf. The only ones surviving and proliferating were the endless number of shops, bakeries, garments, and of course, liquor vends, and now the travel agencies, catering to those desirous of fleeing abroad to the Gulf or to other countries.

Manu ambled around in search of the series of small houses, in one of which he and his friends had lived. Many of those homes had been demolished and some made way for multi-storied flats. After wandering aimlessly through the town, hoping somehow for a miraculous appearance of Pawana, he sauntered into one of the nearby small restaurants like the ones he patronised once. By now these were rather transformed into a newer establishment. He slowly broached the subject of circus and circuses. Some dismissed the very query with 'These days people stick to television sets in their homes. Who probably wants a circus?'. There was another who said, 'Oh, circuses are for kids.' But a middle-aged gentleman recounted with a sparkle in his eyes how years back there was a circus that galvanised these parts. 'There was nothing like that,' he said almost wistfully, wishing its return. It consoled Manu that at least there were some who remembered. The man recalled the wonderful feeling, the hope, and the courage they gave to these townsmen in teaching them independence, how to govern their own destinies by the governance they exhibited, the hospital they had constructed, and the atmosphere charged with energy and love. He said they rightly pitched their tents in the Azad Maidan, where once freedom fighters gave fiery speeches to motivate the freedom movement. 'They were unjustly and unfairly ousted in the name of obstructing the right of parties to conduct political meetings. Now it has been encroached and occupied by the merchants and shopkeepers who finance these parties and local authorities.' He pointed out the spanking-new hospital that the circus had built with such efforts, which had all the people there united. He lamented how it was now in a state of neglect. He learnt how the doctors who had assiduously striven to build a culture of care and cure had been virtually been forced out. Fear and favour had now replaced care and cure. 'And you know, last year there were bomb explosions near the temple at the hill in the outskirts and a mosque. But fortunately, people saw some ruse in it and nothing happened. There have been persistent efforts to drum up some confrontation or the other. Like the loud speakers blaring devotional songs or the processions that are taken out on festivals in the mosque or in the temple. It never was a problem before. People here in the past knew when to do what and when to refrain from. They cared for each other.' He sighed. 'There are those now who create fear and suspicion in the minds of people among each other. Greed, hate, and prejudice is the only factor guiding them. All this shiny stuff around is nothing. It's a nice-looking dead body without a soul. The city has become dead without the circus.' And then he added, 'But I hope one day it will return.'

Manu sighed. The magic that had once enveloped Mayapuram seemed to have vanished and the madness that had spread to Delhi and elsewhere in the world was now permeating back here as well. Though he could not find Pawana, at least he was reassured that the circus and Pawana were no mere figment of his imagination. Manu was gradually attempting to limp back to normal life away from nightmares, yet the seeds of the external manifestations of his madness were taking root.

• •

It was winter in the second month of a new year; he ran into his Sri Lankan friend who proposed a tour of the western state of Gujarat. He was desirous of visiting some places of worship as a way of thanks giving to the gods, and asked Manu if he would accompany him. Ever since the haunting visions and the earthquake, he had this question repeatedly chase him. Was Pawana somewhere there, and had anything happened to her? It was one place that he had missed in his quest for Pawana. As this time of the year travel would be pleasant in there. They set off across to Gujarat. They travelled wide and far to many locations by the sea coast and inland. Manu was combing the depths of his mind, recollecting from what Pawana said, did, his visions, taking notes, and comparing many things. But where was she? Maybe the gods there might give him some answers and soothe his agonies.

They had covered nearly all of those places and were preparing to return, with Pawana not yet in sight. Late in the morning, proceeding to the station, they were suddenly confronted on the way by huge mobs that were setting fire to vehicles, putting up barricades on roads. Even as they were attempting a return to their lodgings, they were waylaid by this bloodthirsty mob. The driver of the autorickshaw carrying them fled the scene. Stones and rocks landed on their vehicle and knocked both unconscious. When he came to, he found himself in a hospital, hung up on drips. His eyes searching for his companion, Karunan, he found him lying in the bed next by the side of his own bed and nearly in the same condition as he himself was in. It was a miraculous save but for a woman and a young man who brought him here; he would not have been alive, he was told. Manu was quite feeble and weak from much bleeding, but the mention of the woman lighted him up. On his persistent enquiry, he was told that they had left as soon as he was brought to safety but only managed a vague description, stating that they appeared a bit like the gypsies, but well-to-do, with a touch of regal bearing.

Even while recouping in bed, he had a relapse of those haunting visions, images of Ashurnasirpal preparing for war, with death and destruction raining on his land and his fleeing from an unknown attacker. Now he saw Saddam flying like some Superman in his military fatigues, suddenly brought down by an antiaircraft fire, while Mr Bush was furiously digging like a gold miner, trying to discover something, maybe the WMD. Then he saw the fearsome figure of that bearded Laden leering at him while Manu shouted, 'No, no, not him!', even as he saw the images of his father screaming at him on his disclosing about Pawana. His agitations would calm down at the image of Pawana or Madman Murali or even some of his friends. But Manu continued hallucinating for months in an asylum when the land between Euphrates and Tigris was again in trouble. The misfortunes of that land and people never seemed to end. There was only a feeble resistance to the American invasion before the in situ regime collapsed and the dictator was on the run, and with that, it took no time before the land descended into chaos, as did Manu's mental state.

CHAPTER X

Two years had passed when Manu was still in and out of therapy, battling the demons in his head, exhausted and gloomy. He was now taking up work assignments intermittently on his own, no longer as an employee. His friend Rajan was with him at times, dropping by, checking on him. Manu was frequently going around to many places of worship, the temples, the Buddha Viharas, and so on. He went around from Kanyakumari, Rameshwaram, Velankanni, the southernmost coastal tips of India, right up to Gaya in the north, and beyond to the shores of Thailand. He felt he was getting drawn to Ruhani more than ever in an inexorable progression of a slow, torturous, yet steady movement, as into some distant vortex. He had this hunch that something momentous was about to happen. But his gloom wouldn't be shaken off. In an aimless attempt to shake off his gloom, he was making the rounds of the monasteries, around where he befriended a young man, discovering him to be a Rohingiya who fled with his family, his native land along the sea coast in a leaky boat. Of the many families who had gone overland, some were shot by border guards, others eaten by wild animals, some lost, never to be found. So the family had decided on the journey by boat. Yet in the end he was the lone survivor, managing to surreptitiously enter this country. While fleeing from some attackers in his native village, he had snatched unwittingly from one of them a small image of Buddha, which he carried with him till he reached safety. It convinced him that the Buddha had saved him. So he became a Buddhist and got sanctuary in this monastery. He was a Rohingiya reborn as a Buddhist. Sometimes Manu wandered around the beaches, finding everywhere Germans, Americans, a few Britons, all on a vacation. All around him he could see revelry. Sitting there, one could forget the real world and think that life was about lazing around on beaches with wave after wave quietly playing out. On that day, Manu sat there, the sound of these waves drowning out his gloom, his eyes transfixed into the distant horizon, lost in thought. It was a long time, a very long time, since he had been to beaches. As he gazed into the distance, he could see Pawana drifting in, smiling, and beckoning at him, a sweet soft music wafting into his ears. As he languidly lay there in the sand, looking afar, mesmerised by Pawana, he didn't quite notice the waves gradually reaching up to him. But he got eager to receive her with outstretched hands. And then the waves were no longer reaching up but racing up and up gathering energy and urgency. A gigantic wave enveloped everything around him, followed by another and yet another, but he saw Pawana advancing towards him, carrying sugar candies and peanuts, which she loved having when they were there together at the beach. He was waving to her, and in an instant she gave him that flash of a smile. She was now hurrying, now running, actually galloping, while his arms were wide open, so wide open. In another moment she was in his tight embrace as he lifted her off his feet, and then both of them together were off their feet as the huge waves closed in. Pawana in his arms was all that mattered. And he was still tight in her embrace when the waves overwhelmed everything in and around that beach and lifted him off his feet.

'Where were you all these years, Pawana? Where were you? I searched for you all everywhere!'

'Oh, just about everywhere and anywhere!'

'But I searched all over and found you only in my visions in the Red Fort, escaping with you from the clutches of the royal troops.'

'Yes, that was a long time back when we were together and you saw your true self in the past.'

'But not being able to find you, I went to Iraq. In my dreams I saw you there among the Assyrians, and then there was the attack on Judea, the sacking, the pillaging, and the killings. And then the great exodus followed and we fled. But I never found you there otherwise.'

'Yes we were there together too, in the very distant past. You have yet to know how long back in time we go together. We were always together from the beginning of time.'

'But I saw you among the onion domes and the grand squares.'

'Yes, after you left for Iraq, we went to the USSR to perform and meet people of our own ilk, some distant relations. We got a rousing welcome, with people there loving it all. It was a wonderful time. But there was turmoil, there was change and confusion, and we were compelled to come back, and some of them came with us. We were carrying on rather well, travelling in the western part of India, till someone complained in the courts about our ill treatment of animals. We said they were our folk, our brothers and sisters, how could we treat them so? Nobody listened. These were confiscated and our circus came to a standstill. It was virtually disbanded. Those poor brothers of ours were put in cages in zoos, starved themselves, pining for us, while we could only watch them in helplessness. And then the blast happened. People ripped apart and then madness followed. Nobody treats even animals that way. Even animals don't treat each other thus.'

At Puzhakkara, Manu's mother was preparing their daily breakfast when for a moment she was reminded of Manu. The cup of coffee she had just picked slipped from her hand and fell, spilling it all on the kitchen counter. Her eyebrows and eyes twitched. Instinctively she felt something amiss. Manu, she felt, was in some kind of danger, something she never had felt all these years. His father was a bit sceptical and calmed her down. Strangely, Madman Murali was seen in the precincts of the village temple in immaculate traditional clothing of mundu, bare chested. Nobody ever had seen him in that temple all those years! And then he vanished. Nobody saw him thereafter.

By this time the waves had long lashed the shores, bringing in everything around floating in the sea and on the shores deep onto the landmass. Boats, yachts, thousands of people, even wooden homes smashed to smithereens were part of a grand pile of flotsam hurrying inland. And then the waves receded, leaving them all stranded. Pawana paused briefly. Manu could clearly see himself lying there amidst these, miraculously intact and even breathing, ever so feebly. He was well above everything, devoid of any material substance, being able to go around freely. It was then he realised that he had detached himself from his physical self and could clearly see himself lying unconscious down there, still breathing.

It was the first time Manu managed anything like that. It was the beginning of his awakening. He was beginning to realise that he was much more than the helpless bundle that was lying down there, endowed with powers that he was unaware of. Pawana continued, 'But I always came back to you! Yes, we went to northern parts of India and had a good time.'

'But I couldn't get you there at all in my time there!'

'No, we were actually passing by through Delhi when that explosion occurred and you were injured. I knew something was afoot, and that is why I insisted to get through that city and came at the nick of the time. And then you were out of danger.'

'Oh! How! Oh! So you went with me to the hospital in Delhi?'

'Yes!'

'But I had visions, so many of them, about distant lands, dream events rooted in the distant past in the very ancient to the more recent past, where I saw you. But I didn't quite manage to locate you in the present.'

'You could not then see the hints. You were confused between what you saw in your actual past and the present and the future. The dreams about the past were real. You saw the now and the immediate future, they too were real. I told you dreams had true meanings. They are not to be treated as trifles. We were always together, going through the ages across continents. I too am past now.'

'What do you mean . . . ? That vision of the caravan . . . in Gujarat? You were in Gujarat?'

'Yes! It was when everything about the circus had ceased! Yes, a mob waylaid us soon after I had managed to put you in that hospital. While our son and my father escaped, I could not, or rather, cared not. My time was up. There was no point in staying back.'

Even as his body lay unconscious amidst the wreckage, he surveyed the damage all around. It was only then the enormity of the catastrophe struck him. For miles around, far beyond the immediate vicinity, he could see the impact the huge waves had left behind, the debris, flotsam, the bodies, and the wreckages. It was quite a while before any help was even seen to be approaching the scene. There was then a swarm of men, machines, and some vehicles like ambulances moving in. Among them was the young monk moving towards his unconscious body.

'What about our son?'

'He is safe with my father. He is studying to be an engineer, like you, but is a trained musician as well as an artist.'

'Did you know that Thomas is no longer with us? He just didn't seem to want to remain.'

'He too had finished his journey. He was no longer needed there.' Pawana again paused.

'And Rema?'

'You will soon realise it yourself.'

'But why did you hurry out of Mayapuram without even giving me a chance?'

'No. I was waiting all long. But I am not ordained to wait anywhere on anything. We have been cursed, if you may say so, to move. It's for me to move, to keep moving like the wind. You could have come along.'

'But—'

'Now we are together,' interrupted Pawana.

'But when will you come back, Pawana?

'When the time is ripe! And then the circus will begin!'

Manu saw himself being carried on a stretcher and the monk hurrying beside him. The ambulance zipped past to the hospital. In fact, he was among the lucky few who were rather found early, while hundreds there lay amidst debris, in difficult-to-access locations, waiting for help. Manu for the moment was now more engrossed in experiencing his new-found freedom than be too overly worried over his physical self. He found from his vantage position the vast expanse of the ocean still in considerable turbulence. He realised that this was a disaster of a unprecedented magnitude. 'Pawana,' he called out to her, pointing at the sea and seashore below. 'What's this?'

At this Pawana smiled. 'You don't seem to have yet realised your own powers. You are capable of witnessing the happenings around the world and about knowing them. Focus and just recall about your true self, and then you will see all that you wish to.' After some silent moments later, slowly the devastation across the Indian Ocean began manifesting before his eyes. The ferocity of the earth and sea was laid bare before him as he saw destruction far and wide. He didn't wish to see further. It was then he demanded of Pawana again, 'What is the use of these powers when one is unable to do anything?'

'You were given enough hints through your dreams of what was to come. But you doubted and didn't act. Each of them there below have the capacity to know all their past and the future. But few realise it. Fewer still use that vast understanding that they have gained. You are among the chosen few who could see far into the past and into the future. You could be even better if you had chosen to use that wisdom. So much of what you saw all through and around you could have been different if the people around had the wisdom to use what all they had learned from their past and when they could see far ahead, the future shaped by what they were doing now, they could change course. But they don't! Their prejudice and miseries are so dear to them that their true selves and of the world are hidden from them.'

Before him all his past, his very distant past, was manifesting. His struggles through the ages, be in Judea, in Assyria, in Persia, in the Sind (in Dilli), in ancient China (in Rajaputana, in Kamboja, or in Suvarnadwipa or in Indonesia) to be with Pawana. Sometimes he succeeded; at others he failed. It dawned on him that the past, the present, and the future were one uninterrupted continuum where Ashurnasirpal, Hussein, or Laden, Ghengis, or Ghazni and the likes marched past, except that one is so engrossed in the current that one cannot see into the past or the future. He was now so clear that Pawana could never be away from him; they were meant to be together. She was always with him, only he couldn't quite recognise the true manifestation of her even though he was moved to his innermost depths in her presence, yet his vision was clouded by peripherals.

He could see the many violent quakes, meteors slamming, volcanoes erupting in the past, and the many violent storms, heat, and dust, the madness and all rising in the distant future. He saw at that moment how his friend Anoop in New York was calmly going about his life, as did he see what his siblings were up to. He could see the doctors milling around him, tending to him. But the monk was always beside him and with the many others who required it. He was firm that Manu would regain consciousness, as would others around there get well.

Manu could see how Hussein was going about his daily routine in Iraq despite misfortunes, hoping those distant magical days would be back. The Americans were there, and so were car bombs going off time and again, sometimes in the Sunni quarter of the city, at other times in the Shia quarter. Yet he hadn't lost hope. He saw Anoop hoping that someday he would be returning to his native village, but for the moment he continued shuttling between New York and Bangalore. Mamu Salman was nearing retirement. But still he was rushing back to Ayodhya at every opportunity, rushing back with sweets, now for his grandchildren. As always, he believed the festivals were invented by man for all to enjoy. His parents were slowly getting to believe that at least their younger son and his family would return, as might their daughter.

He was now getting into the netherworld of the souls, going close to the wailing well where the souls of the universe had gathered around. They were there, heads bowed in silence as though in prayer for redemption of all beings from all the madness in the world, before they departed from there one by one. Among them were Thomas, Rema, Aziz, and Jemima, and then Murali, who came to him straightaway with a smile. Manu turned around to Pawana with a bit of surprise. 'Yes, he is my brother, who was there watching over you. He knew his time was up when despite his warning you got close to the sea. There was no longer any need for him there. And there, Rema and Jemima are my sisters, and Thomas is my cousin, Aziz and Ahmed are your brothers.'

Manu understood that his time too down there was up. He realised that he was now in another dimension, one continuous firmament of space and time invisible to the rest of the world as a black hole. Was a return possible from this or even necessary? As if on cue, Pawana said, 'The circus will come as long as people truly wish for it. It's time will come, as it has over the ages in its many forms. We have always been together, we all.' For the moment Manu was happy to be here with Pawana. He had no desire to be down there right now. There was, anyway, no need for them both in there.

******